Benedict chuckled at that.

There was a warm, earthy sound to his laugh which Effie suddenly found very difficult to ignore. "I enjoy dancing," he told Lady Culver. "So that is no imposition at all."

Benedict nearly took off up the stairs – but he paused thoughtfully and glanced down at his feet. He took one careful step back and pried his muddy boots from them, one after the other.

"There's really no need to make *extra* work for you, is there?" he said to Effie apologetically. He headed up the stairs before she could find the wherewithal to respond.

As his figure disappeared, Effie was struck by a horrified realisation.

"Oh, bother," she said. "I think I've just fallen in love."

By Olivia Atwater

REGENCY FAERIE TALES
Half a Soul
Ten Thousand Stitches
Longshadow

TEN THOUSAND STITCHES

Regency Faerie Tales: Book Two

OLIVIA ATWATER

orbit

orbitbooks.net

Copyright © 2020 by Olivia Atwater
Excerpt from *Longshadow* copyright © 2021 by Olivia Atwater
Excerpt from *Wild and Wicked Things* copyright © 2022 by Francesca Dorricott

Cover images by Shutterstock

Orbit
Hachette Book Group
1290 Avenue of the Americas
New York, NY 10104
orbitbooks.net

First Orbit Paperback Edition: July 2022
Simultaneously published in Great Britain by Orbit
First Orbit eBook Edition: April 2022
Originally published by Starwatch Press in 2020

Orbit is an imprint of Hachette Book Group.
The Orbit name and logo are trademarks of Little, Brown Book Group Limited.

The publisher is not responsible for websites (or their content) that are not owned by the publisher.

The Hachette Speakers Bureau provides a wide range of authors for speaking events. To find out more, go to www.hachettespeakersbureau.com or call (866) 376-6591.

Library of Congress Control Number: 2022931401

ISBNs: 9780316462907 (trade paperback), 9780316463003 (ebook)

Printed in the United States of America

LSC-C

Printing 4, 2024

Dramatis Personae

Euphemia Reeves – irritable housemaid at Hartfield; excellent seamstress

Mrs Sedgewick – housekeeper at Hartfield; at odds with Mr Allen

Mr Allen – butler at Hartfield; at odds with Mrs Sedgewick

Lydia – Euphemia's best friend and fellow housemaid at Hartfield

George Reeves – Euphemia's brother and footman at Hartfield

Cookie – Hartfield's cook; known for her unpleasant remedies for illness

Prudence – Lady Eleanor Ashbrooke's personal maid

Lord Thomas Ashbrooke – the baron of Culver; head of the Family at Hartfield

Lady Eleanor Ashbrooke – Lord Thomas Ashbrooke's wife; also styled Lady Culver; Euphemia's employer; possessed of many gowns

Mr Edmund Ashbrooke – younger brother to Lord Culver

Mr Benedict Ashbrooke – youngest brother to Lord Culver; recently returned from the Continent

Mr Herbert Jesson – a successful tulip merchant; Mr Benedict Ashbrooke's school friend; also known as Mr Tulip

Lord Wilford – Baron of Wilford; head of the Family at Holly House

Miss Mary Buckley – Lord Wilford's sister; Lady Eleanor Ashbrooke's best friend

Mr Fudge – Lord Wilford's butler

Caesar – Lord Wilford's dog; the best boy

Lord Panovar – Baron of Panovar; head of the Family at Finchwood Hall; known for endless complaints to his cooks

Lady Panovar – Lord Panovar's wife; Lady Eleanor Ashbrooke's social rival, who employs several French maids

Lord Blackthorn – faerie viscount of Blackthorn; determined to be helpful

Lady Hollowvale – faerie marchioness of Hollowvale; possesses half an English soul

Stillheart and Gloomfall – brownies; known as the best tailors in faerie; currently pretending to be Lady Hollowvale's servants

Abigail – Lady Hollowvale's teenaged ward

Robert and Hugh – Lady Hollowvale's young wards; deceased but perfectly content

Prologue

uphemia Reeves was a very irritable young woman.

This would have surprised most of the other servants at Hartfield – in fact, if you had asked the esteemed housekeeper, Mrs Sedgewick, she might have told you that Effie was nearly the *ideal* sort of chambermaid. As far as Mrs Sedgewick was aware, Effie never shirked her duties and always conducted herself with perfect composure.

Mrs Sedgewick would have been shocked to hear the words that currently spilled from Effie's lips.

"... no consideration whatsoever, *none!*" Effie hissed to herself, as she scrubbed down the wooden floors of the entryway for the third time that day. Mud caked the floorboards once again, as the men of the Family had come tromping inside one by one from the nasty winter weather outside. "Ought to be against the law to go out ridin' when there's mud an' snow!"

Lord Culver and his younger brother, Mr Edmund Ashbrooke, had little awareness of the spectacular messes that they left behind. Effie would have received quite the tongue-lashing for leaving her boots on back home, but Lord Culver – more than fifteen years her senior! – was so used to messes magically disappearing behind him that he saw little use in peeling off his own boots until he'd already tramped up to his room. Some poor laundry maid would soon have to scrub his entire outfit once he'd pulled it off.

"*There's no use gettin' angry,*" Effie's mother used to chide her. "*It'll just get you into trouble. You can think all of the angry thoughts you want, but they've got to stay inside your head!*"

"Muddy, puffed-up popinjays, the lot of 'em!" Effie muttered at her brush. "Well, birds are smarter, aren't they? At least they clean their own feathers!" The words tumbled out beneath her breath today, instead of staying in her head. *Sorry, Mum,* she thought apologetically. *I've run out of patience again.*

Normally, when Effie became this cross, she went to find some convenient mending – she'd always found needlework to be remarkably soothing. But the Ashbrookes were hosting yet *another* ball tomorrow evening, and the staff was running about like mad trying to prepare for it once again. Lady Culver had only married Lord Culver last year in London, and ever since he'd returned with her, she'd been determined to take charge of the household to run things *her* way.

Unfortunately, Lady Culver's way mostly seemed to involve dismissing any servant who happened to displease her and refusing ever to replace them.

The way Lady Culver goes on, she must think she's hired a bunch of magicians instead of a bunch of servants, Effie thought tiredly. *She ought to put that in her next advertisement – maybe England's court magician will show up and do her laundry!*

This thought, of course, only made Effie even more cross than ever. She sighed and dug into her memory, searching for a nursery rhyme. The cook used nursery rhymes to time her preparations, and Effie had taken to using them as a method of last resort to calm her nerves. She narrowed her eyes and carefully recited at the floor:

> "Wind the bobbin up,
> Wind the bobbin up,
> Pull, pull, clap, clap, clap.
> Wind it back again . . ."

The long frustration of the day dimmed a bit beneath the monotonous rhyme, and Effie relaxed her shoulders minutely. She had just started the verse again, leaning back into the cleaning, when she was interrupted.

"Lydia! Are you about, Lydia?" Mrs Sedgewick's thin, reedy voice snapped through the air in the hallway behind Effie. "For goodness' sake – has anyone seen Lydia? I haven't the time to be tracking down every maid in this household!"

Effie took a deep, steadying breath and tried to erase the scowl from her face as Mrs Sedgewick came around the corner. The stern old housekeeper strode out towards Effie; the wooden soles of her half-boots made a neat clipping noise as she went. Mrs Sedgewick was in particularly immaculate form today, with her dark hair pulled back into a tight bun upon her head. She was dressed in her black silk housekeeper's gown, of course – for she was inordinately proud of the thing, and she preferred never to be seen in any other clothing.

"Effie!" Mrs Sedgewick said. "Have you seen Lydia? Her Ladyship would like the piano in the ballroom dusted again. She says she can still hear the dust in it."

Effie flinched at the suggestion. *We've already dusted that dratted piano twice!* she thought crossly. *Perhaps someone ought to test Her Ladyship's hearing, in case she's going deaf.* But what Effie actually said aloud was, "Mr Allen sent Lydia to air out another of the guest rooms, Mrs Sedgewick."

The housekeeper's eyes flared with irritation. "Mr Allen did?" she observed icily. "Well, well. And since when did the maids of the house start taking orders from the *butler*?"

Effie swallowed down a frustrated sigh. Mrs Sedgewick had been at odds with their new butler, Mr Allen, ever since he'd been hired on at Hartfield. Lady Culver had dismissed the old butler, Mr Simmons – but since Hartfield really could not get by without a butler, Lady Culver's family had insisted on sending Mr Allen to take over the job. He had been a very well-regarded butler in London, before he'd deigned to take over Hartfield. Everyone knew that he was only there by some noble relative's earnest request. Unfortunately, Mr Allen's immediate reorganisation of the household had infuriated Mrs Sedgewick, who was quite used to working with Mr Simmons and not at all fond of this newer, more refined interloper.

Lord only knew who was originally to blame for the initial spat between the butler and the housekeeper – but the rivalry had grown worse and worse as the weeks went by, until even the stable hands found themselves forced to choose an allegiance to one or the other.

"I don't know much more than that, Mrs Sedgewick," Effie said. "But Lydia should be upstairs if you're lookin' for her." Effie scrubbed at a patch of mud on the floor, keeping her eyes carefully on the ground.

"Ordering around the maids!" Mrs Sedgewick huffed again. "Oh, that nasty man, getting above himself! Lady Culver will hear about this – see if she doesn't!"

Effie did not respond this time, though she was sure that Mrs Sedgewick *wanted* her to do so. She had learned that if she did not react to the housekeeper's dramatic pronouncements, Mrs Sedgewick would eventually give up and go seek out one of the more gossip-friendly maids.

"Mr Allen might well spoil the ball at this rate," Mrs Sedgewick added insistently. "I tell you, I shall not hesitate to lay the blame upon him if he does."

"Yes, Mrs Sedgewick," Effie murmured obediently.

The housekeeper thinned her lips to a neat line. "Well," she said. "I am *buried* in work. I cannot simply stand here gabbing at housemaids all day." Mrs Sedgewick said this as though it were *Effie* who had started their conversation, and not her at all.

"Yes, Mrs Sedgewick," Effie repeated carefully. But her mouth had begun to twitch in annoyance, and she knew that she didn't dare look up for fear of showing her irritation on her face.

Mrs Sedgewick turned on her heel and started for the hallway again, the wooden *clip-clop* of her boots slowly fading behind her. As soon as she had gone, Effie let out a long, weary breath.

"None of us has time to gab, of course," Effie muttered at her brush. "Just imagine that! *Time!*" She glanced at the bucket of water next to her and sighed, shoving to her feet. She was going to have to spread fresh sand over the entryway all over again—

The front door opened abruptly.

Effie staggered back with a surprised shriek. Her foot caught on the bucket of water, and she found herself toppling backwards.

"Good God!" a man exclaimed. A strong, sturdy arm snaked around Effie's waist just in time to keep her from plummeting downwards.

Two warm brown eyes blinked down at her. A pleasant, sturdy scent engulfed her – sandalwood, Effie thought, and just a hint of the outside. She coloured as she recognised Mr Benedict Ashbrooke's strong, handsome features.

"Ah!" Effie squeaked. "I . . . I'm so sorry!"

Benedict blinked again. His dark hair was pleasantly mussed and scattered with melting snow. Benedict was the youngest brother of the Ashbrooke family. Effie had always said that he was also the most *handsome* brother – or at least, she had quietly *thought* as much, before he had left a few years ago to travel the Continent. Now that he stared down at her with that sheepish smile, holding her in his strong, warm arms, Effie found herself struck utterly dumb.

"Nothing to worry about," Benedict assured her. "I should be the one apologising, I'm sure." He set Effie carefully back onto her feet – though his hands lingered on her shoulders with a hint of concern. He knit his brow at her. "I swear I know your face, miss. Have we met before? Are you staying here for one of Lady Culver's balls, perchance?"

Effie blinked dazedly. *For the ball?* she thought. *What on earth does he mean by that?*

"I should think you *do* know me, yes!" Effie said. She shouldn't have dared to be so pert – but her heart was still racing in her chest, and her head felt warm and muddled from his nearness.

"I knew I must have," Benedict said ruefully. "Do you know, I am terrible with names – but I normally remember far better when there's such a pretty face attached."

Effie widened her eyes. *I don't know what's going on at all any more*, she thought.

"Benedict, good heavens!" Lady Culver's voice called down from the stairs, and Effie glanced up towards her. The matron of the household was barely older than Effie herself – but the terrible scowl which currently lay upon her fine, aristocratic features made her seem more like old Mrs Sedgewick. "You're back from your tour, then?" Lady Culver asked impatiently. "Why did no one tell me to expect you? And for that matter – why are you exchanging pleasantries with the help?"

Benedict knit his brow again. He glanced back towards Effie, who shrank with embarrassment beneath his gaze. As she did, she caught sight of the old, fraying lace attached to the neckline of her gown.

I am wearing one of Lady Culver's old hand-me-down gowns, Effie realised belatedly. *But really, no one with half a brain ought to mistake me for a lady.*

"Oh," Benedict said. "I see." He managed another helpless smile at Effie. "Well," he told her. "I suppose I have made fools of us both. Do forgive me, miss."

"You're forgiven, of course," Effie mumbled out. It was the only thing she could think to say in the moment.

Benedict cleared his throat and looked back up the stairs

towards Lady Culver. "I sent a letter to Thomas," he told her. "But I suppose he forgot to pass it on, did he?"

Lady Culver narrowed her eyes. "So he did," she said. "Well, Benedict – you are lucky that we have aired out the rooms. The lodge is uninhabitable at the moment, but there may yet be an extra room for you at Hartfield in spite of my husband's oversight." She paused. "There is a ball tomorrow evening, however. You will have to make yourself available to the young ladies for dancing, or else we shall never hear the end of it."

Benedict chuckled at that. There was a warm, earthy sound to his laugh which Effie suddenly found very difficult to ignore. "I enjoy dancing," he told Lady Culver. "So that is no imposition at all."

Benedict nearly took off up the stairs – but he paused thoughtfully and glanced down at his feet. He took one careful step back and pried his muddy boots from them, one after the other.

"There's really no need to make *extra* work for you, is there?" he said to Effie apologetically. He headed up the stairs before she could find the wherewithal to respond.

As his figure disappeared, Effie was struck by a horrified realisation.

"Oh, bother," she said. "I think I've just fallen in love."

Chapter One

"Even Mr Allen thinks Lady Culver ought to hire more servants for the work she has us doin'," Lydia sniffed as she stabbed at the sock in her lap with a needle. She and Effie were settled onto the narrow beds in their shared room below-stairs, working on a quiet bit of mending just before bed. "I heard him sayin' it to George when he didn't see me round the corner. Mr Allen said it's a crime how little she pays the rest of us, too!"

Effie shook her head worriedly. Her brother George worked as a footman for the household, and he was often far too chatty for his own good. "George and Mr Allen ought to keep their voices down better," Effie said, as she stitched up a tear in the silk hem in front of her. "Even Mr Allen's fancy references won't save him if Lady Culver hears he's said somethin' the least bit bad about her."

"Well, Mr Allen's right, isn't he?" Lydia said impatiently. "Look at us, Effie! After midnight, and we're only just now mendin' our own things!" She frowned as she considered Effie. "But ... oh no, what is *that*, Effie? That can't be Mrs Sedgewick's gown! I thought you'd already mended it a few weeks back!"

Effie sighed heavily. "It *is* Mrs Sedgewick's gown," she said. "She wants it fixed for the ball, just in case some guest catches

sight of her. Mrs Sedgewick said she doesn't trust anyone else
to stitch it up for her."

"An' you volunteered to do it, didn't you, Effie?" Lydia
accused her. She wrinkled up her nose in distaste. "You know
what you are, Effie? You're *chronically helpful*. It's a disease. We
ought to call you a physician." Effie wasn't sure what the word
chronic meant, but she was sure that Lydia must have overheard
it from someone recently; the other maid was fond of interesting
vocabulary, and she often plucked new words from the conversations she overheard naturally during her work.

"Is it a bad thing to be chronically helpful?" Effie mumbled.
"Does it really hurt anyone?"

"It's terrible," Lydia informed her bluntly. "You never turn
anyone down, not ever. All anyone has to do is say very loudly
what a problem they've got, an' you'll try to solve it for them.
An' that's why you always end up doin' everyone's mending, Effie, even when they're perfectly capable of doin' it for
themselves."

Effie pressed her lips together at that. Earlier that day, just
after that strange incident with Benedict, she'd had a lovely
few minutes where she'd felt as though she were floating her
way through the manor. But a full day of running breathlessly
to and fro had crushed that tiny sense of elation back into her
usual, miserable frustration.

"I can't just say no to Mrs Sedgewick," Effie sighed. She
stuffed her frustration down with an effort. A few more stitches
calmed her mood slightly, though they did little for the growing
headache behind her eyes. "If either Mrs Sedgewick *or* Her
Ladyship decides they want rid of me, I'll be back at home an'
takin' food off my mum's table. She can't afford that."

Lydia let out a disgusted noise. "Oh, an' they *would* dismiss
you for that, wouldn't they!" she muttered. "You remember when poor Lucy got pregnant an' they tossed her right
out on her behind? I heard Lady Culver gave Lucy not one

farthing – not even a carriage ride home!" Lydia shook her head, as though to rid herself of the unpleasant memory. "Anyway – imagine bein' a housekeeper! We could have other servants doin' all our chores as well, couldn't we? I bet Mrs Sedgewick is already asleep in her bed, while *you* mend her skirts!"

Another shot of anger jolted through Effie at that. She hunched down over the gown, clenching her jaw. *It doesn't do any good to get angry*, Effie reminded herself. *I can't change things, so getting angry will just get me into trouble.*

"It isn't worth complainin'," Effie muttered. "Here, let's talk about somethin' nicer – did you see that Mr Benedict came home today?"

Lydia knit her brow. "Is that nicer?" she asked. "He'll be another member of the Family underfoot for *another* awful ball."

Effie coloured. "He isn't all that bad," she said. "An' at least he's pleasant to look at, isn't he?"

Lydia grinned. "Ooh," she said. "Have you got a *tendre* for him, Effie?" Effie had not heard the word "*tendre*" before, but she was fairly certain of its meaning based on the way that Lydia said it.

"I do not," Effie lied stiffly. "That'd be silly of me, wouldn't it?"

Lydia shrugged and set aside her sock. "I don't know," she said. "It's sometimes nice to dream. An' if we haven't got the time to sleep sometimes, at least we can still *daydream*."

Effie stared down at the gown in her lap. "Yes," she said softly. "I guess there's that."

The single candle on the table soon burned down, and Effie was forced to set aside the gown. As she closed her eyes and tried to sleep, she found herself dreaming of warm brown eyes and a pleasant, heart-tingling smile.

Effie didn't have very long to dream.

Six in the morning came around in no time at all – whereupon Lydia began to shake Effie by the shoulder, hissing about the fireplaces. The two of them rushed to get their usual day-to-day chores out of the way, grimly aware that last-minute preparations for the ball would interrupt their schedule all day long. Sure enough, Lady Culver soon began calling for maids to help with her hair, and Mrs Sedgewick dispatched Effie to polish all of the mirrors in the ballroom one last time.

By the time Lydia joined Effie to lay out the last flowers, neither of them had managed breakfast, or even a quick noon-time snack. But the guests soon began to arrive, and there was still no time for rest.

Mrs Sedgewick hustled into the ballroom from a side door, grasping at Lydia's and Effie's shoulders. "Would someone please go and check on Cookie?" the housekeeper demanded breathlessly. "And where *are* the punch trays?"

Lydia closed her eyes with the slightest groan. Effie fought back her instinctive retort – *Perhaps they got forgotten along with our breakfast!* – and pasted on a polite smile. "I'll go and check, Mrs Sedgewick," she said, with an infinite patience that she did not feel at all. *At least I might pick up something to eat while I'm down in the kitchens,* she thought.

Effie slipped out the side door and down into the passages which led below-stairs. Excited laughter trickled in from the entryway above, where the guests still mingled. A strange stab of longing went through her chest as she imagined herself standing in that front entryway, instead of down below it.

Perhaps Benedict was up there, mingling with the guests. If Effie had truly been the noble lady for which he'd mistaken her, she would be there with him, dressed in her evening best – or rather, she would be dressed in something akin to Lady Culver's evening best. Effie imagined herself in a lovely cream gown, with plenty of lace and embroidered embellishments. Benedict would smile upon seeing her, and ask whether she might save him a dance—

"Out of the way, Effie!" a voice hissed from behind her. Effie's brother George nudged at her back, and she realised that she had paused in the middle of the narrow confines of the servants' passageways, listening to the party above.

Effie hurried forwards, flushed with embarrassment. "I'm so sorry!" she mumbled. "I'm so tired, George; I've lost my mind a bit."

"Haven't we all?" George grumbled behind her. Effie opened the door to the kitchens and entered, stepping aside for him. George coughed harshly into his hand as he passed, and Effie frowned at him.

"That's quite a cough," she said. "Are you all right?"

"Fine," George assured her. "Just tired." Effie rummaged for her handkerchief and offered it over – but George shook his head and pulled out his own. "I've got one," he mumbled. "Yours is so nicely embroidered. I wouldn't want to ruin it."

Effie sighed heavily. "You ought to get some rest," she said.

"Maybe I ought," George said ironically. "An' maybe I ought to be paid more. An' maybe, while we're at it, there ought to be fewer balls. Do you think Her Ladyship would take a meetin' with me about it over tea?"

"You *really* need to watch your mouth, George," Effie told him tiredly. "You know what Mum would tell you."

"Mum's not here right now," George replied bluntly. "I've been up at dawn an' goin' to bed at midnight every night for the last week, Effie. It'd be unnatural if I *didn't* complain at least a little bit." He nudged at her again, more insistent this time. "Now stop holdin' me up. I just want to get through this awful night."

Effie backed herself into the kitchen, and George passed her for the exit before she could pester him further.

The estate's head cook – more affectionately known as

Cookie – was in the process of plating some cold meats and biscuits. Effie saw the punch trays off to one side, and she grabbed one quickly. "I'll just take this one up!" she called to the poor, beleaguered cook. Cookie barely nodded at her, but it was enough to signal her agreement. Effie hurried back out of the kitchen and up to the ballroom.

The guests had begun to filter inside; one of the ladies had sat down at the grand piano, idling her way through a playful tune. Effie headed out among the guests with the tray of punch, keeping her eyes carefully upon her feet. The very last thing she needed was to trip over herself in her tiredness and spill the punch all over some important lady.

"Oh, I'll take one of those, please." A blonde woman in a blue gown reached out to pluck a glass from the tray. Her hair was done up with a golden chain, and her cheeks were tinted faintly pink with rouge.

"I think I will as well." Benedict spoke from Effie's other side, and the sound of his voice froze Effie neatly in place. Benedict took a glass from the tray, and Effie glanced up at him. He was dressed just as finely as the other guests, in a fine golden waistcoat and a black jacket. There was such a warm smile on his handsome face that Effie found herself staring at him.

Her heart sped up in her chest. For just an instant, as his eyes glanced towards her, Effie found herself caught between daydreams and reality. An irrational conviction overtook her: Benedict had recognised her! Was he going to ask her to dance, right here and now?

"Duntham!" Benedict called then, in a cheerful voice. His eyes had fixed upon someone just past Effie's shoulder. "How many years has it been now?" He swept past her with a laugh ... and Effie's heart plummeted all the way down into her feet.

And what was I expecting? she thought wearily. *I have a tray this time. That makes me as good as invisible, doesn't it?*

As a servant, Effie was used to being overlooked. In fact,

being overlooked was considered a crucial skill for someone of her status – noblemen generally preferred their servants to seem as non-existent as possible. But somehow, the experience of being overlooked by *this* particular gentleman stung her unexpectedly. If only Benedict had never spoken to her so charmingly, Effie thought, she would not have got above herself so foolishly.

An awful, jaded disappointment mixed with her fatigue – the feeling rose from her stomach all the way into her throat, knotting there like a stone. Hot tears pricked at the corner of Effie's eyes, and she backpedalled towards the wall with horror.

"Oh, Lydia!" she gasped. "Can you take the tray, please?"

Lydia slumped her shoulders. "You've only just come up with it, Effie!" she whispered plaintively. "Can't you hand out drinks just a *bit* longer?"

"I'm about to cry," Effie informed Lydia, with as level a tone as she could manage. "I need a bit of air, or else I doubt I'll stop."

Lydia took the tray from her with a knowing sigh. "Oh dear," she said. "Well, go an' get it over with. I may need to go have a cry myself by the time this evening is up."

Effie swept past Lydia for the side door, down into the servants' passages. As she did, her tears spilled over, and she found herself weeping with anger and shame.

Crying fits had become somewhat more common among the staff these days, but Effie still had no desire to be caught sobbing in one of the cramped passageways below-stairs. She sought her way outdoors, therefore, just outside the large hedge maze which curled its way behind the manor.

Normally, the hedge maze would have been a source of amusement for at least some of the guests, but the mud and snow had rendered it far less pleasing tonight. As a result, Effie had the bench outside the maze to herself. She settled herself down onto it, wiping at her face and rubbing at her arms. The cold, brisk air tempered her misery, and she took a few deep, steadying breaths.

The faint strains of the grand piano trickled down towards her from the windows above. The dancing had begun, Effie thought. All of those handsome gentlemen would soon invite all of those lovely ladies in their lovely gowns out onto the dance floor. Benedict was probably asking some woman to dance even now.

"That hardly matters, does it?" Effie mumbled to herself. "Why should it matter what he's doin'? Certainly, no one was ever goin' to ask *me* to dance." She blinked a few times and forced out a laugh. "Hah! The very thought!"

"Oh dear." A soft, curious voice came from Effie's right-hand side, and she froze in place. "Is that such a strange thought? But now I am even more compelled to ask than I was before! *Would* you like to dance, miss?"

Effie stumbled to her feet. She turned to look at the man who had spoken ... and found herself even more confused.

He was a tall, lithe man, dressed in a fine, black velvet jacket. His hair was every bit as black as his jacket, and tousled faintly at the ends. His eyes were a shocking emerald-green, like budding leaves in the springtime – they glowed faintly from within in a way which made him stand out in the moonlight. He was not wearing a cravat, Effie thought, but there was a blossoming rose twined around his neck which served the purpose.

"I ... I'm so sorry, sir," Effie managed. "I'd never have come out here if I thought I'd disturb someone—"

"Oh, but I am not disturbed at all!" the man said earnestly. He smiled at Effie, and her aching heart gave a twinge as she thought how handsome it made him appear, even in the semi-darkness. His features were very elegant; his cheekbones were sharp enough that she could have cut her finger upon them.

"I am so very pleased to meet you, in fact," he added. "How exciting this all is!"

Effie swallowed, clasping her hands in front of her. There was something very odd about the way the man spoke to her, but she'd yet to put her finger on just what it was. "Sir," she said slowly. "You are ... aware that I'm a maid here?" She had no wish to repeat her disappointing interaction with Benedict from the previous day.

"Are you?" the man asked. He looked her over, and his eyes lit up. "My goodness, you *are*!" He seemed somehow even more enthused by this revelation. "How delightfully perfect. Please, would you tell me your name?"

Effie blinked. She could not remember the last time that a nobleman had asked for her name. "Er ... my name is Euphemia Reeves, my lord," she said. "But most people call me Effie."

"What a lovely name!" The nobleman beamed at her with such excitement that Effie found herself wondering whether he had ever been displeased by anything in his life. "Well," he said. "I am Lord Blackthorn. And I should ask you again – *would* you like to dance, Miss Euphemia?" He offered out his hand at this, and Effie realised that he truly meant for her to take it.

That is not a good idea, Effie thought. Beyond the fact that she should not be dancing with guests, some part of her had noted that Lord Blackthorn was an uncomfortably strange man – and besides which, Effie had never heard of any land called "Blackthorn".

But Effie's body had run away ahead of her thoughts, and she found that she had already taken his hand. Lord Blackthorn's fingers were very long and fine, and he somehow carried with him the scent of fresh roses, even in the middle of February.

"I believe I know this dance!" Lord Blackthorn said with pleasure. "Why, Lady Hollowvale must have taught it to me only last week!" He took Effie by the waist, even as she struggled to sort out whether she had heard of somewhere called "Hollowvale" or not. Lord Blackthorn twirled Effie about, and she stumbled clumsily over her shoes with a soft gasp. "Now, Miss Euphemia," he said fondly, as though she hadn't just fumbled her very first steps. "I must ask you a very important question: would you say that you are powerless?"

"I – what?" Effie asked dazedly. She stumbled again, now utterly frantic to keep up – but Lord Blackthorn hardly seemed to notice her difficulties. *Something about that question seems like it ought to be improper*, Effie thought. But she couldn't pinpoint exactly *what* about the question was improper, and so she said, "I'm sure I don't know what you mean, m'lord."

"Well," Lord Blackthorn said thoughtfully. "Given the choice, would you say that you are power*ful* or would you say that you are power*less?*"

He spun her about again, and Effie began to feel dizzy. *I don't think this is how the dance goes at all*, she thought. Effie's mind caught up to his words, and her temper surged. "Beggin' your pardon!" she said crossly. "But I'm quite powerful enough to step on your toes if you decide to take liberties, sir!"

Lord Blackthorn tilted his head at Effie, apparently befuddled. As he did, she saw that his ears were gently pointed at the ends.

Effie's heart leapt into her throat with sudden terror.

An elf! she thought frantically. *Oh, lord save me, I'm dancing with an elf!*

"Have I insulted you, Miss Euphemia?" Lord Blackthorn asked. "Oh, that wasn't my intention at all! You see, I have been investigating English virtue of late. I thought that it was all to do with fine boots and expensive jackets – quite tedious, I think you'll agree? – but Lady Hollowvale informed me that it was really to do with being kind to the powerless and cruel to the powerful. And so I have been searching all over for one or the other, so that I might test the concept!"

Effie widened her eyes. "I'm not powerful at all, sir!" she hastened to assure him. "Quite powerless, me!"

Lord Blackthorn laughed with pleasure. "How fortuitous!" he said. "I wondered how long I might need to search – but here you are! In my very backyard, as it were." He spun Effie about, but she couldn't bring herself to take his hand again. Instead, she tumbled into the mud, whimpering with fear.

Cold, wet muck coated Effie's hands and soaked through the knees of her skirt. Under other circumstances, she would have been horrified, knowing that it meant extra laundry. But the terror of her current situation far outweighed even that of an extra, dreaded laundry day. Effie's mother had told her many cautionary tales about the Fair Folk; almost every one of those stories ended quite terribly for the hapless baker or shoemaker or milkmaid who happened to meet a faerie. In fact, many of them ended with the poor protagonist accidentally giving away their very soul.

Lord Blackthorn laughed as though Effie had intentionally flung herself into the mud as some sort of joke. He offered out his hand, but she simply stared up at him from the muddy ground. At her continued silence, he reached down to haul her up by the arms with an unnerving sort of strength, setting her back onto her feet and brushing delicately at the mud on her gown. This, of course, did little to clean the fabric.

"Oh, excellent!" Lord Blackthorn observed. "You have stained your gown! Surely this is a terrible inconvenience. Would you like my help to clean it?"

Effie pressed her lips together helplessly. *People in faerie tales get most into trouble when they say the wrong thing*, she thought. *Perhaps I can just say nothing at all, and he will leave.*

Lord Blackthorn blinked his too-green eyes. "Have you hurt yourself as well?" he asked. "I fear I cannot heal you. Such power is beyond me. But –" He pounded one gloved fist into his hand in sudden inspiration. "– I could remove whichever limb concerns you and replace it with a new one!"

Effie widened her eyes in abject horror. "No!" she cried out, before she could stop herself. "No, no, no, that's ... too generous! Please don't even think of it!"

Lord Blackthorn blinked at this. "But it isn't generous at all," he said. "I would have to ask for some kind of payment in return, no matter how much I might wish it otherwise. I fear that is simply how faeries must do things."

Effie forced a shaky smile at this, kneading her fingers into her palms. "I'm quite poor," she said. "Couldn't pay you even if I wanted to, Your Lordship. I'm afraid you'll just have to find someone else to help."

Lord Blackthorn frowned thoughtfully. "I do not require money," he said. "I could take your happiest memory, perhaps – or else some small part of your name. Really, you would barely miss a syllable or two."

Lord, Effie prayed silently. *Just let me be safely rid of this faerie, and I'll tithe extra to the collection plate this Sunday.* "That's so nice of you," she said, very slowly. "But I prefer to solve my own problems. My mum always told me it builds character."

Lord Blackthorn looked so deeply crestfallen at this that Effie almost felt bad for him. "I was so sure that this would work out perfectly," he sighed. "I was convinced that you had some awful problem that I might solve. But ... " His eyes turned curious. "If I might ask – what *were* you crying about, Miss Euphemia?"

Effie swallowed. She was sure that nothing good could come of telling a faerie about her troubles. But those strange green eyes fixed upon her, and the words rose up into her throat, spilling free without her permission. "I fell in love with someone," Effie said hoarsely. "It was awful stupid of me. An' I was reminded tonight that he can't ever love me back."

Effie cursed her mouth for running ahead without her. *I didn't mean to say any of that!* she thought. *Has he done something magical to me already?*

"How terrible," Lord Blackthorn sighed – though he said it in such a way that Effie wasn't sure if he was pleased or sympathetic. "But why can he not love you back, Miss Euphemia? You seem like a perfectly lovely human being. You have a full soul of your very own, and all of your original fingers!"

Once again, Effie tried to keep her silence – but Lord Blackthorn had lingered oddly on the syllables of her name, and the sound of that name tugged at Effie's very soul, forcing a brand-new answer from her lips.

"He's the son of a baron, Your Lordship," Effie blurted out. "An' I'm just a maid. No baron's son will ever marry a maid. It just isn't done." Lord Blackthorn looked terribly perplexed by this, so Effie added, "It'd be like ... like you givin' me a favour without me payin' you."

This addition brought the light of understanding into the faerie's eyes, and he nodded sagely. "I see," Lord Blackthorn said. "Ah, what a problem. What a *remarkable* problem!" He smiled brightly. "Precisely the sort of problem which requires the most remarkable help!"

"I don't think there's any help to be had there," Effie said warily. "Really, it's fine. I'm feelin' better about it already, Your Lordship."

Lord Blackthorn shook his head at her. "But the matter is simple!" he said. "Tell me, Miss Euphemia – who would a baron's son normally marry?"

Again, Effie felt the overwhelming need to reply. She pressed her lips together, fiercely concentrating to prevent herself from responding ... but the words burst out of her all the same. "He'd marry someone like him, Your Lordship," she said in a breathless rush. "Maybe a baron's daughter, or – oh, *bother!*"

It was her name, Effie realised miserably. She had given the dratted faerie her name, before recognising him for what he was. Dimly, Effie seemed to remember that faeries could do terrible things with one's name. *I've already gone and said the wrong thing*, Effie thought with a rising dread. *But how unfair that is! I had no way of knowing what he was at first!*

Lord Blackthorn smiled at her response. "What a relief!" he said. "Well, that is no trouble at all, Miss Euphemia. I can simply turn you into a baron's daughter, and you shall marry the man you love!"

Effie shut her mouth abruptly, with a loud *clack* of teeth.

For just a moment, all of her fear – all of her wet, muddy misery – evaporated at the touch of that unexpected suggestion.

"You ... you could do that?" Effie whispered. This time, she knew, it was not the mention of her name which made her speak.

"I could indeed," Lord Blackthorn said. His eagerness was painfully apparent, now that he had found something that truly seemed to pique her interest. He reached out to take her hand, patting it fondly. "I could make you any sort of English noblewoman you liked – for all of those purposes which matter to your situation, I mean to say. Why, I could do it right now! Would you like to go to that very ball behind us and dance?"

Effie's mouth went dry. Her throat nearly closed up again with tears. She jerked her hand back from the faerie, pressing it desperately to her chest.

Just minutes earlier, Effie had stood in the passages beneath that ballroom, dreaming that exact, impossible dream. All of those visions now came rushing back to her in an instant – brighter and more alluring than ever before. But this time, the dream was close enough to touch. All she would have to do is say *yes*, and she could walk into Hartfield as an equal rather than as a servant.

Yes. Yes, please. The words were on her tongue. But Effie noticed the surge of wobbly emotion that came with them just in time, and she closed her eyes fiercely.

"*If wishes were horses,*" she recited softly, "*beggars would ride. If turnips were bayonets, I would wear one by my side.*"

Effie opened her eyes and found Lord Blackthorn watching her with a puzzled expression. He was still close enough that the scent of fresh roses came to her with every breath. "I don't understand, Miss Euphemia," he said. "Are you making a wish?"

"No," Effie said softly. "I'm remindin' myself that it's no good to wish." She wrapped her arms around herself. "I fear I must go back inside, Your Lordship. I'm supposed to be workin' at that ball. If I linger here too long, then other people will have to do my work, an' that's not fair.".

Lord Blackthorn knit his brow in obvious consternation. "I see," he sighed. "Helping the powerless is much more difficult than I had first imagined. I should not wonder that English virtue is so rare, I suppose!" He smiled gently at Effie, as though he had understood something very different than she had meant to say. "It's no matter! I shall not give up right from the beginning, Miss Euphemia. Since you have been kind enough to give me your name, I shall give you mine in return. My true name is Juniper Jubilee. If you should ever need the slightest thing – anything at all! – then all you need do is say that name three times, and I shall be back to help you at once."

Effie couldn't help but blink at this. "Juniper Jubilee?" she repeated, before she could stop herself. "What a strange name!"

Lord Blackthorn – or rather, Effie thought, *Mr Jubilee* – merely beamed at her as though she had given him a compliment. "Why, thank you, Miss Euphemia," he said. "I chose the name myself. I am still quite fond of it."

Effie shook her head slowly. "Er, well ... Mr Jubilee," she managed. "You really don't mind that I have to go back an' work? You won't be offended, I mean to say?"

Lord Blackthorn smiled again. "How should I be offended?" he asked. "You have given me your valuable time and conversation, Miss Euphemia. And you were even kind enough to dance with me."

Effie shrank beneath his unearthly green eyes. If any human being had addressed her in this way, she might have been flattered. But there was something about those eyes that reminded her just how dangerous every word of this conversation could be. She averted her gaze uncomfortably towards the ground.

"I'll . . . I'll be goin' then, Your Lordship," Effie said.

But when she looked up again, the elf was already gone.

Chapter Two

$\mathscr{I}$f not for the mud still on her skirts, Effie might have convinced herself that her entire encounter with Lord Blackthorn had been a daydream. In truth, she still wondered whether she had hit her head or started hallucinating from weariness – but she had no chance to remark upon the meeting to Lydia either way. The moment that Effie returned indoors, she was forced to borrow a spare frock from one of the other maids so that she could rush back into the ball to wait on the guests. The rest of the evening was so breathlessly long and tiring that none of them had the time to speak of much, other than punch glasses and courses for supper and the need to find room at the table for someone's inconvenient extra cousin.

By the time Effie finally fell into bed, all thoughts of strange elves had utterly fled her mind. She woke up only a few hours later, as Lydia moaned about the fireplaces. Even the morning after a ball, there was *always* the fireplaces.

"She's goin' to kill us," Lydia mumbled, as they both lurched their way back upstairs to light the hearths. "Lady Culver, I mean. This can't go on for ever, Effie."

"Let's not waste breath complainin'," Effie begged. "I'm so tired today, I don't think I have the energy for it."

Today, at least, the servants below-stairs had the chance to settle down to breakfast, as the Family was all abed sleeping in. But even breakfast came with its own miserable, extra surprise.

"Lady Panovar made mention of her French maid about a dozen times last night," Mrs Sedgewick informed the staff tiredly. "Lady Culver ended the night in a fury. She has insisted that I should find her some French maids at once."

Lydia's mouth dropped open. "What?" she laughed. "Just like that? An' at *her* wages? Aren't French maids rather dear?"

It was a sign of how very exhausted they all were that Mrs Sedgewick did not upbraid Lydia for her impertinence. The housekeeper normally insisted that the staff show strict respect for the Family, even when outside of earshot. "Obviously, there are no French maids to be had in the area, and Her Ladyship hasn't the budget to import one like Lady Panovar," Mrs Sedgewick sighed. "And so, to sum the matter up – you shall all need to *become* French maids."

Effie blinked slowly. "Mrs Sedgewick," she said carefully. "I don't mean to be pert, but ... what does that mean, exactly?"

Mrs Sedgewick shot Effie a tight smile. "It means that you shall need new French names," she said. "At least when you are above-stairs. And you will need to practise a French accent."

"Er," George spoke up, with a slight cough. "Not the footmen, too?"

"No," Mrs Sedgewick said long-sufferingly. "Lady Panovar does not have any French footmen as far as I know, and so Lady Culver does not require any French footmen herself. You may remain English for the moment, George."

"Not," Mr Allen added sharply, "that either Lady Culver *or* Mrs Sedgewick has any say in the matter of footmen, George." The esteemed butler stood off to one side, waiting patiently for Mrs Sedgewick to finish her announcement so that the upper servants might retire to a different room for *their* breakfast. His coat was somehow immaculate in spite of the long evening they'd all had, and his steel-grey moustache was neatly

trimmed. Truly, Effie thought, Mr Allen was every bit the marvellous professional that he had been made out to be upon his
arrival at Hartfield.

Mrs Sedgewick glared openly at Mr Allen, but she did not
contradict him for the moment. "Lydia ... I suppose you shall
be 'Marie'. And Effie – er, let us say you are now 'Giselle'."

Effie sucked in her breath. Somehow the casual name
change felt even more offensive than the entirety of yesterday's
miserable ball. *And just like that*, she thought blearily, *I am suddenly not even allowed to be myself.*

George must have caught the look in Effie's eyes, for he
made a sympathetic face. "The Family still calls me 'James',"
he offered. "I think he was the last footman?"

"We never had a James," Lydia observed glumly. "It's just
what the Family prefers to call footmen. None of them actually
know any of our names. I doubt Lady Culver will remember the
new French names, either."

"*Nevertheless*," Mrs Sedgewick interjected sharply. "I shall
need you to practise your French accent. Do not forget. I will
be testing all of the maids at the end of the week."

Groans went up along the table, but Mrs Sedgewick did not
bother to upbraid the girls. Instead, she turned towards Mr
Allen with a deep scowl and stormed back through the door to
retreat to her own breakfast.

"Practise a French accent," Lydia mumbled at her plate in a
disbelieving tone. "Do *you* know what a French accent sounds
like, Effie?"

"I think I've heard Lady Culver say a few French words
once or twice," Effie muttered back. "You got 'tendre' from her,
didn't you?"

Lydia narrowed her eyes. "One of the gents at the ball started
yellin' in French when he spilled his punch," she said darkly.
"Maybe I'll practise some of *those* words."

Effie didn't reply to this. She knew that Lydia was merely

venting her frustrations – none of them would *really* dare to curse in front of Lady Culver, no matter how upset they were. As she glanced away uncomfortably, however, her eyes came to rest on a tall, prim figure standing near the door to the servants' hall.

Effie froze in horror.

Lord Blackthorn currently watched the gathered servants with a marvellously curious expression on his face. Effie had no idea just when the faerie had appeared – but while he stood out like a sore thumb among the servants, with his fine velvet jacket and his bright green eyes, no one else in the room seemed to pay him any mind at all.

"Lydia?" Effie whispered tremulously. "Do you see that man near the door?"

Lydia turned her head and pursed her lips. "Oh yes, him," she said, as though there were nothing unusual about the elf's presence whatsoever. "What about him, Effie?"

Effie blinked very quickly, trying to square the ridiculousness of the situation with her own expectations. "Well, he – isn't he odd?" Effie insisted. "Look at him again, Lydia! He's got a rose wrapped around his throat!"

Lydia knit her brow. For just a moment, concern flickered across her features ... but it soon smoothed away again into a dazed distraction. "So he does," she said. "Isn't that somethin'?"

Lydia turned back to her food then, and seemed promptly to forget the entire conversation.

"Miss Euphemia!" Lord Blackthorn had caught Effie looking his way, and now he headed over towards her with his usual delighted gait. His bright green eyes sparkled with cheer. "What a lovely morning it is outside! It is very sunny out, you know." He paused, then frowned thoughtfully. "Oh dear! I keep forgetting that English conversation is not always about the weather. Shall we talk of dolphins instead?"

Effie glanced around herself helplessly, searching for anyone who might come to her aid. But, just like Lydia, all of the other servants had entirely lost interest in the elf in front of them. Effie turned back towards Lord Blackthorn with a helpless, terrified sinking in her stomach.

"I thought you'd left, Your Lordship," Effie offered tremulously. She wasn't at all sure how to answer his question about dolphins, and so she swept right past it.

"But why should I leave, Miss Euphemia?" Lord Blackthorn asked Effie. He sounded utterly bewildered now. "Surely you cannot think that I would abandon you while you are in distress! That would not be very virtuous of me at all!"

Effie's stomach dropped all the way to her feet. As exhausted as she had been this morning, she had managed to forget all about her encounter with the elf. And wasn't that arrogant of her! Effie had somehow convinced herself that she had cleverly avoided the faerie's attention for ever, unlike those *other* foolish women in her mother's faerie tales.

"That is ... so thoughtful of you, my lord," Effie said desperately. "But really, I insist. You're an important, er ... elf, obviously. I can't be takin' you from your duties like this."

Lord Blackthorn pressed one gloved hand to his chest. "How noble you are!" he cried. "How humble! Why, you only make me more certain of my choice by the second, Miss Euphemia. Truly, you deserve so much better than your current circumstances!"

Effie sank down into her chair, pressing her face into her hands.

"But what is the matter?" Lord Blackthorn asked her. "Now you are upset again! Is it about the French, Miss Euphemia? I could teach you French in a moment, you know. I would be only too happy to do so."

"N-no," Effie whimpered. "That's all right, Your Lordship. I really ought to learn the French on my own."

"You are very tired-looking," Lord Blackthorn mused. "Has

your sleep been restless? I could help you fall asleep, for certain. How long do you think would be best? I think at least a year is traditional—"

Effie sprang up from her chair. "I have chores I really ought to get to!" she blurted out. "Lots of sweepin' to do, after that big ball!"

Lord Blackthorn blinked at her. "But you have not yet finished your breakfast, Miss Euphemia," he pointed out.

Effie blanched. "I'm . . . not hungry," she lied. She glanced sideways at her breakfast. It was only bread and porridge, mixed with a bit of the leftover ham from the previous evening's ball, but her poor stomach still gurgled plaintively as she thought of leaving it behind. Effie quietly promised herself that she would later sneak down to the kitchens for a snack, once she was safely free of the elf. "Er, why don't *you* have it?" she added on inspiration. Surely, faeries also ate food, didn't they? Perhaps if Lord Blackthorn sat down to eat, he would stay out of Effie's hair for at least a few minutes.

Lord Blackthorn rubbed thoughtfully at his chin. "Are you sure?" he asked her. "You really wish to give me your breakfast, Miss Euphemia?"

There was an odd undertone to his voice as he asked the question, but Effie simply didn't have the energy to parse it. "Yes," she sighed. "Yes, I'm sure. Please have a seat, Your Lordship." She gestured obligingly towards her empty chair.

To Effie's great relief, Lord Blackthorn sat down in her place, still looking thoughtful. "How generous!" he murmured. "Is this what all English maids are like?"

Lydia turned to look at him. "Well, hello!" she said. "Where'd you come from, *monsieur?*" Effie winced at Lydia's half-hearted attempt at a French accent. *Oh, we are never going to be believable*, she thought.

"I come from Blackthorn, of course!" the elf replied cheerfully. "And what is *your* name, young lady?"

Effie widened her eyes at the question. She snatched at

Lydia's arm, hauling her up bodily from her seat before she could respond. "I'll need your help, Lydia!" she gasped. "With all of the ... sweepin'!"

Lydia's mouth dropped open. "What?" she asked incredulously. "But – my breakfast—"

"We've already had enough to eat," Effie hissed to her. "You ought to give His Lordship your breakfast too, Lydia. He's very distinguished company, after all."

Lydia narrowed her eyes – but Effie pinched her side, and she yelped. "Oh, all right!" Lydia huffed. "Take my breakfast too, why don't you?"

Lord Blackthorn stared at them both, looking suddenly overwhelmed. "Must I?" he asked. "Well ... I suppose I must, if you insist."

Effie forced a smile his way, even as she began to drag Lydia towards the door. "Do take your time!" she said.

As soon as they had cleared the door and hurried out into the hallway, Lydia pried her arm free of Effie's grip. "What *is* the matter with you, Effie?" she demanded. "I only got a few bites, and I know you did the same!"

"Did you not see *anything* odd about that man you were just talkin' to?" Effie asked in despair. "His ears are pointed, Lydia! His eyes are strange! I told you before that he was wearin' a rose around his neck, an' it barely seemed to faze you!"

Lydia frowned. This time, however, Effie's words seemed to penetrate somewhat. "I feel like ... like I would have noticed somethin' like that," Lydia said dubiously. But she suddenly seemed less certain of herself than she had been before. "He did come out of nowhere, didn't he? An' I realise now that I don't even know his name."

"He's an elf!" Effie moaned. "I talked to him last night, Lydia. I'm such a fool – I thought he'd gone for good, but he's clearly still here! Whatever you do, you mustn't give him your name or make any deals with him!"

Lydia pressed her fingers to her forehead. "But are you sure?" she mumbled. "Do elves really wander into the servants' hall an' eat people's breakfasts? That seems like such a funny thing to happen."

"Well, hopefully he will take at least a *little* bit to eat our breakfasts," Effie breathed. "I'm not even sure what to do, Lydia. Do we ... do we go an' tell Mrs Sedgewick? Or maybe Mr Allen – he's from the city, isn't he? Surely he ought to know somethin' about dealin' with faeries!"

Lydia shot Effie a sceptical look. "I don't know that even Mr Allen will have dealt with faeries before," she said. "But you're right – we really ought to say *something*."

Effie started heading down the hallway towards Mrs Sedgewick's quarters, where she knew the upper servants would be taking their breakfast. Lydia followed after her, though she dragged her feet reluctantly as they went.

Neither of them particularly wanted to knock at Mrs Sedgewick's door. But Effie knew that it was *her* trouble at issue, and so she forced herself to rap her knuckles there very loudly.

Mrs Sedgewick's wooden soles clip-clopped towards the door. Presently, the housekeeper opened the door, looking tired and peeved. "This had better be an emergency, or else I – oh! Effie!" Mrs Sedgewick's combative tone softened somewhat. "Is something the matter?"

Effie stared at the housekeeper for a moment, speechless. It had seemed only natural to tell the housekeeper about the faerie in their midst, but now that Effie was standing before her, she wasn't sure just *how* to phrase the problem. *I cannot just say, "There is a faerie in the servants' hall eating my breakfast"*, she thought in a panic.

Unfortunately, Effie's tired mind had run away with her, and so she did indeed say, "There's a faerie in the servants' hall eatin' my breakfast, Mrs Sedgewick."

Mrs Sedgewick blinked. Somewhere behind her, Effie

heard the clatter of plates as the rest of the upper servants ate their food.

"Effie," Mrs Sedgewick said slowly. "I do not know what on earth is going on with you. You normally have such a steady head on your shoulders. Surely you haven't let one of the other servants bait you into a silly dare?" Mrs Sedgewick glanced suspiciously at Lydia, who normally *would* have done something of the sort.

"N-no, Mrs Sedgewick!" Effie said desperately. "Oh, I've said it all wrong. But I really mean it, Mrs Sedgewick: there *is* a faerie, and he's goin' to cause all sorts of trouble—"

"We are all very *tired*, Effie!" Mrs Sedgewick said. This time, there was a hint of ice in her voice. "I have neither the time nor the energy to deal with this silliness. Now, I do not want to hear another word on the subject, do you understand me?"

Effie stared at the housekeeper helplessly. She turned to give Lydia a pleading look.

"There ... *is* a faerie, Mrs Sedgewick," Lydia said, though Effie knew that she still didn't entirely believe the words. "He asked me my name, an' everything."

"I *said* not another word!" Mrs Sedgewick snapped. "Not from either of you! And if you persist in this foolish prank, girls, then I will have you in the scullery every day for the next week, so help me!"

Mrs Sedgewick did not give them a chance to respond this time. Rather, she slammed the door shut with a dread sense of finality which made Effie weak in the knees.

"I guess we should've expected that," Lydia sighed. She turned towards Effie. "You don't think we might ignore the faerie an' he'll just ... go away?"

Effie shook her head mournfully. "I thought he'd gone last night," she said. "But then he showed up this morning, an' now nothin' I say can convince him to leave!"

"Well ..." Lydia wrinkled up her nose. "Maybe he's a

helpful faerie? He could be one of those that mends shoes or spins thread."

Effie shook her head despairingly. "No, not at all," she said. "He's a *lord*, Lydia. They're always the worst of the bunch, castin' curses on people an' trickin' them out of their souls!"

Lydia grimaced. "Normal lords is bad enough," she muttered. "*Faerie* lords must be somethin' else entirely." She pursed her lips. "But who else are we supposed to tell? I'm fair certain Mrs Sedgewick would have us whipped if we tried to spin a story for Lady Culver."

Effie rubbed at her face. Mrs Sedgewick was right about one thing: they were all *far* too tired to be dealing with faeries right now. "I don't know," she admitted. "George would just laugh in my face, I'm sure. Oh, this is awful. I . . . I guess I might write to my mum? She does know all of those faerie tales, so maybe she'll know how to keep him out."

Lydia nodded. "Yes, ask your mum," she said. "I'll talk to Cookie, too. She once told me all the herbs to use for a love spell, so she might have a plant to set a faerie straight." Lydia frowned worriedly. "We really do have to get to chores though, Effie, or we won't be workin' here much longer either way."

Effie wilted on her feet at the very thought. "Why must all of this be happenin' at once?" she murmured to herself. "Surely I didn't do somethin' terrible enough to deserve this?"

"What was that?" Lydia asked her, halfway through a yawn.

Effie flinched. "I . . . nothing," she sighed. "I was mutterin' nursery rhymes again."

"You do that at the oddest times," Lydia mumbled.

They walked themselves wearily up the stairs towards the green baize door, searching out the brooms as they went.

But when they came out into the house's front entryway, there was not a single mote of dust to be found. In fact . . . it was already perfectly clean.

"Oh no," Effie said.

"Oh, thank God!" Lydia said.

The entryway ought to have been full of mud and dust from all of those guests trudging in and out of the weather in their booted feet. Effie had noted the awful mess as she'd passed it that morning to tend to the fireplaces.

But the front entryway currently looked as clean as the day it had first been built. All of the floorboards had been scrubbed spick and span – someone had even cast a brand-new layer of sand over it all to finish it off! All of the other surfaces in the entryway had been carefully dusted; the lamp wicks were neatly trimmed; the curtains had been beaten!

"This is a disaster," Effie groaned. "But how did he do it, Lydia? We never made a deal with him! I certainly never promised him anything!"

A broad smile crept over Lydia's face. "Oh, what's it matter, Effie?" she asked. "It's done! All that awful mess from the ball, just magicked away!" Lydia's eyes widened, and she hurried towards the ballroom. There, she threw open the doors and laughed with delight. "Look, Effie! The ballroom's clean, too! We might even have time for a nap, if everythin' is this way!"

"You're not listenin'!" Effie told Lydia. She glanced past the other maid into the ballroom, and her heart sank even further towards her knees. The mirrors had all been cleaned and stashed away somewhere else. It all looked just as it had before they'd set up for the ball at all. "There's goin' to be a *price*, Lydia," Effie said. "An' what will a faerie make us pay for all of this?"

"I don't care, not one whit!" Lydia declared. "I'm goin' back to bed, Effie. I feel like I could fall asleep on my feet."

Effie knew she ought to go after Lydia, as the other maid danced away with her broom in her arms. But she found herself stuck staring into the empty ballroom instead, frozen with an unspeakable dread.

Chapter Three

There was little recourse; Effie could no more undo the cleaning than she could unmeet the elf who had happened upon her. Rather than dwell upon the matter, she went down to the kitchen to beg for some food – and then, with absolute resignation, she took her muddied gown to the scullery to wash it clean.

Thankfully, as it was just one gown and one shift, Effie had only to fetch and boil enough water for one tub. But since the gown was one of Lady Culver's old things, it had some lace at the neckline. This meant that Effie had to unpick the lace and remove it from the collar before she dared to scrub the rest with lye soap. The scullery maid, Alice, complained incessantly about the smell as Effie worked, but Effie knew that she was secretly glad of the company.

Just as Effie finished wringing out as much water as she could from the damp gown, Mrs Sedgewick came clip-clopping down the short stairs of the scullery. "Effie!" the housekeeper said sharply. "There is company. Lady Culver will need you to wait upon her and some guests for tea."

Effie blinked. "Er ..." she started. She had nearly protested that her best gown was still in pieces ... but after Mrs Sedgewick's stern lecture that morning, Effie suspected that this would only gain her another reprimand. "Might I bring this up with me to sew it back together?" she asked instead very carefully.

Mrs Sedgewick had already turned her back to leave the scullery. It was clear that her morning had become much busier. "Yes, fine!" Mrs Sedgewick said. "As long as you keep your eye on the tea. And remember, you are 'Giselle' from now on. I have told Lady Culver, and she has approved the name, so you must not forget."

Effie covered a wince. "Yes, Mrs Sedgewick," she said, as she gathered up her damp gown.

"That is '*Oui*, Mrs Sedgewick'," the housekeeper corrected Effie, in a stilted accent that did not sound French at all.

Effie did not respond again, since she did not trust that she could say it correctly either.

Lady Culver had decided to take tea in the Blue Room that morning – she had three different morning rooms at Hartfield, and so it was always necessary to specify which one. Effie stopped by the kitchen to make a fresh pot of tea, stacking it onto a tray along with the good silver, which Mr Allen had already been kind enough to fetch. "Lady Culver is visiting with her friend Miss Buckley," Mr Allen informed Effie brusquely, as they both exited the kitchen. "They are on very good terms, and so Lady Culver will desire everything to be at its best."

"I swear, I don't know how you keep track of it all, Mr Allen!" Effie marvelled. "I thought you'd be most concerned with Lord Culver's affairs."

"All of the Family's well-being is my affair, Euphemia," Mr Allen informed her in a grave, professional tone. "Only very foolish men in my position presume otherwise."

Mrs Sedgewick thinks that you are meddling in her *position, though*, Effie thought. Thankfully, Mr Allen was already

heading off in the opposite direction before the words could
spill from her tired lips. Effie sighed, and hoisted the tea tray a
bit higher. She dared to peer into the servants' hall on the way
to the stairs ... but it was utterly empty, and especially devoid
of any faeries.

For just a moment, Effie wondered if she'd imagined the
entire morning. But there was no time to dwell upon it.

Lady Culver was only just settling down into the Blue Room
with her guest when Effie headed inside with the tea. The
young, blonde woman in question *did* seem familiar, and Effie
was sure that she'd seen Miss Buckley before, at least in passing; had she been at the ball just the evening before, wearing a
blue gown? As Effie passed the door frame, however, she was
jolted from her surreptitious study of the room by the realisation
that the youngest male Ashbrooke had stopped by to join the
gathering.

Benedict was clearly dressed for the outdoors, in a green
wool coat and buckskin breeches. There was a dashing,
breathless air to him – somehow, Benedict's brown hair already
looked wind-tossed, though Effie was sure that he had yet to
step outside.

"We're just going out for a ride," Benedict was saying to Lady
Culver. "I hardly think you should change your plans for *us*.
Besides, you know how roughly Thomas likes to ride. I'd worry
that one of you ladies might take a fall."

"You are so thoughtful, Benedict," Lady Culver said. There
was a sweetness to her tone that had not been there only the
day before. "We shall spare you the worry, then ... but you *must*
promise that you will join us for tea when you return. You only
danced once with Miss Buckley last night, and I had so hoped
to introduce you better."

If Benedict was at all fazed by Lady Culver's sudden amiabil-
ity, the emotion did not show in his smile. "If you are still here
when we return, then I certainly shall," he promised. "Though

please do not wait too long on my account." Benedict nodded towards the other woman. "Miss Buckley," he said, in a polite dismissal.

And then, Benedict turned towards Effie.

His warm brown eyes met hers. He smiled in such a broad, friendly manner that Effie nearly looked to see if one of his brothers had come up the stairs behind her. But surely she would have heard their heavy footfalls if that was the case.

"And goodbye to you too," Benedict added, with a hint of humour. "Miss ... I really must get your name, mustn't I?"

Effie's heart skipped a beat; she flushed deeply. "Er," she said eloquently.

"Her name is Francesca!" Lady Culver informed Benedict, before Effie could answer for herself. There was an unmistakable irritation in the lady's tone now. "She is French, Benedict. She probably has no idea what you are saying. Now, have mercy and leave her be."

Effie dropped her mouth open before she could catch herself. Mostly, she realised, it was the pure indignity of it all. Lady Culver knew quite well that Benedict had said hello to Effie on his entrance to the house – all three of them were therefore aware that Effie was *not* a French maid. But Lady Culver was the matron of the household, and it would not do for Benedict to call her a liar, no matter how patently ridiculous the whole situation was.

Benedict's smile turned rueful, and Effie was sure that he had angled himself so that Lady Culver could not see the shocked look on Effie's face. "Of course," he said. "She does have that refined French look about her, doesn't she?" Benedict inclined his head towards Effie. "*Pardonnez-moi, mademoiselle.*"

He had a far better French accent than Lady Culver did.

Effie did not trust herself to attempt a French reply. She nodded silently, sidestepping out of his way as he headed for the hallway.

"Would you be quick with the tea, Francesca?" Lady Culver asked sharply.

Effie quickened her steps, setting down the tray and arranging the table for them.

I'm quite sure I'm supposed to be Giselle, Effie thought. Lady Culver had clearly forgotten which silly French name Effie had been assigned, and had simply made up a new one on the spot. *Francesca must be the least creative French name I have ever heard.* Effie swallowed the words, along with her growing fury and misery. It would not do to get angry.

Thankfully, Lady Culver was far more preoccupied with her guest than she was with her servant. The lady quickly forgot Effie's presence entirely, turning towards Miss Buckley as though Effie were invisible.

"I know that I promised to make arrangements for you with Benedict," Lady Culver sighed, "but you see what I mean about him? He is simply ridiculous, even at the best of times. If I weren't here to keep him in line, I swear he would gossip with every maid in this household!"

Effie slunk over towards a chair near the wall, pulling the pieces of her gown from her side bag and searching out a needle and thread. Sewing the lace back onto wet material was hardly ideal – but Effie had waxed the thread, at least, and so she hoped that she might have the gown back in working order by the end of tea, if she was very deliberate about her stitching.

"Oh, surely Mr Benedict isn't as bad as all that," Miss Buckley remarked to Lady Culver cheerfully, as she picked up her teacup. "He has a sense of humour, is all."

"I do not exaggerate, Mary!" Lady Culver huffed. "Not a second after Benedict entered this house for the first time, he was talking with *another* maid! Before he'd even said so much as hello to his own brother!"

Effie pricked at her thumb with the needle. She stifled the resulting gasp – something halfway between pain and fury. *She really doesn't remember who I am!* she thought. Lady Culver had not even identified that Effie was the same maid who had been scrubbing her muddy entryway only two days prior. And now – the nerve! – the lady was going to continue talking about Effie as though she were not sitting right there in the corner, forced to listen to every word.

Do not get angry, Effie reminded herself. She had to grit her teeth against the emotion that choked her throat, however. Effie could not recite English rhymes in front of Lady Culver's guest if she were to be a French maid – but there was stitching in her lap, at least, and so she focused herself upon it with renewed fervour.

"I believe you," Miss Buckley laughed. "But what of it? Are you not taking this a bit far, Eleanor? I know you have always been very serious about etiquette, but men must be permitted *some* allowances. They are all boors to some extent or another."

Lady Culver's tone darkened. "Well, this *is* quite serious, Mary," she replied. "Benedict dallied for quite some time in Venice during his tour – and I assume we both know what *that* means." She paused. "Are you certain that you still wish me to arrange things between you? I will do it, of course. I would much prefer to have you as a sister. But I cannot help but wonder if you will be miserable with the man."

Effie clenched her teeth, focusing ever more keenly upon the gown in her lap. She imagined her anger as part of the thread in her needle: with each careful motion, Effie imagined that anger leaving her body, stowing itself within the stitches of the gown where it could not bother her any longer.

"Oh, why should I worry either way?" Miss Buckley asked. "Mr Benedict has a sizeable portion to his name. He is young and charming, and if I marry him, I shall get to see you more often. I cannot imagine that a better prospect shall come along. I am quite content with the matter, even if he were the worst scoundrel in the world. It's not as though I must love him, is it?"

Effie listened to all of this with a sense of weary misery. Her anger *had* drained away, now that she had soothed herself with a bit of sewing – but without it, she was merely tired again.

What awful accident of birth had led her to this point – sitting in the corner of another woman's morning room, sewing another woman's damp hand-me-down gown together, while better people discussed the man she loved in such an awful, mercenary manner?

And what will I do about it? Effie wondered dully. *There is nothing that I can do about it. I am a maid. The best that I shall ever be is a housekeeper, perhaps. At least I will be able to keep my own silk gown in good condition.*

Lady Culver and Miss Buckley chatted so long over tea that Effie had to refill the pot twice more. Their conversation ranged over a plethora of woeful topics, from the boredom of country life to the difficulty of finding good help. Effie numbed herself to it with her stitching – and at the very least, she had a whole gown once again by the end of the visit.

Benedict did not return in time to say goodbye to Miss Buckley. Effie vaguely hoped that he was as smart as he seemed, and that he had spotted the trap for what it was.

Once Miss Buckley had left, Lady Culver returned to the morning room to pick up a book from the side table. Her eyes caught on the garment in Effie's arms, and she frowned. "Is that my old gown?" Lady Culver asked archly.

Effie took a careful breath. "Yes, Lady Culver," she said carefully. "You gave it to me at Christmas."

Lady Culver narrowed her eyes. "That embroidery on it is new," she said. "The leaves and the flowers. Did you add those yourself?"

Effie chewed at her lip. "Yes, Lady Culver," she said. "I enjoy embroidery."

"Well, it is not proper," Lady Culver said. "You have improved the gown too much. People will mistake you for a lady." She tucked her book into her arms and turned away. "Hand that gown back to Mrs Sedgewick. She will have to find you something less eye-catching to wear."

Before Effie could even think of a response, the lady of the house had disappeared through the doorway.

Effie stared after her in silence.

For once, her anger failed her. In its place was a cold, hollow spot in her chest.

There is nothing I can do, Effie thought again.

But . . . no.

There *was* something that she could do, wasn't there?

Just that morning, a noble elf had reminded Effie that he was very keen to be kind to the powerless. And oh – Effie was feeling *very* powerless right now.

"That is a terrible idea," Effie whispered to herself. "Mum would be horrified."

But Effie's mother had *also* told her that faeries were nothing but dangerous trouble . . . and so far, Lord Blackthorn had not brought any trouble down upon Effie's head, had he? The worst that the faerie had done was clean a few rooms. And he *did* seem so genuinely interested in helping her.

Effie looked down at the gown in her arms. She had spent an embarrassing amount of money on the silk thread she'd used to adorn it; the leaves and flowers had taken months of idle work. It was, she thought, the one pretty thing that she owned. But because of who she was – because of how powerless she was – Lady Culver had decided to take it away from her in the space of a heartbeat.

That isn't right, Effie thought suddenly. *None of this is right. Do I really deserve all of this simply because I was born in a village instead of in a manor?*

"Juniper Jubilee!" The name tumbled from Effie's lips in a scared little whisper. "Juniper Jubilee! Juniper Jubilee! I – I hope you're still here? I'd like to talk to you, if you please—"

The scent of roses flickered through the morning room. There was something both sweeter and wilder about the smell than the bouquets that Effie sometimes handled in the summer. This, she thought, was the heavy scent of an entire winding briar of roses, woody thorns and all. Soon, she became fearfully aware of the tall man now standing behind her.

"Miss Euphemia!" Lord Blackthorn greeted her, with that same ever-present delight in his voice. "What a pleasure! Oh – I do hope my payment was sufficient? I will admit, I was not sure how to match the value of two breakfasts. I am sure that the food did not cost very much *money*, but since you were both so hungry, your breakfasts must have been very dear to you indeed."

Effie knit her brow, turning upon the elf with confusion. He was smiling in his usual manner, but there was a hint of self-consciousness to the expression this time.

"I don't understand," Effie said slowly. "Are you talkin' about the entryway an' the ballroom? But I never asked you to clean anything for me."

Lord Blackthorn sighed. "Oh, mortals," he said, with a hint of fondness. "You really do not know how things are done at all, do you? You gave me a gift, Miss Euphemia, but I cannot simply accept something for nothing. I am therefore obliged to remedy the shortfall." He smiled distantly at this. "I have never had a mortal give me a gift before. What a lovely idea – giving something over without expecting anything else in return. I would love to try it for myself, but I am afraid it is beyond me."

Effie's heart softened just a bit at that, though she knew she shouldn't allow it to do so. "Well, er. As you said, Your Lordship . . . I wasn't expectin' anything in return. You really shouldn't have gone to the trouble." Against her better judgement, Effie began to wonder whether *all* lords of faerie were really so terrible. Surely, there had to be just one story about them that didn't end so awfully. And if there wasn't a story like that . . . well, perhaps hers could be the first?

"But I really *must* go to the trouble," Lord Blackthorn assured her. "I know that it is merely your kind, selfless soul that leads you to deny my help, Miss Euphemia, but it is incumbent upon me to return your gifts to you threefold. Other faeries might of course interpret this maliciously – but I have set myself in pursuit of English virtue, and I would never do such a thing!"

Effie hesitated at this. She turned herself to face him fully now. "You're sayin' that, er . . . you want to be more virtuous?" she hazarded. "You're tryin' to be a better person by helpin' others?"

Lord Blackthorn beamed at her. "Yes, precisely!" he said. "Does that not sound entertaining – to become something that you were not before? What a challenge it is! I am enjoying every moment of it so far!"

Effie pasted on a nervous smile. The oddly worded sentiment did not terribly encourage her. But as Effie thought of what her life must be like otherwise – slinking downstairs to hand her gown over to Mrs Sedgewick, and practising abominable French in between more endless balls – she knew with dreadful certainty that she could not bring herself to do it. Anything, she thought, had to be better than that.

"If I were to ask for your help," Effie said carefully, "what would that entail? Let's say . . . let's say I *did* want to marry Mr Benedict. That would have to cost me somethin', wouldn't it?"

Lord Blackthorn's expression lit up, somehow, with even further pleasure. In fact, Effie thought, one might describe him as full of . . . yes, *jubilation.* "Oh, how exciting!" he breathed. "Then you *are* asking for my help? How wonderful! You will not regret it, Miss Euphemia, I assure you!"

I already halfway regret it, Effie thought wearily. *But I suppose I mustn't say that aloud either.* "But the cost, Your Lordship?" she reminded him carefully.

"Yes, yes," Lord Blackthorn said distractedly. "I suppose we mustn't get ahead of ourselves. But I am sure that we can work out something reasonable." He had begun to pace thoughtfully now, rubbing at his chin. "I cannot simply snap my fingers and have him marry you, of course – he must do the asking himself. But I am sure that it is within my skill to encourage one foolish mortal to fall in love." The elf paused, and then nodded to himself. "I shall give you every bit of aid within my power, Miss Euphemia. You may be sure that I shall do everything I can to see it done. But there is one remaining problem! I suspect that you have little to offer me of equal worth . . . " He straightened abruptly, and his green eyes flashed with inspiration. "Aha! We shall make it a wager. A wager that you are sure to win, of course."

Effie frowned. "What ought I to be wagerin', exactly?" she asked warily.

"Oh, it hardly matters," Lord Blackthorn said, with a careless wave of his hand. "I shall be helping you to win the wager myself, after all! And isn't that clever? Why, it is *almost* like a gift that way!"

Something about this statement set Effie's teeth on edge . . . but she had come too far simply to shrink away from the idea now. "But I still need to know just what it is that I'm agreein' to," she insisted gently.

Lord Blackthorn nodded distractedly. "Well . . . let us say that you have a hundred and one days to marry the man that you love," he offered. "We will see it done, of course. But if something should go awry – and I tell you, Miss Euphemia, it is vanishingly unlikely – then I suppose that you shall simply have to come back with me to faerie and serve me as a maid instead, for the rest of your days." He laughed at this as though he had just made a joke.

Effie swallowed hard. "And that's a fair wager?" she asked. "Doesn't it seem a bit . . . lopsided?"

Lord Blackthorn frowned at that. "It *does* seem correct, doesn't it?" he observed. "You are asking to become something that you are not. If you fail, then I must somehow make you more of what you already are, mustn't I?"

Effie took a deep breath. She squared her shoulders. "I would rather serve a faerie than serve Lady Culver," she said. "Then . . . that's the deal? You'll help me marry Mr Benedict, or else I go back to faerie with you?"

"Well . . . not quite," Lord Blackthorn admitted. He looked sheepish now. "I will have to see to an *awful* lot. You will not easily become a lady, Miss Euphemia – I will need to borrow someone else's elocution for you, and find you gowns, and . . . my goodness, you will need to learn to dance a bit better, since we would not want you ending up in the mud again." His bright green eyes glanced down towards the gown in Effie's arms for some reason, and he smiled to himself. "But I know what I shall ask in return. For every minute that you are a lady, you shall add one stitch to my coat. I am sure that you can embroider something quite fetching upon it, if you set your mind to it."

Effie blinked. "You want me to embroider your coat?" she repeated, uncertain that she had heard him correctly. The idea seemed terribly tame compared to the threat of being dragged back to faerie for the rest of her days.

"Most desperately!" Lord Blackthorn assured her. "What fine work you have done on this gown! I have never seen its like before, Miss Euphemia. I was never fond of Lord Hollowvale's far-too-many jackets – but a jacket with stitching such as *that* would truly make me the envy of every faerie I know. Why . . . it is still possible to be virtuous *and* fashionable, don't you think?"

Effie smiled nervously at that. She couldn't help but be at least a *bit* gratified by the compliment. "If that's all," she said, "then I'll accept that deal, Your Lordship." Surely, Effie wouldn't need to be a lady for more than a few hours every other day – balls did not happen all the time, and she could not spend *every* day trying to catch Benedict's attention. At a hundred and one days, at perhaps a hundred stitches a night . . . that couldn't end up more than ten thousand stitches, all told.

Lord Blackthorn smiled at her. "But you have given me your name, Miss Euphemia," he said. "It is only fair for you to use my name as well – especially since we have made a bargain. You should call me Jubilee at the very least."

Effie winced at the idea. "Perhaps we could split the difference," she offered, "since I might well end up sweepin' your floors someday. I could call you Mr Jubilee?"

Lord Blackthorn laughed – not because the idea was funny, Effie thought, but because he was so pleased to have secured his bargain. "If you must," he said. The elf reached out to take Effie's hand with an exaggerated bow. He brushed his lips across the back of her skin, and she shivered involuntarily; for with that gesture, a strange and uncomfortable hook had settled deep into her soul.

"And now, between us," Lord Blackthorn declared, "we shall surely make you the most desirable lady in all of England!" He straightened with a broad smile. "If you will kindly excuse me for a time, Miss Euphemia . . . I must go and borrow you a few things."

Chapter Four

*F*or the entire rest of the day, Effie did not see Lord
Blackthorn again.

As the hours went by, she became less and less certain that
she had done the right thing by making the bargain. A hundred
and one days? It had seemed like so much more time when
Lord Blackthorn had said it out loud. But really, Effie had
barely three months to make Mr Benedict Ashbrooke fall in
love with her and propose!

Had Lord Blackthorn tricked her into accepting an impossible deal? But he had seemed so genuine on the point! *"I shall do
everything I can to see it done,"* he had said. And Effie had truly
believed that he was sincere. But then why had he disappeared
for a full day?

Effie meant to unburden her woes to Lydia when she
returned to their room that evening – but Lydia was already
fast asleep, and the moment that her own head hit the pillow,
she found herself asleep as well. When Effie woke up the
next morning – *the fireplaces!* Lydia hissed again – they
were immediately so busy that she could not get a word
in edgeways.

Today, at least, Effie managed a few decent meals – though
she found herself constantly checking the doorway to the servants' hall, worried that she might see Lord Blackthorn's tall

figure looming there. The fact that the elf did *not* appear for another full day only made her even more nervous.

Effie was further confounded when she returned to her room that evening to find Lydia perched precariously on top of a side table, hanging mistletoe above their doorway.

"What are you *doin'*, Lydia?" Effie asked, bewildered.

Lydia gasped in surprise and nearly tumbled from the table entirely. Somehow, she managed to clamber down without turning an ankle. "I talked to Cookie today," she said breathlessly. "She said mistletoe keeps away faeries, so I went out to find some!"

Effie flinched at the reminder. "Oh," she sighed. "Lydia, I've done somethin' *awful* thick-headed."

From there, Effie had little choice but to explain the situation. To her surprise, Lydia was more outraged by Lady Culver's demand about Effie's gown than she was about Effie's deal with Lord Blackthorn.

"Well, of *course* you'd ask for anyone's help after that bit o' business!" Lydia said hotly. "What an awful woman! She's got worse manners than our scullery maid – only no one ever notices cos she says it nicer! Can you imagine any one of *us* givin' a gift an' then snatchin' it back again? We'd get us a stern lecture about Christian values, you can be sure!"

"I'm upset about the gown, of course!" Effie said desperately. "But, Lydia, I've gone an' made a bargain with an *elf*!"

Lydia crossed her arms uncomfortably. "Well ... I figure what's done is done on that score," she admitted. "But we can put up more mistletoe, an' maybe he won't come for you? If he can't get in to hold up his end, then the deal goes all wrong, doesn't it?"

Effie was just contemplating the wisdom of this particular approach when there came a polite knocking at the bedroom door. She opened it a crack ... and her heart sank. Lord Blackthorn was standing on the other side with a paper-wrapped package in his arms.

"I have all sorts of ideas!" the elf informed Effie cheerfully, as though there had been no pause at all between their conversation the previous morning and their conversation now. "I do hope that you don't mind the lateness – I have been out all this time gathering the necessities, and it took me somewhat longer than expected."

Lord Blackthorn strode confidently through the doorway, as though the mistletoe hanging above it was no impediment at all.

Effie pressed her hand to her mouth. "Er," she said carefully. "Apologies, Mr Jubilee. But there's mistletoe above the door. Is that a problem for you?"

Lord Blackthorn turned to glance upwards with a bemused expression on his features. "So there is!" he said. "I appreciate your concern, Miss Euphemia, but no – mistletoe is only overprotective when it comes to children, you see, and there are no children here. If I were trying to steal an English child, however, then I would certainly be in trouble!"

Effie glanced worriedly towards Lydia – but her friend's face had once again gone distant and uninterested, and she had now settled herself upon her bed as though she were contemplating sleep.

"The household will be attending a ball tonight," Lord Blackthorn told Effie, as though Lydia were not even present. "Lord Culver told me himself on my way down to look for you. Isn't that convenient? We shall have to see that you are ready for it yourself."

"Of course the household's goin' to a ball," Effie responded dimly. "It's why we don't have to make supper – wait, you talked to Lord Culver? But didn't he see anythin' funny about some stranger walkin' around in his house?"

Lord Blackthorn chuckled. "Humans *do* react in the strangest way when I go about normally," he admitted. "But I have taken to wearing a small glamour so that they all find me horribly ordinary. It makes things so much simpler, don't you think?"

Effie glanced towards Lydia, who was now plumping her pillow and humming to herself. "But I don't seem to be affected," she said. "How does that work?"

"Oh, you have never been affected," Lord Blackthorn said. "I was very confused at first, but I think that it must have something to do with your marvellous stitching. Does it bother you? Shall I release the glamour for the moment? I should have thought to ask!"

Effie wanted to ask what on earth her stitching had to do with glamours – but she cast another sideways glance towards Lydia and decided that it was far more important to answer the elf's question. "I would appreciate that, Mr Jubilee," Effie told him carefully. "It's very strange havin' poor Lydia act as though you aren't here at all."

"As you wish, Miss Euphemia." Lord Blackthorn snapped his fingers, and the rose at his throat curled inwards just a bit.

Lydia shrieked and leapt up from her bed, staring at the elf as though she'd never seen him before.

"Quiet, Lydia!" Effie urged her quickly. "Keep it down, or else Mrs Sedgewick will put us in the scullery!"

Lydia clapped a hand over her own mouth – but she kept her eyes fixed upon Lord Blackthorn, with a terrified expression on her face.

Lord Blackthorn now offered out the paper-wrapped package to Effie, and she took it with wordless resignation. The package was far heavier than it appeared, however, and she buckled beneath its weight. Effie quickly set it down onto her bed, blinking at it in astonishment. "What on earth is this?" she asked.

"It is your gown!" Lord Blackthorn said. His tone was now a mixture of pride and self-consciousness. "I do hope that it will suffice. I know that you could sew something much grander on your own, but we only have so much time, after all."

Effie undid the knot on the package and pulled the paper back curiously. The very edge of the fabric showed, and she dropped her mouth in astonishment: the garment inside was a creamy, parchment sort of colour, with embroidery of inky-black and bright golden thread. "Are you havin' me on?" she managed. "I couldn't possibly sew anything like this!"

"I was worried that was the case," Lord Blackthorn sighed heavily. "No matter! I will go back and ask the brownies to redo it! Perhaps they will be more adept with a different material—"

"No, no!" Effie hastened to correct him. "It's beautiful, please! I meant that I couldn't sew somethin' this lovely if I tried, is all!"

Lord Blackthorn laughed with relief. "Oh, is that all?" he said. "How silly! I keep mistaking your humility, Miss Euphemia. I should know better by now, I am sure. But do not worry – this gown is merely temporary until a better one can be made."

Lydia crept her way slowly over towards the package, still watching Lord Blackthorn with a careful expression. As she came within sight of the garment inside, however, she gasped audibly. "Oh, how pretty!" she said. "What's that material, then? I've never seen it before!"

Lord Blackthorn waved a hand dismissively. "The gown is only made of dignity," he said. "There are better materials to be had, of course, but this is what the brownies had on hand. They were only too happy to rid themselves of it – they consider it quite useless, for all of the trouble that it brings."

Effie blinked uncertainly. "Er," she said. "But . . . it *is* very lovely, isn't it?"

Lord Blackthorn chuckled. "I suppose it is that," he agreed. "Which should suffice for our purposes, at least for tonight." He glanced curiously around the room then, as though searching for something. At first, Effie found herself self-conscious about

the dour, cramped state of the bedroom which she shared with
Lydia – but the furnishings did not seem to concern Lord
Blackthorn, who merely shook his head and pulled a small
glass vial from his jacket pocket. "I was going to suggest that
you should take this with tea," he advised Effie, as he pressed
the vial into her hand. "But there is no time. I fear I have little
idea how it will taste."

Effie glanced down at the vial with trepidation. It was filled
with a scintillating liquid which glowed with golden light.
"Apologies, Mr Jubilee," she said. "But what is it I'm supposed
to be drinkin'?"

"That," Lord Blackthorn said triumphantly, "is one hundred
days' worth of proper elocution! It is not a local accent, I fear,
but I believe that it should more than suffice."

Effie hesitated and glanced towards Lydia, who shook her
head minutely. But really, what was Effie to do other than
drink the strange liquid? Lord Blackthorn seemed so proud of
his acquisition, and Effie was sure that she could not win this
bizarre wager if she didn't *sound* like a noblewoman.

It's far too late to be having qualms now, Effie thought with a
sigh. She popped the cork from the vial and downed it in one
smooth swallow.

The golden liquid wasn't really liquid at all – in fact, it felt
a bit like swallowing light. Effie's throat tickled strangely, and
she coughed a few times to clear it. "That is an exceptionally
odd feeling – oh!" Effie pressed her hand over her mouth in
shock. The voice that had spoken was hers – but the words and
accent sounded suddenly much closer to something she might
hear from Lady Culver.

Lydia widened her eyes. "You're a toff, Effie!" she gasped in
delight. "Say somethin' else, quick!"

Effie floundered, oddly at a loss for something to say. Finally,
she settled on a nursery rhyme:

"Oranges and lemons,
ring the bells at Saint Clemens.
When will you pay me,
ring the bells at Old Bailey.
When I am rich,
ring the bells at Fleetditch—"

Each sentence was perfectly formed, with round vowels and an elegant lilt. Effie dissolved into elated laughter before she could continue – and even *that* was a pleasant sort of laughter, compared to her normal, snorting giggles.

"I *am* a toff!" Effie laughed, in that perfectly proper accent. "Would you just listen to that?"

"Excellent!" Lord Blackthorn said. "Everything seems to be in working order. Now, if you will only put on your gown, Miss Euphemia, we can be off before the party has gone for too long."

Lord Blackthorn stepped outside for a moment while Effie unwrapped the garment. The material was so heavy that she had to get Lydia's help just to pull it over her head – but once the gown settled somewhat, it was easier to walk about in it. There were slippers with it, but these were heavy as well, and Effie had to walk very carefully in them in order to keep her balance.

"You look like a proper princess," Lydia sighed. "Only ... your *hair*, Effie. We really have to do somethin' about it."

Effie reached up towards her hair self-consciously. She had brushed it through already, but it was still a bit tangled and ragged at the ends. There was no way they were going to be able to put it up properly in time for the ball.

"Can you stick it up with a ribbon, Lydia?" Effie asked in a small voice. "I can't see it for myself, is all."

Lydia did her best – but even as Effie stepped outside the room, she knew it wasn't enough. Her hands were rough from housework too, and the gloves she'd used to cover them were tatty at the edges.

Still, Lord Blackthorn's face lit up as he saw her, as though he had created a work of art.

"Perfect!" he crowed. "You shall woo your baron's son for certain, Miss Euphemia!" He offered out his arm, and Effie took it with more than a little bit of discomfort. The scent of roses that he carried with him should have been overwhelming up close, but it was actually quite pleasant.

"You ... you're escorting me, Mr Jubilee?" Effie asked worriedly. The sound of her perfect elocution startled her again, but she recovered herself quickly. "That really isn't done, I have to say. Most ladies show up to balls with a proper chaperone."

Lord Blackthorn's smile lost a bit of its lustre. "Of course!" he sighed. "Foolish me! It is far too late to ask for Lady Mourningwood to accompany us. I am so sorry, Miss Euphemia, I have made a mess of this first attempt – but we will make do, as I said, and the next time will be far better, I assure you!"

Lord Blackthorn turned towards the bedroom, where Lydia still stood, watching after them with horrified fascination. "Miss Euphemia requires a proper chaperone," he said gravely. "I would be most obliged if you could serve that role, miss."

Lydia widened her eyes. "Me?" she squeaked. "But I – I'm not – I *can't*."

Lord Blackthorn shook his head thoughtfully; it seemed that he was barely listening to Lydia's protests. "There is nothing to do for *your* gown – I say, what an addle-pate I am! – but I should be able to glamour you both. It will not sort out your elocution, but it will smooth away the strange edges of things. You shall simply have to be a *silent* chaperone."

Lydia backed away through the door, as though to take shelter beneath the useless mistletoe that she had hung there. "I really can't, sir," she pleaded. "I'm just a maid."

"But of course you can!" Lord Blackthorn exulted. "Why, I ask for your help *especially* because you are a maid! All of the maids that I have met have been the very best examples of

English virtue, and so I consider it a high recommendation!" He offered out his other hand to Lydia with an encouraging smile. "I do hope you will save me from my foolish mistake, miss. I will owe you a favour for the trouble, of course. I will be only too happy to pay it, in return for your kindness."

Lydia pressed her lips together at this. Her eyes were now uncertain, though Effie suspected that she was more tempted by the earnest sincerity in Lord Blackthorn's voice than by anything else.

Effie shook her head at Lydia. *This is my own foolishness,* she thought. *It's bad enough I made a deal with a faerie without dragging Lydia into it as well.* "Lydia and I are both very tired," Effie said. "And there will be the fireplaces in the morning. I appreciate your efforts, Mr Jubilee, but perhaps I could go to a later ball –"

"You've only got so much time on your wager," Lydia interrupted. "Isn't that what you said, Effie?" Her voice was small and worried. "I think . . . I ought to go. I can be your chaperone if it's just for tonight."

Effie winced. "I just don't think it's the best idea—" she started.

"How kind of you, truly!" Lord Blackthorn interrupted. "I am so pleased to have met you both. I can already tell that I will learn much of English virtue from you!"

Effie felt something wind around her wrist then, and she jumped with a gasp. When she glanced down, she saw that there was a rose vine there, quite similar to the one that Lord Blackthorn wore himself. Its thorns prickled uncomfortably at her skin as it climbed its way up her arm to coil around her neck – but the single yellow rose which blossomed there set the same wild, refreshing scent into the air that his did, and she found herself breathing its perfume in deeply.

Lydia squeaked again, and Effie knew that the other maid had been gifted a similar flower.

"There now!" Lord Blackthorn said with satisfaction. "That is as good as we shall get for tonight. Do remember not to speak this evening, miss, or people will notice that your accent is strange for a chaperone."

Lord Blackthorn took them along the servants' passageways, as though there were nothing strange at all about their departure. They came upon Mrs Sedgewick in the passages, puttering worriedly about in her silk gown, and Effie sucked in her breath with fear – but the housekeeper merely blinked at them and nodded vaguely, and they passed her without incident.

Whatever else Lord Blackthorn had forgotten, he *had* remembered to procure them a carriage. The one that awaited them outside was made of tightly woven rose vines, with blossoms peeking out from every angle. It was a bit fierce-looking, in fact, with all of its impressive thorns, but Lord Blackthorn helped them each into the carriage in a gentlemanly manner, and Effie discovered that it was perfectly comfortable inside. The cushions were all made of velvet like Lord Blackthorn's jacket, and the ride was surprisingly smooth – though Effie preferred not to dwell too much upon the fact that the carriage moved without the aid of any horses.

"Now, as to our strategy," Lord Blackthorn said, as soon as the two of them had settled inside. "I am sure that you will catch Mr Benedict's eye all on your own, Miss Euphemia – but let us be certain! I can rid us of all of the other ladies at the ball so that you are the only one left—"

Effie widened her eyes. "No!" she burst out. "No, that's ... quite all right! I would rather you didn't do anything to the other ladies, Mr Jubilee." Effie did not need to ask the faerie how exactly he intended to *rid* them of an entire room full of women – she already knew she would not like the answer.

Lord Blackthorn frowned at that. "I see," he sighed. "You would prefer a fair playing field. I do wish that you were less noble, Miss Euphemia, but I respect your desires nonetheless.

Do let me know if you change your mind – I must also practise being cruel to the powerful, and I have yet to approach the matter at all."

"Cruel to the powerful?" Lydia asked. "What d'you mean by that?" The other maid had been sitting in the corner of the carriage with a quiet, wary manner, but she couldn't seem to help her interest in the current conversation.

Lord Blackthorn smiled at Lydia. "I am trying to be more virtuous," he said. "I am told that it entails two parts. I believe I have done a passable job of being kind to the powerless, but I have not yet thought on how to be cruel to the powerful."

Lydia snorted. "I've got endless thoughts on *that*," she said. "All you had t'do was ask."

Effie shook her head quickly at Lydia, but Lord Blackthorn had straightened with interest. "Well!" he said. "I shall ask, then! How would *you* go about being cruel to the powerful, miss?"

Lydia glanced past him, towards Effie's stricken face. "I … I'll think more on it," Lydia demurred hastily. "I ought to give you the *right* thoughts, after all. An' we're here for Effie right now."

Lord Blackthorn nodded seriously. "Yes, quite right," he agreed. "Let us first see Miss Euphemia happily married!"

The carriage came to a pause. Lord Blackthorn exited first in order to offer them each a hand down.

They had stopped on a cobblestone drive, just in front of a sprawling manor with many windows. A flat, well-manicured lawn surrounded them, broken up only by the display of a single impressive fountain – in the darkness, Effie was barely able to make out three chubby angelic forms, each cradling a water basin in their arms. Off to either side of the manor house stretched more pastoral landscapes, carefully crafted to appear tastefully overgrown.

Effie had never been to the manor herself, but she recognised it by description. "Why, this is Finchwood Hall!" she said. "I heard that the angels on the fountain have to be scrubbed every morning, or else they go an awful green colour!"

Lydia nodded sagely. "Our Cookie used to work here," she said. "She told me Lord Panovar sends his supper back every night sayin' it's not spiced enough. His cooks *always* quit a few months in."

Effie squinted at the doors, which had been left open to the evening air. "Was it Lord Panovar's son who kicked his governess into the pond?" she wondered aloud.

Lydia shook her head. "Definitely not," she said. "That was Lord Gelborn's son. I remember cos Mrs Sedgewick was tuttin' about it. She said, 'Never you go work in a household with ill-behaved children, Lydia. I've regretted it every time.'"

Lord Blackthorn was still holding onto Effie's hand. He frowned thoughtfully as the two of them spoke. "Is this what the English call gossip?" he asked. "I thought it was considered impolite – but I have been wrong before."

Effie flushed with embarrassment. "Oh," she said. "You are right, I think. How awful of me."

Lydia rolled her eyes. "If we didn't talk about our employers, we'd never know what we were walkin' into on a job," she said. "Besides – nobles talk about *us* all they like. I guess they figure it's different, since it's always over tea and biscuits."

Effie remembered the way that Lady Culver had complained to Miss Buckley about the difficulty of finding good help. The conversation had involved several detailed accounts of overly vain footmen and maids with nasty attitudes. *I suppose that was also gossip*, she thought.

Lord Blackthorn nodded seriously. "I see," he said. "That does seem practical."

Lydia shot the elf a narrow-eyed look. "I wonder what your servants would say about *you*," she mused.

Lord Blackthorn blinked. "I, too, would be curious to know," he admitted. "But I have never had any servants."

This was such an outlandish statement that both Effie and Lydia nearly stopped in their tracks – but the footman at the door interrupted them. "Your invitation, my lord?" he addressed Lord Blackthorn.

Lord Blackthorn smiled pleasantly. "I really don't require one," he assured the footman.

The footman nodded agreeably at this, as though it should have been self-evident. "Of course," he said. He brought them into the entryway, and suddenly Effie felt as though she were caught halfway in a dream.

Most of the guests had long since moved on to the ballroom, but there were a handful still lingering near the door, all wearing their lovely suits and gowns, with their clothes freshly ironed and their hair neatly done. Some of them turned from their conversations to smile at their group as they passed; a lady met Effie's eyes directly, and she felt a strange shiver go down her spine.

I'm not invisible any more, Effie realised. *No one is looking away from me.*

It was far more shocking than it should have been – but the reality of it nearly overwhelmed her. In Effie's daydreams, she had blended in effortlessly with the nobility, laughing and smiling with them; but now, she found herself clinging to Lord Blackthorn's arm with a mixture of terror and delight.

"Someone's goin' to have to sweep this entryway again," Lydia sighed under her breath.

Effie glanced down. The entryway had probably been freshly swept and sanded only a few hours ago. Already, it was showing the dirt and wear of so many feet.

The realisation only compounded Effie's dreamy confusion.

Lord Blackthorn was speaking to the footman just next to her. He, in turn, had introduced them to another serious-looking man with thinning grey hair. "Good evening, Miss Reeves," the man said, and it took Effie a moment to understand that someone had already introduced her. "Here is your dance card. Please do enjoy yourself."

He turned towards the ballroom – all full of dazzling candles and lovely music and colourful people – and then he announced their group in a strong, booming voice. "His Lordship, the Viscount of Blackthorn, and his companion, Miss Euphemia Reeves!"

A roomful of eyes turned their way, and Effie tried her very best to sink into the floor.

Chapter Five

Effie had never had so many people look at her at once. Murmurs mixed together indistinguishably within the crowd. Surely, they were all noticing her ratty gloves and barely done hair?

"Your Lordship!" A tall, older man in a faded green coat approached them, oddly breathless. "How good it is to see you!" The gentleman kept his gaze fixed upon Effie as he spoke to Lord Blackthorn – a circumstance which she found both odd and unnerving. "I find it . . . difficult to remember. Have you introduced your companion to me before?"

Lord Blackthorn smiled. "I have not introduced her before," he said. This was the truth, Effie noted, but she had also begun to suspect that the poor man before them had never met Lord Blackthorn before either – the elf's glamour was terribly persuasive that way. "This is Miss Euphemia Reeves. She is my ward, and I am hoping to see her married." Lord Blackthorn gestured back towards the older man. "Miss Euphemia, this is . . . " He paused with embarrassment. "Well, what *is* your name again?"

If the older gentleman took offence, then at least he did not show it. "Lord Panovar, of course," he said distantly. He took Effie's hand and kissed the air above it. "But this is your ward, Lord Blackthorn? And you say she isn't married yet? How strange!"

Effie flushed with confusion again. "Er . . . why strange, my lord?" she asked hesitantly. She glanced down at the gloved hand he still held, distressed by the sight of a stray thread hanging off its wrist.

"Please take no offence," Lord Panovar assured her hastily as he dropped her hand again. "I had simply thought . . . well! You are far too dignified a lady to be *unmarried*, Miss Reeves! Surely, you have at least been out in society for a while? Perhaps Lord Blackthorn has been hiding you in London?"

Effie knit her brow at this. For a moment, she worried that Lord Panovar was somehow having fun at her expense – surely, this was his way of pointing out her shabby accessories and questionable manners – but she remembered belatedly that Lord Blackthorn had given her a gown made of dignity. *How queer!* she thought. *I don't feel at all dignified, but Lord Panovar seems to believe that I am, all the same.*

Lord Blackthorn had been worried over the gown, but Effie suddenly found herself grateful for it.

"I have not been in London," Effie assured the man. "But how kind of you to say all of that, Lord Panovar."

"Not at all, Miss Reeves," Lord Panovar replied. An odd expression had formed on his weathered old face, and Effie began to notice that they had created a small knot of people among the crowd. "If you would pardon an old man's curiosity for a moment – I have been dwelling on a question of late, and I suspect you might be just the woman to help me. Do you mind?"

Effie forced a smile at this, though she was already feeling overwhelmed. "Of course, my lord," she said. "I will do my best."

Lord Panovar held her eyes with deep interest. "Lady Panovar has hired on these French maids, you see," he said. The words spilled from him with unnatural fervour, as though he could barely contain them. "She insists that they are of higher quality than a normal English maid, but I cannot much see the difference – and they are *terribly* expensive. Are French maids truly worth the extra cost? Surely, a woman of your dignity has an opinion on the matter?"

Effie froze, wide-eyed. The question itself was terrifying – she had a feeling that if she gave the wrong answer, she might be putting some innocent French maids out onto the street – but there was something strange about the way that Lord Panovar spoke to her, so instantly eager for her opinion. It reminded her, she realised, of the way that she'd felt obliged to answer Lord Blackthorn's every question.

But Lord Panovar was still looking at her expectantly, and Effie knew that she would not escape the conversation without giving an answer.

"I am sure that you handed domestic matters over to Lady Panovar because you trust her to see to them," Effie replied weakly. "Surely, she knows her business well."

Somewhere behind her, Lydia gave a sarcastic snort.

Lord Panovar nodded seriously at this, as though Effie had blessed him with some uncommon pearl of wisdom. "Oh yes, quite," he said. "I see what you are at, young lady. Certainly, the matter is not worth causing marital strife. A peaceful home is worth the money."

Effie had not meant to imply this at all, but she was not about to contradict their host.

"It seems that I must continue introductions," Lord Blackthorn interrupted cheerfully. "There are so many people hoping to meet you, Miss Euphemia."

As the elf said this, Effie realised that they had slowly been surrounded during the course of their conversation by a small army of well-dressed guests, all sneaking glances towards Effie while trying not to look very interested in her at all.

All of them, she soon discovered, were in desperate need of her opinion.

A young Miss Chester wished to know how to fairly handle

two sisters both pursuing the same gentleman (Effie found this question even more alarming than the first, but she managed to put it off with the observation that surely the gentleman in question would have some say in the matter). Lady Tilley very seriously enquired whether she could still get away with planting roses in late spring, or whether that was gauche (at this, Effie carefully enthused that roses were appropriate at all times, since Lord Blackthorn was standing just behind her, and since she suspected that this was a matter near and dear to his heart).

"Miss Reeves," a Mr Herbert Jesson soon asked, "might I dare to ask for a dance? If your card is not completely full, that is."

Effie gratefully seized upon the opportunity, accepting his gloved hand. "Yes," she gasped. "I would greatly enjoy a dance. If – if my chaperone approves, of course." She glanced back towards Lydia, who crossed her arms and nodded sternly in what Effie suspected to be an imitation of Mrs Sedgewick's usual behaviour.

Mr Jesson was not an attractive man – his face was a bit too round, his hair was unflatteringly cut and his eyes were a kind of watery-blue colour – but he was so aggressively inoffensive as to be nearly charming, especially when compared to the veritable crush of more charismatic people around them. As he guided Effie onto the dance floor, she let out a soft sigh of relief. There was still a smothering press of people there with them, but at least, she thought, they were not all pausing to ask her *questions*.

As they walked, Effie took the chance to glance around the room, searching for Benedict. For a moment, she thought she saw him across the dance floor with another young lady on his arm – but the music began then, and Effie was forced to return her attentions to her current partner.

Unfortunately, Effie soon realised that her gown and slippers were so heavy that dancing was nearly untenable. She stumbled clumsily through the steps, wincing each time that she stepped on poor Mr Jesson's feet. To the man's credit, he did not seem at all upset by her fumblings; more than once, in fact, he *complimented* Effie's dancing, which she found admittedly odd. Mr Jesson was not himself a very accomplished dancer – but Effie so rarely got to dance at all that she found the deficiency did not bother her.

He smiled weakly at her. "I am very pleased that you were willing to come out onto the floor with me, Miss Reeves," he said. "Now that we are here, I must admit to a somewhat shameful hope. I have had a longstanding problem, you see, and for some reason I am sure that you will be able to advise me."

Effie slumped her shoulders. "Oh," she sighed. "Yes, of course you do." Mr Jesson's expression took on a hint of distress at this, however, and Effie immediately felt discourteous. "I don't mean to be rude, sir," she assured him. "I am just very confused that everyone seems to think I can solve their problems for them. The only thing most people know of me is that I am wearing a very fine gown – and that hardly qualifies me to speak on such a broad range of topics!"

Mr Jesson looked sheepish at this. "It is a *very* dignified gown," he admitted. "But is that really the secret? For I had hoped to ask you how to be more confident, Miss Reeves. You must admit, at least, that you are quite good at commanding a room!"

Effie blinked at this. "Well, I . . . Do you know, I suppose that *is* relevant," she replied. "But yes, Mr Jesson, it is absolutely to do with the gown. I am afraid I do not have an extra, or else I would lend it to you."

Mr Jesson laughed at this – and for a moment, the expression lit up his face so that the sum of him seemed more attractive than his parts. The genuine display softened Effie towards him, and she found she could not help but smile in return.

"I think that you should do *that* more often," she advised him. "Whatever it is you are doing now, it is very flattering on you."

This made Mr Jesson's eyes crinkle upwards at the edges. "That is better advice than I have had so far," he observed. "Thank you very much, Miss Reeves. Is there anything I might do to repay you?"

Effie looked at his face, trying to parse his expression. From someone else, the overture might have been flirtatious, but poor Mr Jesson was far too clumsy to attempt such a subtle implication – the offer was quite sincere.

"I don't suppose you are acquainted with Mr Benedict Ashbrooke?" Effie asked him hopefully.

Mr Jesson nodded. "We went to school together," he said. "Oh dear – were you hoping for an introduction?"

Effie winced. "You may forget that I asked," she assured him hastily.

Mr Jesson shook his head. "I am not offended," he said. "I am simply concerned. Mr Benedict is very popular with women – he has that confidence which I lack. But he is not well-known for *settling*, if you take my meaning."

At this revelation, Effie felt a hint of worry; it had not occurred to her that Benedict might be entirely uninterested in marriage! "But every man must settle eventually," she insisted.

"This is true," Mr Jesson admitted. "And you *are* uniquely compelling, Miss Reeves, even if you would prefer to blame your dress rather than your manner. If you would really like, I can arrange the introduction."

Effie gave him a relieved smile. "I would appreciate that very much, Mr Jesson," she said.

Mr Jesson was kind enough to endure Effie stepping on his toes a few times more, as the song wound down. When the dance was over, he took her by the arm and led her to the edge of the dance floor, peering about for Benedict. As Effie helped him search, she caught sight of Lady Culver standing with a crowd of people around Lord Panovar and Lord Blackthorn – but she did not see Benedict among the company. Lydia was standing next to Lord Blackthorn, looking particularly miserable, and Effie winced as she remembered that the other maid was supposed to avoid speaking.

"There you are!" Mr Jesson said brightly. Effie turned around, forgetting the scene. The crowd had parted – and, just like fate, Benedict was standing right in front of them, holding a glass of punch. Somehow, he was looking even more handsome than usual, in a forest-green waistcoat which made his eyes seem more golden than brown. Benedict smiled at Mr Jesson with genuine pleasure, and the expression made Effie's heart feel faint with longing.

"Why," Benedict declared, "if it isn't Mr Tulip himself!" The nickname sounded affectionate, rather than dismissive, and Mr Jesson beamed at hearing it. "I've been meaning to invite you for a brandy – but wouldn't you know it, the family's been claiming all my time."

Mr Jesson's eyes wrinkled with humour again, and Effie thought how flattering it was. "Family is hardly a burden, Mr Benedict," he said. "I am sure they're all very pleased to see you after so long. We shall have our brandy whenever you are able." Mr Jesson turned to nod at Effie then. "I have had a charming dance with the new young lady, Miss Reeves – she is Lord Blackthorn's ward, you know. If you are not otherwise occupied, I would recommend her company for the next dance."

Effie flushed at the high praise. Benedict turned his eyes towards her with interest, and she inwardly marked down a debt to Mr Jesson, to be paid at a future date.

"Have we met before?" Benedict asked her curiously. "My memory really must be going. I keep getting that impression lately."

Effie widened her eyes. Surely, he wouldn't recognise her as a house maid with Lord Blackthorn's excellent glamour at her throat? "Oh," she said. "I think we may have met, yes. But I cannot remember where."

Benedict smiled again, and the sight was very nearly dev-astating. "Well, I hold Mr Tulip's opinion in very high regard, Miss Reeves," he said. "I would be eternally in your debt if you were to take the next dance with me—"

A hideous noise echoed across the room, interrupting him.

All three of them cringed at the sound – it was something like a donkey's braying, except that it was far louder and more grating. Effie whirled to search for the source, unable to stop herself.

At first, she had trouble pin-pointing the origin. Clearly, the sound had come from somewhere within that group sur-rounding Lord Panovar and Lord Blackthorn, for everyone in the vicinity had turned to look in that direction with their hands clasped to their chests. Even as Effie watched, however, Lady Culver opened her mouth to speak to Lord Panovar – and another awful, ugly braying noise escaped her.

Just behind Lady Culver, Lydia let out a gasp, somewhere between horror and delight. Lord Blackthorn alone continued smiling politely, as though women brayed like donkeys all the time where he was from.

"I suspect we shall need to postpone our dance for another time," Benedict said grimly, as he hurried past Effie and Mr Jesson. "My apologies, Miss Reeves."

What on earth is going on? Effie thought desperately. Soon, both Benedict and Lord Culver had joined Lady Culver and taken her by the arm. Lord Culver looked to be making effusive apologies for his wife as the three of them made to abruptly depart.

"Oh dear," Mr Jesson said. "Is Lady Culver ill?"

Effie's heart sank as she watched the entirety of Lord Culver's household head for the exit. "I suppose she is," she mumbled. "How awful."

"I am sorry that your introduction was ruined," Mr Jesson told her apologetically. "If it would please you – my family will be holding a breakfast in our gardens when the first tulips bloom, and I am sure that Mr Benedict will be there. You and Lord Blackthorn would be marvellously welcome as well, and it would give me a second chance to introduce you."

Effie shot him a piteously grateful look. "Truly, you are a gem among gentlemen, Mr Jesson," she told him.

Mr Jesson patted her arm reassuringly. "For now," he said, "I suppose I must get you back to your chaperone."

Effie soon rejoined Lydia and Lord Blackthorn, while people murmured about Lady Culver's strange outburst. Some small, selfish part of Effie was satisfied to hear people laughing and making fun of the woman – but the greater part of her was confused and morose. She had been so close to dancing with Benedict – and now, her very first attempt at catching his attention had been utterly ruined!

Lord Blackthorn looked oddly guilty as he took Effie by the arm again, leading her away from the crowd. "Perhaps I should introduce you to a few more gentlemen?" he asked. "Or else *we* could dance, Miss Euphemia! I believe I have finally caught on to the minuet!"

Effie stared at him, and a sudden suspicion rose up within her. "Did *you* steal Lady Culver's voice, Mr Jubilee?" she whispered. Effie meant to keep the words carefully polite, but a thread of real anger slipped through in spite of her efforts.

Lord Blackthorn winced. "Oh, I didn't mean to," he explained worriedly. "Or else – I did *mean* to, but I hadn't realised that it would interfere with your own designs. I am so very sorry, Miss Euphemia. I have made a mess of things again."

Effie's mouth dropped open. "Surely, you aren't attempting to prevent me from winning our wager—?" she started hotly.

But Lydia grabbed Effie by the other arm, interrupting her. "It's not his fault," Lydia whispered with a miserable look on her face. "It's mine. I'm so sorry, Effie. Lady Culver was goin' on about her new French maids an' how much better we were

than Lady Panovar's French maids. She'd just got on to sayin'
we recite French *poetry* for her at night, an' I just couldn't take
it any more!"

Effie blinked at Lydia. "I don't understand," she said. "What
did you do, Lydia?"

Lydia shifted on her feet. "Lord Blackthorn said he wanted
to be cruel to the powerful," she said. "So I might've . . . made
a few suggestions."

Effie closed her eyes in despair. Everything had seemed
much simpler before, when she had been the only one making
deals with Lord Blackthorn – but her own willingness to
barter with the faerie had clearly convinced Lydia that he and
his offers were harmless. "You didn't *trade* him for it?" Effie
whispered, keenly aware that Lord Blackthorn could hear their
every word.

"I didn't!" Lydia promised. "He owed me for bein' your
chaperone – isn't that right, Lord Blackthorn?"

"Quite right," Lord Blackthorn assured them both. "I was
merely fulfilling an existing debt."

The tightness in Effie's chest eased very slightly at that revelation – though not by much. "Well . . . what's done is done," she
said uncomfortably. "And it's not all bad. Mr Jesson has invited
us to breakfast when the first tulips bloom. He said that Mr
Benedict is sure to be there too."

Lord Blackthorn looked relieved at this. "How fortunate!" he
said. "Oh, I'm still very sorry, Miss Euphemia, but don't worry –
this time, we shall have the opportunity to properly prepare!"

Effie smiled tremulously at him. "I'm very sorry for suspect-
ing you of ill intentions, Mr Jubilee," she said, though some
part of her still worried that the elf had somehow engineered
the whole debacle. "I hope you can forgive me."

Lord Blackthorn waved a hand. "It is already forgotten," he
assured her. "I have botched this evening's ball, after all, and
so we may call it even."

Effie sighed. "I suppose there's not much point in staying longer," she said morosely, "since Mr Benedict and all his family have left."

"An' we've gotta be up in the mornin'," Lydia groaned. "There's always the fireplaces."

There were always the fireplaces.

$\mathscr{B}$y the time Effie and the others returned to Hartfield, the Ashbrookes were still awake – and having quite the argument. The incessant sound of Lady Culver's braying filtered down the stairs as they snuck inside. Effie cringed each time, but Lydia had to cover her mouth to prevent herself from bursting into giggles.

Not a moment after Effie and Lydia had returned to their room and tucked their glamours into the drawer in the bedside table, Mrs Sedgewick called Lydia away to handle a late-night pot of tea for the Family, thoroughly oblivious to the presence of the elf in the corner. Effie tried to volunteer in Lydia's place, worried she might laugh at an inopportune moment, but Lydia gleefully insisted that it ought to be her. Thus, Effie found herself, now dressed in her shift and housecoat, alone with Lord Blackthorn.

She glanced worriedly towards the faerie, blinking away her weariness as she sat down on the edge of the bed. "Lady Culver won't sound like that for ever, will she?" she asked.

Lord Blackthorn shook his head. "The lady shall have her normal voice back with the rising of the sun," he assured her. "I could have cursed her for ever, I suppose, but Miss Lydia's debt was far too limited."

Effie bit at her lip. She didn't *want* to enjoy Lady Culver's distress – there was something unchristian about the sentiment, she was sure – but now that she knew the curse would disappear, she just couldn't bring herself to feel bad for the woman. "I suppose it's not the worst thing in the world," Effie murmured. "But people will surely laugh at her for months."

Lord Blackthorn considered this thoughtfully. "If everyone is laughing at her," he said, "then I suppose she will have fewer opportunities to speak of French maids."

"There is that," Effie said, feeling heartened. "And she probably won't be throwing any balls for a long while!" The thought was so deeply relieving that Effie found she had forgiven Lydia entirely for the incident. She rubbed her eyes and refocused herself, remembering that there were other things that still needed doing. "But your jacket," she mumbled. "I still need to start the embroidery. I shouldn't embroider it directly – it is far too fine for that – but I've already pounced a pattern on some linen. I can do the work there first, and then sew the linen onto the jacket—"

"Oh no, I fear that won't do at all, Miss Euphemia," Lord Blackthorn replied worriedly. "Our deal was that you would embroider the jacket, and not some other fabric. Perhaps it *was* poor wording, but since we have agreed upon it already, we must truly stick to the terms as described."

Effie winced. "Well," she sighed. "If we must. You will have to give me your jacket if I am going to embroider it, however. There is no way around that. I was thinking of embroidering a rose, by the way. I hope that suits you, Mr Jubilee?"

Lord Blackthorn tugged his coat thoughtfully from his shoulders. "I am sure that whatever you embroider will be marvellous, Miss Euphemia," he assured her.

Effie smiled at his response in spite of herself. Whatever the elf's other qualities, he *did* have a way of making one feel very important and appreciated. She took the black velvet jacket from him, settling it into her lap. The velvet was lush and well-piled, and the longer she looked at it, the more worried she became.

It will be so difficult to embroider this without ruining it, she thought. But then it occurred to Effie that she was embroidering an elf's jacket, and that this fact surely ought to have concerned her more than the choice of material.

She reached into the drawer in the small bedside table, carefully collecting both the hooped linen and what remained of the precious silk embroidery thread she'd used for her own work. Briefly, Effie wished that she had the means to purchase gold thread – a jacket this fine really *ought* to be embroidered in gold.

"I hope you will not be upset if I stitch the linen *into* the velvet?" Effie asked Lord Blackthorn warily. "Velvet does not take embroidery very well all on its own, and I really don't know how else it could be done."

Lord Blackthorn nodded. "As long as you are stitching into the jacket," he said. "Any stitches which do not touch the velvet would not count, I fear."

As Effie basted the linen on top of the velvet, it occurred to her that Lord Blackthorn could have just as easily kept silent about all of these technicalities, if he had truly wished it. *I would have embroidered on the linen and not on the jacket at all, if he hadn't told me otherwise*, Effie realised. She smiled tiredly at that.

"You really are trying to help, in your way," Effie said. "Isn't that funny?"

Lord Blackthorn blinked. "But of course I am trying to help," he said. "I have told you as much, Miss Euphemia – and faeries cannot lie."

Effie's smile curved a bit further upwards at this. The night had not gone *quite* as she had hoped, but the revelation that the elf was indeed sincere did much for her state of mind. "I cannot fathom it," she told him. "Even if you were not an elf, Mr Jubilee, you are still a lord – and I cannot think of the lord who has cause to be helpful towards a maid."

Lord Blackthorn looked troubled at this. "English lords do not sound very useful," he observed. "Perhaps I should not be

a lord, after all. It sounded quite fanciful at first when Lord
Hollowvale described it to me, but I have found English maids
far more useful and admirable so far."

Effie laughed. "You can't just stop being a lord," she said.
"And you certainly cannot be a *maid*. Well – the very thought!"

Lord Blackthorn nodded seriously. "I would not dare to
lay claim to the title of maid," he assured Effie. "I have not
worked nearly hard enough to do so. But I cannot see why it
should be difficult to stop being a lord. I only became one in
the first place because someone called me a lord and no one
else objected. I expect that *unbecoming* a lord would be rather
the same, wouldn't it?"

Effie was now very confused. She set aside the jacket to stare
at Lord Blackthorn. "But . . . don't you own land in faerie?" she
asked carefully. "You said you don't have servants – but surely
you have a manor or an estate?"

Lord Blackthorn laughed. "Own land in faerie?" he asked
incredulously. "The nerve of it! Not at all, Miss Euphemia. In
faerie, the land owns *you*. Blackthorn suffers my presence only
because it hasn't any hands of its own, and because I do a passable job of serving its interests with mine!"

Effie rubbed her face. "This is all very different from
England," she told him. "Lords do own land here. And they
cannot simply *claim* to be a lord. They're appointed by the
king – or, well, I suppose that is a bit of a childish explanation,
but it is still mostly accurate."

Lord Blackthorn shook his head. "It is quite the same," he
said. "The king calls someone a lord, and no one argues. If
enough people were to argue, then the person in question could
not possibly be a lord any longer."

Effie opened her mouth to protest . . . but she could not
find a simplistic enough reply to debate the elf's strange logic.
She shook her head and returned her attention to the linen in
front of her.

"I really must be a lord in order to see you married off, however," Lord Blackthorn continued to muse. "I shall therefore wait until you are engaged in order to unbecome one. Perhaps, if I am very dedicated, I can become something more useful afterwards – like a butler or a footman."

Effie snorted. "Footmen aren't *that* useful," she muttered. Much as Effie loved her brother George, she was well aware that he had been hired primarily because he was a full two inches taller than the next tallest candidate. She refused to entertain the rest of Lord Blackthorn's words; whatever the elf might have believed, one could not simply discard a title in the same way that one discarded a piece of clothing.

Now buried beneath a layer of linen, the fine velvet jacket looked a little bit less daunting. Effie threaded her needle and sucked in her breath. "I suppose I should get started," she said. "How many stitches do I owe you so far, Mr Jubilee?"

"Only one hundred and thirty-two," he informed her helpfully. "I am very sorry for that, Miss Euphemia. Surely next time, you will have longer."

"I am sure that I will," Effie said distractedly. She focused herself on the embroidery work as she spoke. A hundred and thirty-two stitches was really very little, but her eyes were just as tired as her feet, and the candlelight was not ideal.

Effie tried very hard to get through all of the stitches – but at some point, she found herself blinking up at the ceiling from her own bed, unable to recollect quite how she had got there. It *was* clear that someone had tucked her neatly into bed and put out the candle on the bedside table.

Lydia snored lightly from the next bed over, and Effie decided that it was best to pick up speculating in the morning when she was better rested.

Effie's back and feet both ached even worse when she awoke the next morning. *It's a good thing I didn't stay out too late*, she thought tiredly. *I'm already feeling halfway useless as it is.*

Unfortunately, while Lady Culver had indeed regained her normal voice, she was certainly in a *mood* after last night's debacle, and the entire household could not help but know it. Naturally, because Lady Culver was in a mood, Mrs Sedgewick was also in a mood – and since misery does love company, Mrs Sedgewick had made sure that the maids were all in a mood with *her* as well.

Effie only became aware of just how dire the situation was when she saw Lydia storm below-stairs, dripping fresh tea down her face.

"That woman!" Lydia hissed. "I swear, I felt bad for her for just a moment – an' then she had to go an' ruin it. D'you know, she tossed a teapot at my face? Told me the tea was too cold!"

Effie cringed. "Perhaps you shouldn't have asked Mr Jubilee to embarrass Lady Culver," she mumbled worriedly.

Lydia narrowed her eyes. "Far from it," she said. "I think he didn't embarrass her *enough*, Effie. She hasn't learned a bit of humility." Another dark drop of tea trickled down the maid's nose. "I swear, if I had another favour from him—"

"But you don't!" Effie told her quickly. "So you must not even think of it, Lydia. It can't lead anywhere good."

Lydia considered Effie for a long moment. "You know," she said, "you still sound like a toff, Effie. It makes me annoyed with you, even though I know it's not your fault."

Effie sighed. "I can't just switch accents as I like," she admitted. "I've already tried to use my old voice – I just sound like a poor imitation of myself. I'm not sure there's anything to be done about it until this wager is over with."

"Effie!" Mrs Sedgewick's voice preceded her as she clip-clopped down the stairs. Her tone was terse and frosty. "Lady Culver has found a rip in one of the lace tablecloths. Drop whatever else you are doing and get to mending it."

Effie glanced up at the housekeeper as she came into view. For a moment, she worried that Mrs Sedgewick might expect her to reply – in which case, her accent would surely become an issue – but the housekeeper merely shoved the offending table-cloth into Effie's arms and hurried back up the stairs. Even the formidable Mrs Sedgewick looked harried today, as though the furies themselves were snapping at her wooden heels.

"I suppose I won't be airing out the bedrooms after all," Effie mumbled, looking down at the lace tablecloth. "Really, everyone keeps asking me to sew things, Lydia. I ought to be a seamstress and not a maid at all."

"Don't complain to me!" Lydia snapped. "I'd murder some-one to sit down an' sew right now. My back hurts from standin' all last night, an' I've still got tea all over me."

The whipcrack in Lydia's voice sent a twinge of answering irritation through Effie – but she stopped herself from snapping back at her friend just in time. *It's no good to get angry,* Effie reminded herself. *And Lydia did go to an awful lot of trouble for me just last night. I've got to keep my temper.* She closed her eyes and muttered beneath her breath:

> "Polly put the kettle on,
> Polly put the kettle on,
> Polly put the kettle on,
> We'll all have tea."

"Are you makin' fun of me?" Lydia demanded. Her voice rose an octave at the idea.

Effie blinked. "What?" she asked. "No, I—"

"Well, that just tears it!" Lydia declared. "I'm goin' to get changed. Enjoy your tablecloth, why don't you?"

And then, before Effie could protest, she was gone.

Effie's irritation surged back at that. It was one thing to be accused of having fun by Lydia, and another thing entirely to be prevented from defending herself. "Fine!" Effie snapped at the empty air where the other maid had been. "Don't listen, then. No one *else* ever bothers to listen, so why should you?"

Effie stomped back to her room with the tablecloth, settling onto the bed to search it over for tears. It took some time, but she did eventually find a run in the lace. As she set herself to repairing it, she forced her anger down again, taking comfort in the repetitive nature of the task.

Partway through her work on the tablecloth, however, Mrs Sedgewick knocked at her door.

"Fresh tea for the study!" the housekeeper called through the door. "Quickly, Effie!"

Effie set the tablecloth aside with a quiet hiss of frustration, swallowing down the remnants of her anger as she stormed back for the kitchen to grab a tray. By the time she reached the upstairs study with a fresh pot of tea, she was already searching for a new nursery rhyme to calm her nerves.

"That was terribly quick!" Benedict's voice sounded from the chair next to the desk, where he'd seated himself with one of the leather-bound books from the shelves. A hint of pleasant surprise coloured his words, mixed with just a bit of guilt. "I didn't mean to imply that anyone should hurry. It's really just tea."

Effie's anger drained away somewhat beneath those warm brown eyes. She flushed with embarrassment and confusion. She was suddenly keenly aware of their conversation just the evening before, and was a bit ashamed of the fact that Benedict was missing full knowledge of the situation. "It's just fine, sir," Effie said softly, glancing at her feet. "Happy to do it."

Benedict shot her a wry smile as she settled the tea tray next to him. "Amazing," he said. "You sound so very English. I never would have guessed you were from France at all."

The words stabbed into Effie's chest unexpectedly. Her distress must have showed on her face, however, for Benedict quickly backtracked. "I didn't mean to insult," he assured her hastily. "I was trying to make a joke. I've never understood the obsession with everything French."

Effie took in a careful breath. Benedict was looking at her with concern now, which she thought might be even worse than being invisible. "Please don't mention it to anyone, sir," she said carefully. "I'm supposed to be sticking to French. It will get me into trouble."

"You will get in trouble?" Benedict asked blankly. "For speaking English in England?" When Effie failed to contradict him, he shook his head in amazement. "I swear, this is why I don't run a household. If there's a sense to any of this, then I simply cannot see it."

He poured himself a measure of tea, still frowning at the cup. As he did, Effie felt the awkward distance between them. Lady Culver always seemed to look straight past Effie when she was around – but while Benedict did not ignore Effie in quite the same way, he still did not *see* her in the way that he had done just the evening before. He was perfectly polite – gentlemanly, even! – but Effie had the vaguest hint that Benedict was hoping to get back to his book just as soon as he'd finished the bare minimum of pleasantries with her.

You promised me a dance, only last evening, Effie wanted to blurt out at him. *Won't you still dance with me, even though I'm just a maid?*

But she held her tongue, just barely, aware of how ridiculous the idea was.

Benedict looked up at her again after a moment, and Effie realised that she had lingered just a bit too long in one spot. He smiled sheepishly. "Oh, of course," he said. "I promise I will not tell anyone about the English. I should have said that first."

This time, Effie had the sense that he expected their conversation was done. She nodded morosely, ducking back out of the study with a lead weight in her heart.

She returned to her room, picking the tablecloth back up

with a sigh. At least, she thought, she would have the chance to stitch a few more of her woes into the lace.

Presently, however, she became aware of Lord Blackthorn's tall figure peering at her curiously from the doorway.

"My!" the elf said. "What a thoroughly miserable tablecloth that is! I do not know if I have ever seen its like before!" His voice was deeply admiring rather than derisive – as though he found the tablecloth to be an exotic curiosity of great interest. Effie knit her brow.

"It's not *that* awful," she said. "I've seen far worse." She glanced up towards him and set the tablecloth aside for a moment. Lord Blackthorn was not wearing his customary black velvet jacket, of course, since that was neatly folded up inside the drawer of her bedside table. As he was without his jacket, she could see his green and gold waistcoat more clearly. It was a flattering cut, and her tired mind wandered to the stitching along its top before she caught herself. "How might I help you, Mr Jubilee?" Effie asked, blinking away her tiredness.

"You needn't help me at all!" Lord Blackthorn assured her. "I am here to help *you*! Mr Jesson has had his invitation delivered to Mr Benedict. There is going to be a breakfast next week, and so we must prepare you to attend! I wanted to be sure that we find you the perfect gown this time, and so I thought that I would come retrieve you directly!"

Effie blinked. "You mean to say ... you want me to come with you right now?" she asked. "But I can't possibly do that, Mr Jubilee! I'm in the middle of work!"

Lord Blackthorn waved a hand. "It will only take an hour or two to get you safely there and back," he assured her. "You can bring your tablecloth with you, in fact, so that you are still working the entire time!"

Effie gave him a wary look. "*Safely* there and back?" she asked. "Where is it that you would like to take me, Mr Jubilee?"

"Why, to faerie, of course!" Lord Blackthorn replied

enthusiastically, as though this were a perfectly normal suggestion. "The brownies in Hollowvale have procured new materials for us to peruse, and they have been kind enough to make time to measure you in person! Lady Hollowvale has been ever so helpful – I can barely wait for you to meet her!"

Effie widened her eyes and tightened her hands on the table-cloth. "I . . . that is very generous indeed," she stuttered out. "But surely, I couldn't impose on a fine faerie lady—"

"Lady Hollowvale is really only *half* a faerie," Lord Blackthorn told Effie brightly. "Her other half is a fine English lady. I am sure that you will have much in common with one another, since you are also English."

Effie was so flabbergasted by all of the different implications here that she could not figure out which one she ought to reply to first. By the time she had come up with a response, however, Lord Blackthorn had taken the tablecloth from her hands and folded it up, then offered out his arm.

"I *will* be coming back from faerie again if I go with you, Mr Jubilee?" Effie asked him carefully. "For instance – what if Lady Hollowvale decides that I ought to stay in her realm for much longer?"

Lord Blackthorn shook his head. "Why, keeping you in faerie for too long would defeat the entire purpose of making you a gown!" he said. "You have my word, Miss Euphemia – you will be back in time for your breakfast!"

Effie glanced towards the tablecloth, which he had tucked beneath his other arm. She sighed and got to her feet. "I will rely entirely upon you, Mr Jubilee," she told him, "since I know that you so sincerely wish to help."

These words had a pronounced effect upon Lord Blackthorn; his ever-present smile broadened even further, and his vivid green eyes sparkled with sudden pride. "I do wish to help," he assured Effie, as he tucked her hand into his arm. "Very sincerely. Why, with all of this practice, I feel I am getting better at it already."

Effie smiled back at him. Though the morning had been hard, it was difficult to be upset in the presence of someone so effusively optimistic. She was especially surprised to find that she was growing used to the comforting warmth of the faerie's arm beneath her hand, and the scent of wild roses which he carried with him all of the time.

"You seemed awfully upset again before I came in, Miss Euphemia," Lord Blackthorn observed, as he escorted her through the servants' passageways. "I hope last night is not still distressing you?" A few of the other servants passed them by, but none of them looked up – Lord Blackthorn's glamour had broadened to protect them both.

Effie chewed anxiously at her lip. She tried to formulate a diplomatic answer in her head – but since Lord Blackthorn had used her name, her mouth opened without her permission, and she found herself responding with brutal honesty instead. "I just saw Mr Benedict," Effie told him. "He was perfectly pleasant, but for some reason, I've been feeling upset since I left him." She paused. "I could just be out of sorts from earlier this morning."

"I see," Lord Blackthorn said, though it was clear that he did not entirely understand just yet. "What happened this morning, if I might ask?"

Effie flushed, thankful for the change in subject. "Lady Culver threw a teapot at Lydia," she told the elf. "She said it was because the tea was cold, but it's really just because she's still embarrassed about last night. Then Lydia got cross with *me* – and I tried very hard not to get angry back at her! – but she still seems to think I was making fun of her, and she wouldn't stay to find out otherwise."

Lord Blackthorn frowned at that. "Oh dear," he said. "Is Lady Culver perhaps aware of the favour that Miss Lydia requested? I had not meant to get her into trouble."

Effie shook her head emphatically. "I am *quite* positive that Lady Culver would not believe there was an elf in her home, even if someone were to tell her outright," she said. "Lady Culver doesn't believe that Lydia is responsible for what happened to her voice – she was just angry in general, I suppose, and it made her feel better to be angry with Lydia specifically instead of with the world."

"How interesting!" Lord Blackthorn mused. "Why, it's almost like a plague, isn't it? Lady Culver became angry, and then Miss Lydia caught her anger, and then you – well, *are* you still angry, Miss Euphemia?"

Effie blinked at that. "I'm not angry at all any more, actually," she said. "How curious! I'd normally need to do a few more stitches before I felt any better, but I'm in quite a lovely mood now that you're here." She flushed at the admission, though she couldn't have kept the answer inside herself even if she'd tried. "You have such a wonderful attitude, Mr Jubilee. I hadn't realised it before, but you are unlike the rest of us in more ways than one. Everyone below-stairs is just so angry all the time. It's lovely to be around someone who is *happy*, no matter the cause."

Lord Blackthorn beamed at her. "I am so pleased to have lifted your spirits," he said. "But to be fair, Miss Euphemia, I am still a lord today – I have yet to unbecome one, as I promised – and so I have little to be unhappy about. If I were a hardworking maid having teapots thrown at my head, I am sure that I would be angry as well."

Effie frowned at this. "Getting angry doesn't ever help, though," she said. "All it does is get you into trouble."

Lord Blackthorn paused to open the green baize door for her. "I cannot see how that would be the case," he said solemnly. "If anger never helped, then why would you have it at all? Some humans are born with extra fingers or toes, yes, but *all* of you are born with at least a little bit of anger. It must do something of use."

Effie took his arm again as they headed into the main house

and towards a back door. "Maybe it helps for lords and ladies to get angry," she observed slowly. "But when servants get angry, we are just dismissed from our jobs. So I suppose … anger is useful for everyone else."

"How troubling," Lord Blackthorn murmured. "How puzzling! I must give this some thought. But I should think on it later — we are heading into Blackthorn first, after all, and it would not do to have a clouded mind while we are walking through the maze."

Effie noticed then that Lord Blackthorn had been angling them towards the hedge maze behind the manor — the very same one where she had first met him. As he led her outside, into the half-dry mud and lukewarm sunlight, Effie realised belatedly just how much she'd missed the light.

When was the last time she'd walked outside during the day, just for the pleasure of it? She couldn't rightly remember. It was rare that she was able to leave the manor at all, except to walk to church. But here she was, strolling into the hedge maze in the cloud-dappled sunlight, listening to the whispering of the wind between its branches. The feeling of freedom — of breathing fresh air and walking out of doors without first begging for permission — lifted a weight from her soul which had crept there slowly and insidiously without her notice.

The company, Effie decided, was quite pleasant as well.

"Oh!" she said, as something occurred to her. "You told me when we first met that Hartfield was right in your backyard! Were you perhaps being literal, Mr Jubilee?"

Lord Blackthorn beamed at her. "I was indeed," he told her. "Your hedge leads directly into Blackthorn. It is one of many places in England where the veil to faerie is thin."

Effie turned wide eyes upon him. "Do you mean to say that I could have accidentally wandered into faerie at any time if I'd ever gone inside?" she asked in shock.

Lord Blackthorn laughed. "No, certainly not," he assured

her. "I can come and go from Blackthorn at my whim, of course – but mortals must use a trick in order to pass the veil. *You* shall need to spin yourself three times counterclockwise and walk backwards into the maze." He paused them just before the entrance to the maze and settled one hand on Effie's shoulder. "If you would do the honours, Miss Euphemia – we do want to get you home in good time, after all."

If she had been with anyone else, Effie would have felt at least a little bit embarrassed to spin herself around in circles like a child playing games. But it occurred to her now that she had yet to hear Lord Blackthorn make fun of anyone at all within her earshot – nor indeed had he ever said anything less than complimentary to her, no matter how awkward or unwieldy she felt herself.

The sunlight was warm on her skin, and the air was fresh on her face. Effie smiled at the feeling. "Must it be *exactly* three times, Mr Jubilee?" she asked whimsically.

As she had expected, Lord Blackthorn did not seem at all fazed by the question. "It could be far more than three times, of course," he replied in a helpful tone.

Effie spun herself around in a whirl of skirts and trampled grass. She kept spinning, over and over, until she was nearly too dizzy to stand. Finally, she swayed on her feet with a helpless giggle, drunk on the feeling of *out of the house.*

As Effie stumbled sideways, Lord Blackthorn caught her upon his arm. He smiled down at her as though she had done something splendid. "Well done!" he congratulated her. "That was far more than three times, Miss Euphemia!"

Effie smiled back dazedly. "That was most fun," she confided. "I haven't done anything like that since before I left home."

"Oh dear," Lord Blackthorn sighed. "Don't tell me lords and ladies are also averse to *spinning*? I become less enamoured with my title by the day."

Effie giggled. "Lords and ladies and servants are all very serious," she said. "We mustn't do anything that does not have a point. I am certain that if a lady had to go to faerie, she would spin around exactly three times – no more and no less."

"But nothing has a point!" Lord Blackthorn protested incredulously. "All of life is absurd to some extent or other!" He frowned at Effie. "Being a lady sounds dreadfully bleak," he declared. "Must you really go through with it, Miss Euphemia?"

Effie's laughter faded a bit at that. "I really must," she reminded him. "If I am *not* a lady, then I cannot marry Mr Benedict."

Lord Blackthorn sighed heavily at this. "A tragic sacrifice," he murmured. "But yes, you are right. Well then – let us be on with it." He took her by the hand and went ahead of her into the hedge maze. "No, stay facing forward, Miss Euphemia," he said, as she turned instinctively to face him. "I will lead you safely backward."

He paused, then added, "Keep your goal firmly in mind as we walk. We must keep our wits about us while we are in Blackthorn!"

Chapter Seven

Effie did her best to fix her mind upon Benedict as she stumbled backwards through the hedge maze with Lord Blackthorn. She envisioned Benedict's warm laugh and his charming smile; she imagined what it would be like to finally dance with him, to have his undivided attention for just a few minutes. *I only want the chance*, she thought. *Just one chance, at least.*

As they walked, Effie became aware that the hedges around them had grown greener and wilder. Great big roses of every colour threaded their way between the leaves, bursting with the same natural scent that Lord Blackthorn always carried with him. Slowly, the hedges transitioned into towering trees, such that they were soon walking in an impossibly large forest. The branches wound tightly together on either side of them, forming passageways through the overgrowth; above them, a broad canopy blocked out most of the sun, though the occasional shaft of light glinted through to brighten their way.

Finally, Lord Blackthorn released Effie's hand and turned her around by the shoulders so that she was facing the front once more.

"We are properly in Blackthorn now," he told her, "so you may walk normally from here on out." There was a hint of self-consciousness in Lord Blackthorn's tone as he spoke, and Effie realised that he was anxious to see what she thought of his realm.

Before them, the tightly wound passageway had opened up into a forest clearing. Standing at the very centre of the clearing was a single prominent table, upon which burned a cheerful candle. A silver tray next to the candle had a handful of calling cards spread out upon it.

Effie stepped uncertainly towards the table. One of the cards on the tray had on it the name *Lady Hollowvale* written in neat, flowing cursive. Another card next to it had the name *Lord Longshadow* written in a tall, ominous hand.

"Is this . . . your entryway?" Effie asked curiously.

Lord Blackthorn smiled with relief. "It is!" he said. "I am always worried that people will walk past it, since I do not have a butler to guide them."

Effie looked around the forest clearing again. There were a few exits among the greenery, leading into more of those tightly woven tunnels of branches. Just beyond one of those tunnels to the right, she saw another forest clearing with a large pianoforte standing at its very centre, surrounded by chairs. Slowly, it began to dawn upon her that there was no Blackthorn Manor in the usual sense – all of the rooms were *outside*.

I could never clean this place if I were to become Mr Jubilee's maid, Effie thought with horror. *I could spend all day working from dawn until dusk – but one can't sweep an entryway clear of dirt when it's in an actual forest!*

Lord Blackthorn was still looking at her anxiously, though, and she couldn't bring herself to dash his perennially cheerful mood by worrying about her own future. "It's . . . very lovely," Effie told him weakly. "I have never seen anything quite like it before."

This response instantly relieved whatever worry Lord Blackthorn had been carrying; he relaxed into his usual bright smile. "But this is nothing!" he told her excitedly. "You must at least see the Green Room while you are here!"

Effie bit her lip. She was keenly aware of every second that ticked by – each one was one more second in which something more urgent than the tablecloth might come up, and Mrs Sedgewick might discover that Effie had left the manor entirely. But Lord Blackthorn's enthusiasm was even more contagious than Lady Culver's anger in some respects . . . and the breeze was so fragrant, and the leaves were so very *green*. Effie had been indoors for so much of her life at a time that this first real taste of the wild stirred a dangerous yearning within her soul.

"I suppose we can see the Green Room then, Mr Jubilee," Effie sighed. "As long as we are quick about it, of course."

"Of course!" Lord Blackthorn echoed her. "Yes, we shall be very quick!"

He took Effie by the arm, leading her proudly between the great clearings which made up Blackthorn. Against her will, Effie found herself thoroughly enchanted. There was the drawing room with the pianoforte, all tangled up within the roots of an impossibly large tree. (Neither Effie nor Lord Blackthorn knew how to *play* the pianoforte, of course, but Lord Blackthorn assured her that the instrument was perfectly in tune.) After that, there was a library full of freestanding bookshelves, all open to the sky. ("But don't the books get wet, Mr Jubilee?" Effie asked him. "Blackthorn is very polite with my things," Lord Blackthorn assured her. "It always chooses to rain elsewhere.")

Finally, they came out into a clearing all full of moss, with a trickling creek running through it. A broad oak table was dug into the centre of the creek; somewhere beneath the ivy that clung to it, Effie caught the glint of a silver tea set. Mismatched chairs in various styles surrounded the table – some of them leaned awkwardly forward due to the uneven ground, but the ivy had grown so thickly around the chair legs that none of them had yet toppled over.

Effie considered the scene with a tilt of her head. "Is this the Green Room, then?" she asked Lord Blackthorn.

"It is!" Lord Blackthorn replied. "Er – but not *the* Green Room."

Effie frowned. "But shouldn't there only be *one* Green Room?" she asked.

Lord Blackthorn shook his head. "Not at all," he corrected her. "This is the Greene Room – there is an extra *e* on the end to distinguish it."

"I see," Effie said. She pressed her fingers to her forehead, trying not to imagine a future where she had to learn the difference. "Because . . . so many of your rooms are green, of course."

"Precisely!" Lord Blackthorn said. "I thought at first that the rooms here would not be well-suited to English naming conventions – but this is a clever solution, don't you think?"

Effie stumbled through the ivy, clinging tightly to his arm. "But perhaps you needn't name your rooms as the English do at all?" she suggested carefully. "If I might ask, in fact – why *have* you taken such an interest in the English, Mr Jubilee?"

Lord Blackthorn helped Effie over a fallen, moss-covered log. "But why shouldn't I take an interest?" he asked her keenly. "You are all in my backyard, after all! How can I be a good neighbour if I do not try to understand the English?"

Effie smiled at this, even as her half-boots scrabbled against the log. "Somehow," she said, "your answers still manage to surprise me, Mr Jubilee. In a good way, I mean. Is that why all of the Fair Folk visit England? Are you all simply being good neighbours?"

Lord Blackthorn frowned thoughtfully at this. "I think that we are all curious to some extent," he said. "But the reasons for our curiosity vary. I would not deign to assume that I know how all of the rest of my cousins think."

Effie had to steady herself against his hand as she came back down to the ground. "I suppose I *had* been assuming that you all think alike," she admitted. "That's silly of me, isn't it? I'll admit, Mr Jubilee, the stories that we hear about you are fearful. But they are stories in the end, and I probably shouldn't have believed them so wholeheartedly."

Lord Blackthorn patted her hand fondly. "If it makes you feel any better," he said, "Lady Hollowvale says that most faeries are very wicked indeed by English standards. She tells me that I am a pleasant aberration."

Effie did not know what the word *aberration* meant, but she was sure that Lydia would love to use it in a sentence. She noted it down for later, before remembering that Lydia was probably too cross with her to talk.

She was distracted from the thought by a flash of orange and a flutter of movement to her right. A butterfly nearly the size of Effie's hand had flown lazily past her, brushing against her hair. Even as she watched, it wavered its way towards one of the tunnels of branches which led out of the Greene Room.

"Oh, thank you very much," Lord Blackthorn addressed the butterfly. "It seems that the Green Room is *this* way today."

"Today?" Effie echoed. Another dull stab of worry hit her at that: *The rooms move around?* she thought in despair. But Lord Blackthorn was moving briskly again, pulling her along next to him, and so she set the thought aside and let him lead the way.

They walked through both a Greeen Room and a Green Roome – each one with a handful more of those burnt-orange butterflies settled onto different surfaces. Just as Effie was beginning to think they would need more *e*s, however, Lord Blackthorn brought her out into a broad, sunny meadow without much of a canopy at all.

This meadow had no furniture – but Effie could not imagine where one would *put* any furniture, even if it had been available.

The tall grass was peppered with pale pink flowers, upon which rested a veritable blanket of black and orange butterflies. Thousands of colourful wings quivered delicately in place, as though the meadow itself were breathing.

Effie stopped in place at the very edge of the meadow, marvelling at the sight. She held her breath, worried that the slightest movement might disturb the moment.

"*This* is the Green Room," Lord Blackthorn told her proudly. "Though ... to be fair, I suppose it is very orange right now. Perhaps I shall temporarily change its name."

"It's beautiful," Effie whispered. "I've never seen so many butterflies before. Are they always here?"

"Not always," Lord Blackthorn mused. "They often pass through on their way to somewhere else, however. The flowers are a particular favourite of theirs, I suppose, and Blackthorn enjoys having them here."

As he spoke, one of the butterflies rose from its perch, floating lazily into the air. Another butterfly joined the first – and soon, the air was awash with black and orange wings. The butterflies swept towards Effie, and she stepped back against the faerie with a gasp. Lord Blackthorn steadied her reassuringly, with an arm around her shoulders.

"They're just curious, I expect," he told her cheerfully. "They might not be from England at all, you know – perhaps they've never seen a housemaid before!"

Effie held onto him more tightly as the butterflies swarmed them both, pressing her eyes into his shoulder. Still, she caught glimpses of the swirl of colour from beneath her lashes – and slowly, she found herself so awed by the sight that she lifted her eyes again. Soft wings brushed against her frock, her cheek, her hair; the touches were delicate and feather-light. The butterflies seemed perfectly content to inspect her only briefly before continuing past her, darting onwards into the branches behind them.

Slowly, their numbers began to dwindle, until only a few of them remained, lazily fanning their wings upon her person.

"I'm sorry," Lord Blackthorn said softly. "Are they very frightening?"

"No," Effie sighed. "No, not at all. I'm only scared to hurt them. They're ever so fragile-looking."

Lord Blackthorn reached out to brush a finger through her hair, and Effie blinked up at him. A moment later, she realised that he had offered out a finger to one of the butterflies caught in her tresses. A strange light came into his leaf-green eyes as the creature crawled obligingly onto his hand, and the fingers of his other hand tightened on Effie's shoulder. "Oh," he said. "Yes, they ... they are rather fragile, aren't they?" He looked at her then, and Effie had the impression that he might not be thinking of the butterfly as he spoke. She became acutely aware of his comforting warmth against her, and of the fond way that his frown furrowed his features; because he frowned so rarely, there was always a hint of thoughtful kindness about the expression on him.

A strange fear gripped Effie suddenly. It was not the same fear that she had felt when she had first met Lord Blackthorn, nor the same fear she'd felt upon agreeing to his wager; rather, it was an uncanny sense that she had mistaken something very important, and that it was none of the elf's fault at all.

"We must not delay you too badly, Miss Euphemia," Lord Blackthorn said suddenly. He let her go, and Effie found that she missed his arm around her quite unaccountably.

She forced a smile, though she suddenly did not feel like smiling. "Thank you for showing me the Green Room, Mr Jubilee," she said. "It's quite as you said – I would have been sad to miss it."

Lord Blackthorn smiled in return – but Effie wondered whether there was something missing from it this time. "We should still make good time to Hollowvale," he assured her. "We are not very far at all, as long as we stay on track."

He took Effie's arm again – a bit more delicately, she thought – and some odd worry in her chest loosened at the reassurance.

As Lord Blackthorn led them through the wooded passageways, a hazy fog began to swirl about their feet; soon, the air became clammy, and the leaves and flowers faded away into whiteness. The fog made Effie's fingertips tingle and go numb – but Lord Blackthorn did not seem concerned, and so she did her best to ignore the feeling.

Effie had not noticed that they had left the forest at all – but as a tall, imposing English-style manor rose out of the fog, she realised that they must have long since left Blackthorn behind them in order for the sky to be so clear of trees.

"Oh, excellent," Lord Blackthorn said with a hint of relief. "Here we are at the Hollow House!" Effie wondered whether he had been expecting some sort of further delay – but a high-pitched scream from the fog ahead of them made her jump in surprise.

"Get back here, you!" a young boy's voice demanded. "I know I just touched someone!"

Giggles trickled through the fog towards Effie and Lord Blackthorn, drawing closer and closer. Soon, a tall adolescent girl in breeches hurried down the path, dragging a younger boy behind her by the hand. The girl's blonde hair was stiff and simply cut, tied back with a lovely green taffeta ribbon which contrasted sharply with her style of dress. The dark-haired boy behind her was very handsome and dignified in his perfectly tailored vest and polished shoes – but the silk kerchief he wore about his head had momentarily slipped to reveal one missing eye.

The blonde girl came up short as she saw Effie and the faerie. Surprise registered on her features – but a moment later, a cunning expression came over her face, and she pressed her finger to her lips, pulling the boy behind her as she ducked behind Effie's skirts.

Shortly after this, a last young boy came blundering through the fog, wearing some gentleman's neck cloth tied around his eyes. "I hear you both!" he called out confidently. "You're not s'pposed to leave Hollowvale, you little blighters! Them's the rules!"

The little boy behind Effie's skirts couldn't quite repress his giggle at this; the boy with the neck cloth over his eyes lunged towards the sound with a sharp *aha!*, and his hand came down upon Lord Blackthorn's arm, where Effie still held it.

"It's Hugh!" the blindfolded boy called triumphantly. "I've caught Hugh!" He reached up to tear the neck cloth away from his eyes – and immediately startled backwards, falling back onto his bottom.

The girl behind Effie burst out laughing. "You've caught a faerie's what you've done, Robert!" she taunted. "You're lucky it's just Lord Blackthorn, aren't you?"

Lord Blackthorn offered a dignified hand out to the boy on the ground, who took it with only the slightest grumble. "You *have* caught me, though," Lord Blackthorn offered helpfully. "You are a very skilled blind man, Robert, I must say."

Robert rolled his eyes at this. "I wasn't *aimin'* to catch a faerie," he said. "But look here! Did I catch a lady too?" His eyes flickered towards Effie, and she blushed.

"I'm not a lady," she admitted. "But you don't seem to be a faerie yourself. What are you doing in Hollowvale?"

Robert knit his brow as Effie spoke, as though he was trying to place something familiar about her. She nearly checked to be sure that she wasn't wearing one of Lord Blackthorn's glamours before she realised that Robert had seen the *faerie* perfectly well too. "You *sound* like a lady," Robert said finally. "Just like Mum used to sound, actually. Where is it you're from?"

Lord Blackthorn cleared his throat politely. "This is Miss Euphemia Reeves," he addressed the young boy. "She is my ward for the next little bit." He then turned towards Effie and gestured at the boy. "This is Master Robert. He was an English child, but I fear that he is now deceased. He is one of the stolen souls that Lady Hollowvale adopted when she inherited her father's realm. Behind you are Master Hugh and Miss Abigail Wilder."

Effie widened her eyes at this. "*Deceased?*" she repeated faintly. She stared intently at Robert, searching him for any awful signs of death – but none seemed readily apparent.

Robert grinned broadly at this. "Boo!" he said. "I'm a ghost, I am."

"*I'm* not a ghost," Abigail said from behind Effie. "I'm just visitin'. But Hugh's dead too. It's not the worst thing ever."

"*Is* your mother about?" Lord Blackthorn asked Robert curiously. "I would stay and take a turn with the blindfold, but I fear that we are on a time limit today."

"Huh!" Robert said. "You'll owe us a game next time then, toff!" He grinned at the two of them and turned down the path, with the neck cloth wound up in his hand. "Mum's on the piano-fort again, last time I checked. Hope your ears are made of strong stuff, m'lady." He addressed this last part to Effie, mispronouncing the word "pianoforte" with a contemptuous scoff.

Robert led them through the entrance to the grand manor and up a spiralling flight of marble stairs, as the other two children trailed behind. Effie found herself searching for signs of faerie servants – *Surely, they've got to clean this marble all of the time*, she thought – but if they were present, then she did not have the faculties necessary to find them.

As they headed down one of the many darkened hallways, lit by eerie blue candles along the walls, an awful, cacophonous noise began to echo back towards them. It had the semblance of a pianoforte, it was true – but each note seemed chosen at random, mangled with an almost vicious glee.

"Lady Hollowvale's skill with the pianoforte is unmatched in all of faerie," Lord Blackthorn told Effie sagely. "She used to spend days at a time learning to play it, without even sleeping."

Effie winced as another awful, clanging note struck her ears. "I see," she said, because she was not sure she could manage anything more polite in the moment.

Robert took them around a last corner and through an open doorway, and Effie finally saw the source of the hideous noise. At the very centre of a black and white chequered ballroom, a perfectly proper-looking, auburn-haired lady in a ragged grey gown had settled herself at a grand pianoforte. Even as Effie watched, the woman slammed her hands down upon the piano keys with wild abandon, mashing at them with her palms. Lady Hollowvale laughed madly in between notes, with a terrible joy upon her fine features.

They stood there in audience for a few moments longer as the faerie lady continued to abuse her poor instrument. Effie had to work not to cover her ears – but she couldn't possibly hide her winces. Eventually, Robert must have taken pity upon her, because the boy strolled out towards the piano to catch Lady Hollowvale's eyes and yell at her over the din.

Lady Hollowvale stopped her playing abruptly, tilting her head at him. "Did you say somethin', Robert?" she asked, in a familiar lower-class accent. "I didn't hear, on account of the music."

Effie stared at the faerie lady in shock. *That's my old accent*, she thought. *It's not my voice, but it's surely my accent, right down to every syllable!*

Robert grinned at Lady Hollowvale. "I said, we've got *guests*, Mum," he repeated. "Figured you didn't invite 'em just to play all day."

Lady Hollowvale turned to look at Effie and Lord

Blackthorn. Her stare was even more uncanny than the rest of her – for now that Effie was looking directly at Lady Hollowvale's eyes, she saw that the woman had one grey eye and one green one. As the faerie lady fixed her gaze upon Lord Blackthorn, her face broke out into a brilliant smile, and she bounded up to her feet.

"You're here!" Lady Hollowvale declared, with a fervent joy that surpassed even Lord Blackthorn's usual, ever-present enthusiasm. "Oh, it's just grand seein' you again!" She bounded towards the other faerie with very unladylike strides, throwing her arms around him. Effie's stomach did a strange turn at this for some reason – until she too found herself the beneficiary of an overly fond hug.

"His Lordship *was* here only a few days ago, Mum," Hugh observed shyly.

"He was, of course," Lady Hollowvale agreed. "But he's here now too, an' isn't that lovely? An' he's got a guest this time! I'm just over the moon!"

Effie closed her arms awkwardly around the faerie lady, a bit embarrassed by her bountiful affections. "Er," she said. "It's a pleasure to meet you, my lady."

Lady Hollowvale pulled back at that, staring at Effie with awe on her face. "You're the one!" she said excitedly. "You've got my elocution, haven't you? How are you enjoyin' it, then?"

Effie blinked quickly. "I ... I hadn't realised that it was *your* elocution I'd been borrowing," she admitted. "It's very lovely. I don't think I could ever speak this well, even if I practised for a hundred years."

Lady Hollowvale's eyes filled up with tears at that for some reason. She released Effie with a sudden sniffle. "You could, though," she said. "You *could*, if someone made you practise for a hundred years. You ought to be more careful what you say in faerie, or you might end up doin' just that!"

Effie stared at her, taken aback by the abrupt change in

emotion. Next to her, Lord Blackthorn calmly offered out a handkerchief, which Lady Hollowvale took without comment. "I'm so sorry," Lady Hollowvale sobbed into the silk. "I gave all my patience to my other half, and she left me with all the violent emotions. It's like this all the time, but especially when she's upset. Her an' her husband are stayin' up workin' into the night lately, an' it's done a number on my nerves."

"There, there," Lord Blackthorn said soothingly. "Miss Euphemia will not be trapped in faerie for a hundred years of elocution practice, I assure you. We shall get her a very fine gown while we are here, and then she will marry the man she loves."

I will? Effie thought. *Oh. Yes, I will. That was the plan, after all.* For just a moment, she was struck by that uneasy feeling again – but Lady Hollowvale's attitude had shifted abruptly once again, and Effie found herself caught off-guard by the faerie lady's sudden, joyful smile.

"A gown, that's right!" Lady Hollowvale crowed. "Yes, I did promise that. The brownies are still playin' servant, so they'll be happy to oblige." The faerie lady spun on her heel and began to stride towards the door, walking with Lord Blackthorn next to her. Effie hurried to keep up with them, blinking away her confusion.

"Playing servant?" Effie asked the children, who'd scurried along next to her.

"Faeries aren't actually ever nobles or servants," Abigail informed Effie, with all the haughtiness of a teenager who's discovered she's an expert. "They're only ever playin' at one or the other because it suits 'em. An' you should know they get it all wrong most of the time, anyway."

Effie frowned. "My goodness," she muttered. "I wish I could stop being a servant whenever it suited me."

Abigail raised an eyebrow at her. "Well, *can't* you stop whenever it suits you?" she asked. "Maybe faeries get it wrong a lot, but they do tend to notice the obvious."

Effie worked very hard not to roll her eyes at this. "I don't have any other means of income," she said. "If I stopped being a servant, I wouldn't have anything to eat or anywhere to sleep. I might have to go to a workhouse if that were the case."

All three children shivered so violently at this suggestion that Effie wondered if she'd accidentally uttered a curse word. Robert crossed himself, and Hugh shrank behind Abigail just a little bit.

"I'll be married soon, though," Effie said quickly, feeling oddly impelled to quell their fears. "I won't be a lady, but I'll have enough to live on that I could stop being a servant *then*. And I very much doubt that any Ashbrookes have ever ended up in a workhouse, or ever will do."

"Guess your gown is for the weddin', then?" Abigail asked carefully.

Effie winced. "Well . . . not quite," she admitted. "I still have to make Mr Benedict fall in love with me. I am currently doing a rather poor job of it, but Mr Jubilee is convinced that a better gown will help."

"Mr Jubilee?" Robert asked. "Who's that?"

Effie bit her tongue with a wince. *I suppose Lord Blackthorn doesn't give out his real name all of the time*, she thought. "No one," Effie said hastily. "Just a . . . friend. Lord Blackthorn brought me here to get a gown made, however, and I suppose that's what is important."

Abigail nodded seriously. "Mum will sort you out," she said. "This half of her can seem a little much, but she's actually got a good head on her shoulders. It's why I came back to Hollowvale to learn magic from her instead of Dad." She wrinkled up her nose at this. "That, an' he's always terrible busy. I feel bad askin' most of the time."

This inspired a whole slew of new questions in Effie – but before she had the chance to ask any of them, Lady Hollowvale whirled about to usher her into another room, full of draped fabrics and sewing accoutrements of all kinds. Robert wrinkled up his nose at the sight, and Hugh edged back another few feet. Abigail looked a bit more interested – but she glanced back towards the other children with a heavy sigh and shot Effie a long-suffering look.

"It's my turn to be the blind man, I guess," Abigail said. "Good luck with your gown, then."

Effie blinked at her dimly. "Good luck with your magic," she replied, since it seemed the only polite thing to say.

Abigail headed out towards the other two, snatching the neck cloth from Robert and pulling the door closed behind her.

"What sort of gown were you lookin' for?" Lady Hollowvale asked, in Effie's own accent. Effie opened her mouth to respond, before she realised that the faerie lady had actually been addressing Lord Blackthorn.

"Certainly nothing made of dignity," Lord Blackthorn said. "I knew it was a terrible idea before, but I simply didn't have the time for anything better."

"It was far too heavy," Effie added in a small voice. "And everyone kept asking me *questions*."

Lady Hollowvale shook her head angrily. "Ugh," she spat. "Dignity. I'm so glad this half doesn't have to worry about *that* any more. Never you mind – we won't be makin' you another gown out of dignity." She rummaged through the other bolts of material leaning against the wall before pulling out a shining white satin-looking material. "Mortals are always impressed with moonlight, though, aren't they?"

"This is for a breakfast, I'm afraid," Lord Blackthorn replied. "If anything, it would have to be sunlight."

"Poor idea," Lady Hollowvale responded instantly. "'Less she wants to blind her beau."

"This is why I always ask your opinion on mortal matters, Lady Hollowvale," Lord Blackthorn sighed. "You remember all of the little details."

Lady Hollowvale dug about a little more, before she came up with a bolt of gauzy material which looked rather like muslin. "Oh!" she said. "We could always dress you up in decorum, Miss – Euphemia, was it? There's nothin' lighter than decorum – all that useless nonsense you say an' do just to avoid talkin' about anything important. An' no one'll ask you any heavy questions that way."

Effie looked at the material hopefully. "That does sound helpful," she said. "Perhaps—"

"But no," Lady Hollowvale interrupted with a sigh. "No one'll find you the least bit interestin' that way, either. Good luck catchin' a good man's interest with *decorum!*" She snorted at this and shoved the bolt of material aside.

Effie's face fell. Decorum *had* looked very lovely. "Do you have any other suggestions?" she asked softly.

Lady Hollowvale turned to regard Effie directly with her oddly mismatched eyes. "I might," she said. "Depends what sort of man you're hopin' to marry, I suppose."

Effie looked down, feeling suddenly shy. "Well, I ... I had hoped to marry Mr Benedict Ashbrooke," she said. "I am beginning to realise that I don't know him as well as I thought I did, strictly speaking. But he is handsome, and very kind, and he has the warmest smile I have ever seen."

That, Effie realised, was not *entirely* true. Or at least, it was now less true than it had been when she had first met Benedict – for Lord Blackthorn's smile was even warmer than his, and wasn't *that* a strange thing to be thinking about while picking out a gown to lure Mr Benedict Ashbrooke's interest?

"Very few of us have the luck to marry a man we've known for long," Lady Hollowvale sighed. "My other half was unreasonably lucky to find a decently angry man. I suppose the rest of you may have to settle for kind men instead."

"A decently *angry* man?" Effie asked, bewildered.

"Have you looked around at the state of things lately?"

Lady Hollowvale asked dryly. "Any really decent man ought to be angry, you'd think." She lifted her tattered grey skirts to climb over a pile of folded cloth, angling towards some bolts near the back of the room. "But if you're aimin' for a kind man, I guess you can't go wrong with a gown made out of wishes."

"Wishes?" Lord Blackthorn asked with a hint of worry. "Are you sure, Lady Hollowvale? An entire gown made out of wishes would fetch quite a dear price."

"I'm not doin' anything else with all these wishes, am I?" Lady Hollowvale observed. "An' besides – I generally prefer doin' rather than wishin' these days." She pulled free a much smaller bolt of cloth near the back, and Effie's heart leapt with such a sharp yearning that she clasped her hands to her mouth.

This material looked like a light blue silk – but as Lady Hollowvale turned it in her hands, the colour seemed to shimmer in the light, unveiling a coruscating rainbow of hues.

"Could I please have that one?" Effie blurted out, before she could think to be more polite. There was just something about the sight that made her heart ache, and she suddenly wasn't sure what she would do if she had to leave without at least a *little* square of wishes.

"You can indeed!" Lady Hollowvale replied exuberantly. "But Lord Blackthorn will have to leave if we're goin' to get the rest done, won't he?" She arched her eyebrows at the faerie in question, who politely stepped back towards the door.

"I shall wait with the pianoforte," Lord Blackthorn promised. "Do tell me if you need anything, either of you."

As soon as he had exited the room and closed the door behind him, Lady Hollowvale turned to regard Effie with her mismatched eyes. "I am fond of Lord Blackthorn," she said, "but he's still a faerie, all the same. He hasn't caused you any trouble, has he? You don't require rescuin' from him?"

Effie blinked at this. "No, not at all," she replied. "I mean to say – I don't think that I require rescuing. And he hasn't *meant* to cause any trouble, certainly."

Lady Hollowvale pursed her lips. "Well," she said. "We have some work to do. While we're doin' it anyway, you really ought to tell me everything."

Chapter Eight

*E*ffie spent the next little bit explaining her situation to Lady Hollowvale as she dressed down to her underthings. She was not obliged to explain things – Lady Hollowvale did not know her full name, and therefore could not compel the truth from her – but though the faerie lady *was* prone to strange outbursts, she had a kind of sympathy about her which felt just human enough to be comforting.

As Effie talked, Lady Hollowvale started offering out instructions regarding Effie's gown. At first, Effie thought the lady was speaking to her, and she became confused – but a pair of small shadows detached themselves from the wall, sweeping up the bolt of cloth in their arms, and Effie paused to stare at them in amazement.

"Where are my manners?" Lady Hollowvale said suddenly. "I should've introduced you. Miss Euphemia, these two are Stillheart an' Gloomfall. They're the best tailors in faerie, you know, an' they're in the mood to be servants this week, so you're in luck."

Effie curtsied awkwardly. She wasn't entirely certain how to navigate the social rules of the situation, as strange as it was, and so she settled for addressing the two shadows the way that she might address fellow servants whom she respected well. "It's a pleasure to meet you," she said. "I greatly appreciate your help, just so you know."

The taller of the two shadows bowed towards her, nearly losing what looked like a shadowy bowler hat in the process. The other shadow, perhaps half the first one's size, simply waved a hand impatiently.

"Can . . . can you not talk?" Effie asked with concern.

"Oh, they *can*," Lady Hollowvale said. "But brownies can change shape into just about anything they like, whenever they like. They're playin' at bein' servants, so they're doin' their best to be silent an' invisible."

A shiver of discomfort crawled down Effie's spine. "But doesn't that bother you?" she asked the two shadows plaintively. "Doesn't it make you feel like . . . like every inch of you is unimportant? Like you might as well not even exist?"

The taller shadow quirked its head at Effie as though it didn't quite understand her meaning. The smaller one patted her awkwardly on the shoulder. All in all, she had the distinct impression that neither of them really understood the problem.

"It's always different when you've got a choice," Lady Hollowvale told Effie sympathetically. "Faeries try on lives as though they're costumes. They're like children playin' games of pretend. For just a little bit, it can be fun to go around unseen. But it'd probably turn awful if that was always how it was, wouldn't it?"

Tears welled up in Effie's eyes. "It really is awful," she said. "I don't think that anyone should ever be invisible. It's a terrible nightmare – to know that you could disappear, and that no one with the power to help you would really care."

The two shadows turned to glance at each other consideringly. Lady Hollowvale knit her brow. "But wouldn't Mr Benedict care if you disappeared?" she asked. "You said he's a kind man."

Effie looked down at her half-boots. "I think that he might give it a passing thought, at least," she said softly. "He might wonder where it was I went off to. But . . . that isn't quite the same thing as caring, is it?" She reached up to wipe at her eyes. "I am not entirely invisible to him, though. Mr Benedict talks to me and smiles at me, and he even took off his boots when he came in from the mud so that I wouldn't have to do any extra work."

"Well," Lady Hollowvale said slowly. "That is ... kind of him." She had a dubious tone, however, and Effie became miserably aware of just how pathetic this must have sounded. "At the very least, it's not *unkind* of him."

"I do feel warm when I think of him," Effie said softly. "I desperately want to dance with him, just once. I think that I could be very happy with him – much happier than I am now, for certain. And I would love to make him happy, too."

Lady Hollowvale considered this. "I think there's better reasons to marry someone than the fact they'll look you in the eyes instead of at the wallpaper," she said. "But I've always been at least a 'Miss', even if I *did* sometimes think the faeries here would kill me for usin' the wrong spoon. If you think Mr Benedict will be kind to you, an' marryin' him might make you both happier, then I suppose we ought to get you a gown worthy of lookin' at."

Effie fiddled nervously with her shift. "I worry, though, Lady Hollowvale – the gown made out of dignity made everyone act so strangely, and I am sure that a gown made out of wishes would do the same. I don't want to *charm* Mr Benedict into falling in love with me."

Lady Hollowvale shook her head. "Course not," she agreed. "You'll want to catch his attention, though, won't you? An' once you have, you can make sure you're wearin' somethin' normal an' boring, by the time he proposes."

Effie nodded at this, somewhat reassured. The shorter shadow patted her shoulder again – and for a moment, she thought she heard a whisper on the air. "*There, there,*" it breathed, in a voice like the wind. The faerie servant slid away again, and soon both shadows began pulling the cloth from the bolt. Even as Effie watched, glimmering threads made of wishes unravelled themselves, floating towards her and draping themselves over her arms.

Each strand sent a tiny shiver of longing through her – and Effie found herself thinking of all the things she'd ever wished for. Once, she had wished very badly for an embroidery hoop. They hadn't had an awful lot of money, but somehow George had scraped up the funds anyway. Effie had thanked him by sneaking into his room and embroidering a tiny morning glory onto the collar of his shirt. The memory made Effie smile wistfully, and she thought how amazed George would be at all of the things she had seen in faerie so far.

Benedict's smile soon floated to mind as well, and Effie found herself keenly longing to see it again. But while she still harboured a wish to dance with him, Effie found that another wish had crept up to join this one while she wasn't looking, and she frowned.

"Somethin' else troublin' you?" Lady Hollowvale asked.

"I was just thinking that I would like to dance with Lord Blackthorn again," Effie mumbled. "I did dance with him once, but I was in an awful state at the time, and I ended up in the mud. He keeps saying that he's learned better since then, and – do you think he really *wants* to dance with me? I assumed it was because he was so distractible, but he does keep bringing it up." Effie heard a hopeful note in her own voice, and she looked down in embarrassment.

"Oh, he *is* distractible," Lady Hollowvale laughed. "But he's always sincere. I keep tryin' to teach him to dance better, but I'll be honest – he's a hopeless case." The faerie lady smiled slyly at Effie for some reason. "*Would* you still like to dance with him?" she asked. "Even if he was still hopeless at it?"

Effie nodded at the floor, and Lady Hollowale beamed at her.

"Is Lord Blackthorn really very different from other faeries?"

Effie blurted out at her. "He said that you called him an aberration."

Lady Hollowvale laughed again. There was a strange, triumphant note to it this time. "Lord Blackthorn is quite an aberration," she declared. "He's not nearly as wicked as the rest of us."

Effie blinked at her. "But you don't seem wicked at all!" she protested.

"Oh, villains find me *very* wicked," Lady Hollowvale assured her. "But you're not a villain, so I haven't got any wickedness left over for you. Lord Blackthorn's not wicked at all, or at least not on purpose. I think it's somethin' to do with Blackthorn – with the realm, I mean. It's always growin' an' changin' an' tryin' to be somethin' it wasn't just yesterday. I think it convinced Lord Blackthorn to grow too, an' now he's *almost* become something entirely different."

Effie pressed her lips together. "He's *almost* become?" she asked. "What does that mean?"

"It means that as much as Lord Blackthorn might wish it," Lady Hollowvale said, "he still hasn't got a human soul. He's only got a faerie soul – which is normally quite all right, mind you, but it doesn't grow as well as a human soul does. Every inch of change is very hard for him."

Effie nodded hesitantly. "Then it's an awful lot of work for him to become virtuous in the way that he wants, isn't it?" she asked.

"An *awful* lot of work," Lady Hollowvale confirmed. "But let's just see what happens, shall we? Maybe he'll manage it in the end." The faerie lady gestured towards a different corner of the room, where Effie saw a tall, ornate mirror. "Go an' take a look at your gown," she said. "Only, be careful of the mirror – you never know what you might see in one while you're in faerie."

Effie followed Lady Hollowvale's instructions with a hint

of trepidation – but all she saw in the mirror was a dull maid in a pretty gown.

It had been quite some time since Effie had bothered to look into a mirror, and the revelation of her own reflection was more than a bit depressing. Her brown hair was still ragged and uninspired; she had pulled it back into a tight bun for the day's work, but wild strands had begun to pull loose over the course of her trek through Blackthorn. Her skin was pale in an unhealthy sort of way, pallid from being cooped up underground for so long. Her eyes were the tired colour of mud. Her half-boots were old and covered in dirt. Her hands were rough and calloused from years of housework.

The gown she wore was so splendid that it made her feel dirty and worn out by comparison. Wishes rippled down to the floor in a shimmering waterfall, shifting colour in the flickering blue light of the candles on the walls. The brownies had indeed done unparalleled work. The collar was perfectly even; the lace on the sleeves came to perfect points at the ends, and the seams on the gown were nearly invisible.

The sight of that gown sent fresh waves of longing through Effie. *I would love to be a lady*, she thought. *But even the most beautiful gown in the world can't make me one. How Benedict ever mistook me for a noblewoman is beyond me.*

"Gloves an' slippers," Lady Hollowvale said suddenly. "You'll need those too, won't you?"

Effie looked down at her half-boots. *It hardly matters*, she thought. "I really should get back to work soon," she said quietly.

Lady Hollowvale pursed her lips. "There's not enough wishes left for another whole gown," she said. "Ought to use the last bit for somethin', don't you think?"

A stray thought occurred to Effie as she stared down at her shoes. "Could the wishes be unravelled into thread?" she asked. "I would love to use them to embroider something, if that's all right."

"Could do that," Lady Hollowvale agreed. "Your embroidery's really somethin', accordin' to Lord Blackthorn."

Effie smiled at her boots. "Lord Blackthorn thinks that everything is *something*," she said. "It is part of his charm – but I do not think you ought to mistake his opinion for fact. I could not sew anything half as beautiful as Stillheart or Gloomfall have done."

Lady Hollowvale scoffed. "There aren't any facts when it comes to opinions," she said. "There's only people who like things an' people who don't. If Lord Blackthorn likes your embroidery, then it's lovely to *him*, isn't it?"

Effie warmed at that observation, though she did not reply to it. In truth, it had already occurred to her that Lord Blackthorn's jacket would be much lovelier if it were embroidered with wishes instead of with mere silk thread. She knew that slippers and gloves would not make her nearly as happy as the jacket would make him instead.

As Effie had this thought, she realised that the edges of the mirror in front of her had darkened strangely. She glanced upwards and saw that the image had also changed. Instead of a ragged maid in a lovely gown, there was now a broad forest clearing, all tangled up in rose vines. It was certainly somewhere in Blackthorn, Effie thought, for she had never seen such tall trees or vivid green anywhere else.

At the very centre of the clearing was a giant tree stump, prominently raised above the rest of the greenery. Part of the stump had been carved away so that it somewhat resembled a chair – but it was such a *large* chair that Effie probably could have fit three of herself on it at once and still left room for one or two of the children from Hollowvale.

"I don't understand," Effie said blankly. "Is there a reason that I should be seeing a chair in the mirror, Lady Hollowvale?"

The faerie lady shrugged. "I don't always understand why I see what I see in the mirrors here," she admitted. "But it's

probably related to *somethin'* you're already thinkin' about."
She paused. "Maybe your feet hurt from standin' too much?"

Effie shook her head in puzzlement. "I suppose that might
be it," she mumbled.

"Did the gown look all right, before the chair got in the
way?" Lady Hollowvale asked her.

"The gown is wonderful," Effie assured her. She turned back
towards Stillheart and Gloomfall with a hint of nervousness.
"Thank you so very much, both of you. Do I ... do I owe you
something? Lord Blackthorn said that faeries cannot give gifts."

"I can give gifts," Lady Hollowvale said. "I've got half a
human soul, after all. An' I'm the one payin' the brownies. But
if you *wanted* to give me somethin' for the gown, I do have an
idea in mind."

Effie blinked at this. "I would certainly *like* to pay you back,"
she said. "What was it you were thinking?"

Lady Hollowvale smiled. "You should dance with Lord
Blackthorn before you go," she said. "He needs a partner to
practise with, an' I'm tired of him steppin' on my feet."

❧

"Oh, it's perfect!" Lord Blackthorn exclaimed, when Effie and
Lady Hollowvale returned to the room with the pianoforte.
"How lovely you look, Miss Euphemia. I am sure that you shall
catch Mr Benedict's eye at once!"

Effie smiled ruefully at this. After seeing herself in the
mirror, she was sure that Lord Blackthorn's opinions on her
loveliness were about as accurate as his opinions on her embroidery. But the sincerity in his voice made her *feel* more beautiful
than she knew she was, and she stood a little straighter nonetheless. "Faeries cannot lie," she observed. "So you must really
believe all of that, I suppose."

Lord Blackthorn gave her a puzzled look. "I do, of course,"

he said. "I know that things have not gone quite as planned so far, Miss Euphemia, but that is all simply due to terrible luck. You need only the proper opportunity; Mr Benedict will fall in love with you quickly, as soon as he knows you better."

Effie considered this thoughtfully. She was about to respond when Lady Hollowvale headed over to the pianoforte and settled herself upon the bench. The faerie lady laid her fingers upon the keys, and Effie instinctively flinched – but this time, she played a delicate, sprightly melody, with all of the expertise that Effie might have expected from the best pianist in all of faerie.

"Oh!" Lord Blackthorn said with sudden delight. "This is a quadrille!"

"It is a quadrille," Lady Hollowvale agreed. "I thought you might practise with Miss Euphemia while you're here. You'll have to imagine the other couples, but I hazard that imaginin's no hardship for a faerie."

"It is no hardship at all!" Lord Blackthorn assured her. He set the lace tablecloth onto the back of the pianoforte and turned back to Effie, with an obvious light behind his leaf-green eyes. "Would you like to dance, Miss Euphemia?" Lord Blackthorn asked. He said it in the same tone that he had always used before – but Effie found herself keenly aware this time of the sincerity in his voice.

Lord Blackthorn truly *did* want to dance with her, she knew. In the same way that he believed that her stitching was more precious than a gown made of wishes – in the same way that he believed that she was lovely, with her ragged hair and her worn-down half-boots – he had a genuine desire to join her in the quadrille.

"I would love to dance with you, Mr Jubilee," Effie said softly.

She took his hand, with an odd flutter in her heart. The elf did not shy away from her touch, though her hands were bare and calloused. It was immediately clear that he hadn't the first idea what he was doing; while he did bow to her very nicely at the beginning, everything else was just a terrible mess. Lady Hollowvale cheerfully called out figures from her place at the pianoforte – but even Effie, with her limited knowledge of dancing and balls, was aware that Lord Blackthorn kept mistaking the forms. More than once, Effie bumped into him awkwardly, as she tried to follow Lady Hollowvale's instructions and found herself at odds with her own partner.

Nevertheless, she was smiling so widely that her cheeks hurt.

Far too soon, the song wound down, and Lady Hollowvale lifted her hands from the keys. Lord Blackthorn beamed at Effie. "I think that must be my best attempt yet!" he told her. "It does help to have such a talented partner, of course. Thank you for indulging me, Miss Euphemia."

"I think it *was* your best attempt," Effie told him warmly. "It was certainly the best dance that I have ever had." For just a moment, Effie thought she understood Lord Blackthorn's tendency to treat everything with utter delight – for she meant these words sincerely as well, even if most people would have considered the dance to be terribly unskilled.

Lord Blackthorn's eyes lit up again at the compliment, and Effie's heart grew so light that she began to wonder if it might just fly away. As she considered the feeling, she realised that it was something exactly the opposite of how she normally felt at Hartfield. Much as she normally thought of herself as an irritable young woman, that awful stewing anger was currently nowhere to be found. In its place was a genuine pleasure and a joy for life that Effie had assumed was something you were only allowed as a child.

Surely, this was an unnatural occurrence – a quirk of being in faerie. Effie's joy dimmed at the edges as she realised that she would have to leave it behind. Eventually, her wager would end, and Lord Blackthorn and his endless wonder would disappear from her life.

"Could we dance again?" Effie asked.

She was sure that women were not supposed to ask men to dance. But maids were really not supposed to dance with faeries in the first place, either.

The question caught Lord Blackthorn by surprise – but he brightened and turned towards Lady Hollowvale. "Would you mind terribly?" he asked her. "I have not had so much fun in years!"

Lady Hollowvale replied by settling her hands back to the keys and starting another song.

Effie soon lost track of how many songs there were, or how long they had danced. Every time she began to think that perhaps she ought to get back, a stubborn, furtive feeling stole her resolve. The idea of returning to Hartfield – of going back underground and being trapped there for ages – leached away at her will. Already, she could feel the helpless suffocation of the world beyond the green baize door.

Here and now, Effie was dancing with an elf who enjoyed her company, in a world where Lady Culver could not reach her.

Eventually, however, a knock at the door interrupted Lady Hollowvale's playing. The music stopped, and Effie snapped back to her senses with a jolt.

"Sorry, Mum," Abigail said apologetically. "I do have some lessons, don't I?"

Lady Hollowvale leapt up from the piano. "You do!" she gasped. "Oh, I feel so awful, Abigail, I went an' forgot—" And here, Lady Hollowvale began to sniffle and cry. "There I go cryin' again! You'll have to give me a second while I sort myself out."

Lord Blackthorn released Effie's hand to go pat Lady Hollowvale comfortingly on the shoulder. "I'm so sorry to have kept you," he said. "But thank you for everything. It really has been a lovely afternoon."

Well, Effie thought sadly, *all good things come to an end.* A last worry occurred to her as Lady Hollowvale hurried for the doorway. "I do need to put my frock back on!" Effie said. "And I – I would like to take the rest of the wishes with me, if I may?" Lady Hollowvale nodded through sniffles. "What a fool I am," she mumbled. "I've lost my head today. Go an' grab your things, of course."

Effie returned to the room where she had left her normal frock – but even more than her frock, she was relieved to have remembered the wishes, which Stillheart and Gloomfall had helpfully unwound into spools of thread.

I wouldn't have wanted to forget these, she thought, as she changed back into her usual clothing and folded up the gown made of wishes.

Lord Blackthorn met her at the bottom of the stairs. He immediately offered to carry Effie's gifts from Lady Hollowvale, which was very kind of him.

It did not occur to Effie, somehow, that they had both forgotten something *else* behind them.

Effie and Lord Blackthorn had only just exited Hollowvale's foggy environs and returned to the towering trees of Blackthorn when suddenly, the faerie stopped in his tracks and said the word "Drat."

"Whatever is the matter?" Effie asked.

Lord Blackthorn winced. "I was afraid of this," he said. "It seems that we have entered Blackthorn's Folly." He gestured ahead of them, and Effie turned her eyes in the direction he had indicated. Between the last wisps of fog, she caught sight of a familiar tree stump, which was shaped like a chair.

"Oh!" Effie said. "That's the chair that I saw in Lady Hollowvale's mirror!" She gave Lord Blackthorn a puzzled look. "But why is that a problem?"

Lord Blackthorn shook his head mournfully. "Blackthorn always means well," he told Effie. "But it can sometimes be *too* helpful, if you understand my meaning. It is why I said we should be careful to keep our goals firmly in mind. Blackthorn will always try to take you wherever it is you wish to go – but if you do not *know* where it is that you wish to go, it assumes that what you really need is to sit down and think for a while."

Effie felt a guilty stab at that. Even as Lord Blackthorn said the words, she knew that it was *her* mind that had strayed. *I have been having such a lovely afternoon*, she thought. *I don't want to return to Hartfield at all.*

"I appreciate the thought," Effie told Lord Blackthorn. "But I really do need to get back. I've already stayed here longer than I ought to have done."

Lord Blackthorn nodded, but there was a hint of unease on his face as he did. "Thank you very much!" he called out to the clearing ahead of them. "But we do not need a chair! We'll just take our leave now if you do not mind!"

Lord Blackthorn turned back around the way that they had come, forcing a firmness into his steps. Effie followed along with him, thinking furiously of all the chores she really needed to get done. But somehow, even though they had walked directly away from Blackthorn's Folly, they soon ended up right back in the same spot, staring at the chair in the clearing.

"Bother," Lord Blackthorn said.

Effie knit her brow. "Won't Blackthorn listen to you if you tell it that we are fine?" she asked him.

"I'm so very sorry, Miss Euphemia," Lord Blackthorn sighed. "As I told you before – Blackthorn owns me, and not the other way around. We are friends of a sort, and so I might try to explain the situation – but I suspect that Blackthorn is feeling particularly helpful today."

How familiar, Effie thought dryly. *Blackthorn really is an awful lot like its lord.* But she did not speak the words aloud. "It is probably my fault," she admitted. "I really do not want to go back to working for Lady Culver. Every time I think about it, I find it a little bit hard to breathe."

Lord Blackthorn frowned at this. "That does not sound healthy," he advised. "I have heard that mortal sicknesses travel in the air. Do you think that there is a miasma beneath Hartfield?"

Effie shook her head. "I didn't mean that," she said. "Though ... I suppose it *is* quite stuffy down there. No, I meant ... " She sighed. "I feel so trapped, knowing that Lady Culver might upend my life at any moment. It makes no sense, of course – I applied for the job myself some time ago, and I am paid for it. Why should I feel so awful doing exactly what I promised to do? And conversely, if I am so miserable, then why am I even *more* miserable at the thought that Lady Culver might dismiss me? Why can't I just be grateful that I have a job at all, Mr Jubilee?"

Lord Blackthorn furrowed his brow with greater and greater concern as Effie spoke. "If all of your options are terrible," he said slowly, "then that is a trap of a different sort, isn't it?"

Effie looked down at her boots. Misery had flushed her face now. "Sometimes," she confided, "I have thought about quitting, even if it meant that I might starve. But only for a moment, Mr Jubilee. I always remember at the last instant that thinking about starving and *actually* starving are two very different things."

Lord Blackthorn went quiet. For some reason, the chair in the clearing loomed very large in the silence.

"Being a maid is very awful, then," he said finally. "I am sorry that I offered you the wager that I did, Miss Euphemia – to be a maid for ever. I would not wish to be the cause of your misery."

Effie crossed her arms uncomfortably. "I did agree to the wager," she told him. "You must not feel bad about that."

"But you had only terrible choices," Lord Blackthorn insisted. "I am no better than your employer, if I have offered you only one *more* terrible choice." He shook his head. "We really must get you back to England, is what I mean to say. Your happiness depends upon it. You will marry Mr Benedict, and everything will be better."

There was an odd note in his voice as he spoke. Effie glanced up at him curiously. Lord Blackthorn had an expression as though he were arguing the matter with someone . . . but *Effie* certainly had no intention of arguing with him. At the end of the day, she knew that she needed to return to Hartfield in order to fulfil their wager. Perhaps Lord Blackthorn was truly addressing the chair in front of them?

But Mr Jubilee is looking at me, and not at the chair, Effie thought. His sharp features had clouded with gloom and confusion, and Effie opened her mouth to ask him just what had upset him so badly – but even as she did, she noticed that the chair had disappeared.

Effie blinked. "Look at that!" she said. "We've escaped Blackthorn's Folly! I must have convinced myself of our destination, Mr Jubilee."

Lord Blackthorn smiled at that, though there seemed this time to be something lacking behind his eyes. "That might explain it," he said. "We should take advantage then, while we are both feeling quite certain."

It did not take them long at all after that to find their way back to England. It was just mid-afternoon when Lord Blackthorn led Effie back out of the hedge maze at Hartfield. The sight of the manor set a dull, leaden feeling into her stomach – but she reminded herself that Benedict, at least, was still inside. At this thought, the weight lifted ever so slightly.

"There is so little sunlight beneath Hartfield," Lord Blackthorn murmured next to her. "Perhaps that is the problem. Don't humans require sunlight in order to grow?"

"You are thinking of trees, Mr Jubilee," Effie told him fondly. But she could not deny that it was hard for her to leave the sun-light, now that she had tasted it.

"Oh!" Lord Blackthorn said suddenly. "Your gown!" He offered out the brown paper package which he had been carrying. "I nearly forgot it entirely."

Effie took the package from him. "I am feeling forgetful today, too," she admitted. "But thank you for everything, Mr Jubilee. It was wonderful to be out of doors for just a while. And I had a very lovely afternoon."

Lord Blackthorn had been looking a bit glum for the last little bit – but he brightened again at this, and his smile strengthened. "The pleasure was all mine, Miss Euphemia," he said. "Do have a good evening. I will be sure to return promptly on the day that you have your breakfast."

Effie had to force herself to leave his company to walk back into Hartfield. But each step was just a little bit easier than the last. *In less than a hundred days*, she thought, *I will either be married to Benedict or else I will spend the rest of my life endlessly sweeping the dirt from Blackthorn. Either way, I shall not be here for ever.*

Only a moment after she had returned to the dark, cramped passageways below-stairs, however, Effie ran into Mrs Sedgewick. The housekeeper's mouth dropped as she saw Effie, and she lifted her hand to her chest in shock.

"Effie!" Mrs Sedgewick gasped, with a mixture of fury and relief. "Where on earth have you *been*?"

Effie blinked. "I ... I'm sorry, Mrs Sedgewick," she said. "I only meant to step outside for a moment, but I seem to have taken an hour or two longer than I'd hoped."

Mrs Sedgewick blinked at this, and Effie realised that she had spoken to the housekeeper with a far more elevated accent than she normally used. "Have you been hit on the head, Effie?" she demanded. "You have been missing for two whole days – and now that you finally return, you're pretending to be a lady?"

Effie stared at the housekeeper. "I don't understand," she said. "I can't have been gone for two days. That simply isn't possible."

But Mrs Sedgewick's expression was so genuinely infuriated that Effie knew the housekeeper was not lying. Effie thought back to her time in Hollowvale with a slow, sinking feeling of dread. *I danced with Lord Blackthorn for an awfully long time,* she thought. *And all of the stories say that time passes strangely in faerie.*

"Is that the tablecloth you were supposed to fix?" Mrs Sedgewick asked sharply. "Don't tell me you walked to town with it, Effie!"

The tablecloth.

Effie pressed her hand to her face with a moan. "Oh no," she mumbled.

Lord Blackthorn had left the lace tablecloth sitting on top of Lady Hollowvale's pianoforte.

Chapter Nine

$\mathcal{M}$rs Sedgewick was rightfully furious.

Effie endured quite the tongue-lashing – all the more so because she could not explain to Mrs Sedgewick where it was that she had been. Effie suspected that she might have convinced the housekeeper of her story if she had shown her the gown made of wishes ... but she was suddenly very fearful that either Mrs Sedgewick or Lady Culver would take the gown away from her if they knew of its existence. As such, Effie spent much of the hour waiting to be told that she would be dismissed – but Mrs Sedgewick instead exhausted herself yelling, and then told Effie that the lace tablecloth would be deducted from her year's wages, and that she would spend every night from now until the end-times taking her supper in the scullery while she washed it top to bottom.

And so, Effie found herself in the scullery that very evening, scrubbing at dirty dishes.

Effie was used to being irritable when things like this happened – but this time, she could not dredge up even a lick of anger. All she felt instead was a sense of failure. What maid in her right mind ever expected that gallivanting off to faerie would turn out for the best?

Someone knocked softly on the door frame to the scullery. Effie cringed instinctively, expecting another dressing-down from some other angry upper servant – but it was only George, who had stopped by with her food.

"I can't believe you disappeared without tellin' me," he sighed. "Mrs Sedgewick wouldn't say where you were. I thought you might have finally quit the place an' run away."

Effie took the bowl from him with a worried frown. She set it aside just long enough to hug him tightly. "I didn't mean to scare you, George," she said softly. "I feel so awful about it, I promise."

George laughed at this for some reason. Halfway through, the laugh turned into a hacking cough, and he had to release Effie to catch himself against the scullery counter. "Mrs Sedgewick tells you to practise your French, an' instead you've gone an' practised your English!" he wheezed. "What *have* you been doin' the last two days, Effie?"

Effie knit her brow at him. "That is *quite* a cough," she told him again. "I don't like how it sounds on you."

George waved her away. "Cookie's been givin' me some awful tea to drink," he said. "She told me to put orange peels up my nose too, but I wasn't so keen on that idea."

Effie looked down at her food. "My disappearing must not have improved your health," she mumbled. "Won't you go to bed, George? I feel more wretched every moment that you're here."

George waved her off. "I'll sleep better now that you're back," he said. "Don't work too hard on the scullery though, Effie. Mrs Sedgewick was never goin' to dismiss you – we're too short-staffed as it is, and we all know Lady Culver won't hire a replacement if you go."

Effie pursed her lips. "I wondered why Mrs Sedgewick didn't dismiss me on the spot," she admitted. "I had hoped for a moment that she really cared about me, but that makes a lot more sense."

George cuffed Effie affectionately across the shoulder.

"You've been the perfect maid since you got here," he said. "She'd be mad to let you go, either way. I'd say you're due for a mistake or two, Effie, if only so the rest of us don't feel so rubbish by comparison."

Effie smiled at him wanly. For a moment, it occurred to her that she might try to tell George all about her wager with Lord Blackthorn, if only so he knew the truth – but as he was even more tired-looking now than he had seemed before she'd left two days ago, she worried that the revelation might well trouble him anew. "Do go to bed, George," she told him instead. "We'll talk more in the morning." She took him by the shoulders then and shoved him physically out of the scullery.

Only a quarter-hour after George had gone, however, someone else slipped through the doorway.

"I suppose you *haven't* been abducted to faerie, then," Lydia mumbled. She looked tired and guilty. "I really thought . . . well, I worried that I'd somehow run you off an' convinced you to give up your wager."

Effie winced. "I *was* in faerie," she said. "But I was only supposed to be there for an hour or two. I lost track of time, exactly as people do in the faerie tales. I'm only lucky that I didn't lose an entire year."

Lydia grabbed at a dirty plate, shaking her head. "*Faeries,*" she muttered. "All kinds of trouble, aren't they? I don't guess Lord Blackthorn warned you that might happen, did he?"

Effie sighed heavily. "If he knew that it was possible, then I'm sure that he forgot," she said. "The strangest thing is that he really does mean well, Lydia. He simply doesn't understand certain things, or . . . or else he doesn't think far enough ahead."

Lydia pursed her lips. "He won't be much help winnin' your wager then, will he?" she said.

Effie felt a pang of worry at the observation. "I am sure that he will continue to *try,*" she replied weakly.

"Tryin' won't matter if he gets you dismissed," Lydia told her

matter-of-factly. "We've got to take this into our own hands."
Effie shot her a surprised look, and Lydia smiled ruefully.
"I'm sorry for thinkin' you'd make fun of me, Effie," she said.
"You've never done it before, an' you're just not the sort. I was
upset, an' I took it out on you. At the end of the day, though,
we're friends, an' we have to watch out for each other."

Effie realised then that Lydia had begun scrubbing at the
dirty dishes right alongside her. A warm spot of hope and affection blossomed in her chest, pressing back against the miserable
self-loathing which had settled there.

"Mrs Sedgewick won't want to let you out again," Lydia continued. "But you've got to get to Mr Jesson's breakfast without
her gettin' angry afterwards. Cookie still owes me a favour or
two, so I'll see if she can't send us off for errands in town that
day. I don't know what else I can manage, but I can at least come
with you again an' watch your back."

Lydia stayed through supper to help Effie with the scullery.
It was hard work, but by the end of it, Effie was feeling far more
optimistic than when she'd first returned.

Oddly, when she laid her head down on her pillow and closed
her eyes, she did not dream of dancing with Benedict. Instead,
she dreamed she was wearing a gown made of wishes, dancing
with a handsome elf in a distant faerie ballroom.

For the next few days, Mrs Sedgewick kept Effie very busy
indeed. Effie addressed all of the chores she was given with as
much energy as she could muster, keenly aware that Mr Jesson's
breakfast was just around the corner. Lydia did her best to help
where she could; whatever anger the other maid felt towards
Lady Culver, she seemed to have channelled it into helping
Effie to win her wager.

"It's a kind of revenge," Lydia told Effie, as she snuck in to help her strip the sheets from one of the beds. "Just one of us gettin' away from Her Ladyship an' livin' well would be worth it."

This statement struck Effie a bit badly – it had not occurred to her that she was essentially running away and leaving the other servants to deal with Lady Culver – but Lydia had such an air of determination now that she couldn't dredge up the fortitude to broach the subject. Instead, Effie let the observation simmer within herself, wondering silently on its existence.

Meanwhile, the situation between Mr Allen and Mrs Sedgewick seemed to grow worse and worse by the day. This time, Effie found herself in the strange position of listening to Mr Allen's woes as she mended a tear in his coat.

"I have never known another woman in my life who takes everything so *personally*," the butler sniffed. "I have stopped asking her for anything at all, even when it is to do with the household. She always says she is too busy, or that I ought to handle it myself, even when it falls directly within her purview!"

Though Mrs Sedgewick had been the cause of an awful lot of Effie's work lately, Effie still could not help but feel a sense of kinship with the woman. Since Mrs Sedgewick had to report directly to Lady Culver – who was still quite upset over her incident at the ball – the housekeeper had lately endured all sorts of sudden, furious requests. No matter how unreasonable Lady Culver was feeling, however, she never dared to harass Mr Allen in the same manner, since he reported to her husband.

"Mrs Sedgewick *is* very busy," Effie told Mr Allen politely. "We could greatly use another maid on staff – or maybe even two."

Mr Allen frowned at this. "I agree, of course," he said. "When I first arrived, however, Mrs Sedgewick accused me of trying to steal her duties from her. *Now*, she is upset when I keep strictly to our roles. I cannot seem to make peace with her, no matter what I do. I am growing very weary of trying."

Effie sighed heavily. Somehow, the fact that she always ended up doing the mending *also* meant that she had to listen to everyone's woes. This time, however, Mr Allen's miseries struck her in a particular way, and she paused over his coat.

Lord Blackthorn had observed that Lady Culver's anger was a plague – and Effie had been unable to reason with Lydia at all once she had caught that anger. It was only when things had calmed that Lydia had found her senses again.

We are never allowed to be angry with Lady Culver, Effie thought. *So we are always taking it out on each other, even when it makes no sense.*

"Mr Allen," Effie said. "I am not the person to ask about Mrs Sedgewick's moods. But in general, I have noticed that it is impossible to make peace when *everyone* is under pressure at once – and we have all been under pressure since well before you arrived. You would not ask a woman with a broken leg to be more reasonable, I hope, until the leg was set. This strikes me in much the same way."

Mr Allen knit his brow. For a second, Effie thought that he might reply – but instead, he stayed in thoughtful silence until she was done with his coat.

A few days after this, the day of Mr Jesson's breakfast finally arrived. True to her word, Lydia convinced Cookie to send them both on an errand around that time. "We'll have only an hour or two," Lydia told Effie, as they went back to their room to change. "And *not* in faerie time. I might have to leave even earlier if we're to get our shoppin' done."

Lydia was still musing on their timetable when Effie pulled the gown of wishes from its wrappings. The other maid gasped and stared, entirely broken from her previous thoughts. "An' here I thought your other gown was beautiful," Lydia said. "Oh, this one reminds me so much of your stitchin', too!"

Effie blinked at this. "It does?" she asked. "But this is a gown made out of wishes, Lydia – and it was sewn by the best tailors in faerie. What on earth has that got to do with my stitching?"

Lydia knit her brow. "I don't know," she admitted. "It was just the first thing that came to mind for some reason. I was lookin' at the gown, an' suddenly I found myself thinkin' about that embroidery you did for me a few months back." Effie gave Lydia a blank look, which the other maid must have misconstrued for forgetfulness. "I got upset, cos Lady Culver yelled at me an' told Mrs Sedgewick I was an awful maid," Lydia reminded her. "I was bawlin' my eyes out. You said Lady Culver was just bein' a bully, an' you stitched a little thistle on my handkerchief to cheer me up."

"I *do* remember that," Effie assured her. "But I suspect that really wasn't my finest work. I was upset on your behalf as well, and the stitches were probably uneven."

Lydia shook her head slowly. "It meant somethin'," she said. "For the longest time, whenever I started feelin' like I wasn't worth anything, I pulled out my handkerchief – an' then, just like magic, I remembered that I ought to be angry instead."

Effie winced. "I didn't mean to make you *angry*—" she started.

"Well, you did," Lydia said matter-of-factly. "An' it wasn't a bad thing, Effie. I miss that handkerchief. I used it all the time, until it ended up in pieces. It made me feel like I wasn't crazy for feelin' like we all deserve better."

Effie looked at the gown in her hands. It was undoubtedly superior to her own work in every possible way. But for some reason, both Lydia and Lord Blackthorn had now evinced a preference for Effie's sewing.

I suppose one truly can't account for taste, Effie thought, as she changed into the gown.

By the time Lydia had helped Effie put her hair up, there was a polite, familiar knock at their bedroom door. Lord Blackthorn was waiting outside, with his usual barely leashed excitement. As his eyes lit upon Effie, he broadened his smile in a way that made her stomach flip-flop strangely.

"Right on time!" Lord Blackthorn exclaimed. "This is already going much better than the first attempt, Miss Euphemia, don't you think?"

A small, bitter part of Effie wanted to point out that she had not returned *on time* the last time she had gone anywhere with him – but the elf's good cheer was infectious, and she could not really bring herself to be angry with him. *He does mean well,* Effie reminded herself. Lord Blackthorn took her arm very delicately, and Effie found herself smiling again at the scent of wild roses which suffused the air around them.

"Don't run off just yet!" Lydia gasped from the bedroom. She rummaged within the drawer in the bedside table, then hurried out to press a rose into Effie's hand. Lord Blackthorn's glamour wiggled its way obediently up Effie's arm to curl around her throat, and she let out a sigh of relief.

"Thank you for that," Effie said. "I might have gone all the way to Mr Jesson's breakfast and then discovered I was still a maid!"

"How silly of me!" Lord Blackthorn sighed. "Yes, I would have forgotten as well. Thank you very much, Miss Lydia."

"I *figured* you might have forgotten," Lydia muttered beneath her breath. But she shot the elf a rueful smile and twined the other rose around her neck. "An' I don't see a chaperone this time either. You're just lucky I've cleared out my schedule."

Lord Blackthorn now looked terribly sheepish. "That is very kind of you, Miss Lydia," he said. "I did try to secure Lady Mourningwood's aid as a chaperone, but Lady Hollowvale warned me that Lady Mourningwood's ideas of propriety are a bit too strict for a casual breakfast, and she strongly suggested that I should discard the idea."

Lydia straightened her back and took Lord Blackthorn's other arm firmly in hers. "Fewer faeries is better, I think," she said. "Respectfully speakin', Your Lordship, but things get mad enough when *you're* around – I hate to think what two faeries would do to a little breakfast like this. Just remember that we're hopin' to keep things calm enough that Effie can have a conversation or two."

Had Lydia been addressing any other faerie, Effie was sure that she would have been courting danger with such a straightforward statement – but Lord Blackthorn merely nodded at this, as though the other maid had blessed him with a rare and valuable wisdom. "Quite right!" he said. "I am glad that Miss Euphemia has such a competent chaperone! I will owe you another favour, of course, for your trouble."

Lydia pursed her lips at this, and Effie knew that she was thinking of how wildly unpredictable Lord Blackthorn's favours could be. "I'm sure that's not necessary," she said.

"I fear that it is," Lord Blackthorn told her gently. "I cannot accept gifts, Miss Lydia. I shall owe you a favour for certain."

Lydia sighed. "One favour, then," she mumbled. "I suppose we'll see if I use it."

Chapter Ten

They departed once again in the carriage of roses – this time, it took them to Mr Herbert Jesson's family estate. The land there was far less curated to appear wild and untamed; in fact, almost every inch of the grounds was covered in flowers of vibrant shape and colour, many of which had only just begun to bloom. The small manor that they approached was really poor and unremarkable-looking when compared to the flush of red and yellow tulips that overtook the lawn before it.

"Well!" Lord Blackthorn said approvingly, as he helped Effie and Lydia from the carriage. "It is no Blackthorn, but it will do. At least Mr Jesson has a proper sense of decoration!"

"Mr Jesson's family sells flowers," Lydia told Effie, from Lord Blackthorn's other side. "Mainly tulips, of course – a good tulip is awful expensive. I asked Mrs Sedgewick, an' she said we buy most of our flowers from Orange End, right here."

Effie considered the small line of other carriages which had arrayed themselves outside Orange End. "I am sure that Mr Jesson has never kicked any governesses into ponds," she said. "But I haven't heard much about him otherwise."

Lydia looked thoughtful. "I don't know any of his servants," she said. "He doesn't socialise much, so I haven't run into any of them."

Effie now found herself even more curious about Mr Jesson's

servants than she was about Orange End itself – but to her surprise, though the front door had been left open, there was no servant there to greet them. In fact, the entryway was entirely empty except for a table near the front, on which a bright orange tulip and a handwritten note had been left.

Breakfast is in the garden just behind the house, it said helpfully.

"Mr Jesson *does* have servants, doesn't he?" Effie murmured to Lydia, perplexed.

Lydia frowned. "He must," she said. "You couldn't keep a house like Orange End without them."

Effie found herself inspecting the entryway for clues. The floors were a bit dirtied, but they had surely been swept within the last few days, at least. The table near the front had been spot-cleaned, but it did not shine with quite the terrible perfection that Lady Culver always required at Hartfield. The lace which laid beneath the note was visibly frayed at the edges, so that Effie's fingers itched with the need to mend it.

"We'd be dismissed if we left the entryway like this," Lydia muttered.

"We'd be dismissed for a lot of things," Effie said. But she couldn't help feeling at least a hint of professional distaste at the slight mess. In fact, she had to remind herself that she was currently a lady and not a maid, so that she didn't stop to wipe the dust from the table with her gloves.

The sound of distant laughter drew them deeper into the house, however – and soon, they found another door at the back of the manor which had been left open to the outside.

The back garden was a riot of orange and yellow colour. Neat lines of hedges made the area feel small and private – but pots with tulips had been tucked into every spare inch, so that there was barely enough room for the table and chairs which had been set out for the morning's breakfast. A few other ladies and gentlemen had already found their seats at the table, but it was clear that their company was going to be a relatively small gathering.

Effie did not need to search for Benedict — she heard his laugh from the back of the table and instantly knew that he was there. He was sitting with an older woman whose features reminded Effie very strongly of Mr Jesson. Somehow, fantastically, there was a seat open just on Benedict's other side. Effie released Lord Blackthorn's arm and started towards it with great urgency — but she found herself quickly intercepted by Mr Jesson, who had noticed their arrival.

"Miss Reeves!" Mr Jesson said, with pleasant surprise in his voice. "I was worried that you wouldn't make it! We had a devil of a time trying to find Lord Blackthorn's address in order to send over an invitation."

"I daresay the Royal Post does not deliver to faerie," Lord Blackthorn said with bemusement.

This outlandish statement only made Mr Jesson nod his head in agreement. "It is so obvious now that you say it, of course," he replied, with a wave of his hand. "What was I thinking? But I am glad that you have found your way here regardless. Won't you come and sit with us?"

There was no polite way to refuse such an invitation, of course — but while Effie had been hoping to find her way to the spot just next to Benedict, Mr Jesson settled the three of them just next to him at the very head of the table, a few seats down from where Effie had been aiming. Worse still, Mr Jesson could not seem to tear his gaze from Effie; he began to converse with her almost as soon as they had sat down, with no seeming remembrance of his promise to re-introduce her to Benedict.

"I feel compelled to say," Mr Jesson enthused, "you are even more lovely today than I remembered you before, Miss Reeves. Why, there is a kind of wistfulness about you that simply moves the soul! Surely, you cannot tell me that it is the fault of your dress, since you are wearing a new gown."

Effie flushed at the unexpected comment. "I fear it is still to do with my dress, Mr Jesson," she told him. "Though I do not expect you to believe me." Perhaps Effie was growing used to the strange effect that Lord Blackthorn's glamours had upon people, for she added, "I am wearing a gown made of wishes. The best tailors in faerie made it for me."

"I begin to suspect that you are far too modest for your own good, Miss Reeves," Mr Jesson mused, as though she had said nothing the least bit strange.

"Miss Euphemia is always *very* modest," Lord Blackthorn agreed. "You must not listen to her, Mr Jesson – I assure you, she is lovely no matter what she happens to be wearing. Why, her soul is made of the very finest thread I have ever seen!"

Effie had been about to argue with Mr Jesson once again – but at this odd comment, she paused. "Whatever do you mean by that, Mr Jubilee?" she asked Lord Blackthorn.

Lord Blackthorn looked at Effie with curiosity. "Surely you are aware?" he said. "Oh! But I keep forgetting that mortals cannot see souls. What a shame, Miss Euphemia. Your soul is so full of strength and anger and generosity. If you could only see it yourself, I am sure that you would be less apt to discount yourself."

Effie's flush deepened, and she found herself curving into her chair in a most unladylike manner. Lord Blackthorn had said the words with such earnestness, as he always did. She should have thought: *he is equally fond of my terrible stitching and my terrible dancing.* But there was something about the soft smile on his lips as he said the words that made her heart flutter in a way that it should not have done.

Lydia had settled herself into the chair on Effie's other side, in order to play the part of glaring chaperone – but the more that Lord Blackthorn spoke, the more she began to pay attention to the conversation. Now, she began to look between Effie and the faerie with a very curious expression.

"Just a few days ago, you said that anger was a plague," Effie mumbled. "I cannot see how that would make for very fine thread, Mr Jubilee."

"But we were speaking of Lady Culver's anger at the time, and not of yours!" Lord Blackthorn replied cheerfully. "The two could not possibly be more different. Lady Culver's anger is terribly ugly – it is all selfish and chaotic. I suppose the pattern might appeal to those of a particular persuasion, but I have never been fond of it myself. *Your* anger is bright and focused, and it does not hurt people – instead, I think that it must fill in the places where they have already been hurt." He paused thoughtfully. "Miss Lydia has clearly caught your anger, though, Miss Euphemia . . . so I suppose that it is *also* a bit like a plague."

"I've caught *what?*" Lydia hissed.

The conversation ground to a halt – and Effie remembered a moment later that Lydia's glamour was not strong enough to mask the oddness of her accent.

Lydia clamped her hand over her mouth, now bright red with embarrassment. Effie glanced around worriedly; thankfully, it seemed that most of the table had missed Lydia's outburst. Mr Jesson, however, was staring at her with surprise and curiosity.

"Oh dear," Lord Blackthorn murmured. "How awkward."

Effie shoved quickly to her feet. "Might we take a walk and see the flowers, Mr Jesson?" she asked quickly. "It would be a shame to come all this way only to stay at the table!"

Mr Jesson blinked. He glanced once more towards Lydia, who still had her hand pressed over her mouth. Slowly, he rose to his feet. "Of course, Miss Reeves," he said. "I would be delighted." He offered out his arm obligingly, and Effie took it.

Effie glanced back towards Lydia and Lord Blackthorn, and she lowered her voice. "I really do wish to finish this discussion later," she told them.

To Effie's surprise, Lord Blackthorn rose to his feet. "I

think I will join you for your walk," he said. "I also wish to see the flowers."

Effie chewed at her lip. "I had hoped to speak with Mr Jesson *alone*," she emphasised, since she suspected that anything less straightforward would fly directly over Lord Blackthorn's head. He had a way of derailing delicate conversations, and Effie was suddenly uncertain whether she could juggle both Mr Jesson *and* the faerie at the same time.

Lord Blackthorn glanced between Effie and Mr Jesson, and he knit his brow. "That ... does not strike me as very proper," he said. There was an unexpected hint of stubbornness to his tone that Effie had not heard before. "I am sure that there must be some English rule against it."

Effie blinked. "It is entirely proper, as long as we are within sight of my chaperone," she said. "And I do not intend to stray very far, Mr Jubilee."

Mr Jesson shook his head. "I would never wish to make your guardian uncomfortable, Miss Reeves," he said. "Please – why don't you join us while we walk, my lord?"

Thus, Effie found herself walking arm-in-arm with Mr Jesson among the flowers, while Lord Blackthorn paced just behind them.

"I have only just now realised," Mr Jesson addressed Effie, "that I have not heard your chaperone speak at all before now! Now that I have done, it strikes me that she sounds a bit more like a housemaid than she does like a lady. But that cannot be right, can it?"

Effie could not entirely hide her cringe. "I must implore you as a gentleman, Mr Jesson," she said. "If I tell you the truth, will you keep it a secret?"

Mr Jesson frowned. "I would never tarnish a lady's reputation on purpose," he assured Effie. "I am sure that whatever the explanation, it is a sound one. Your guardian is such an august figure, after all."

Lord Blackthorn – the guardian in question – was currently frowning at Mr Jesson's back in a worrisome manner. Effie quickly decided that she ought to speed the matter along, before the faerie decided to vent whatever frustration had recently occurred to him.

"Lydia is my housemaid," Effie told Mr Jesson quickly. "But she is also my friend, and I do not like to go to these events without her. I feel so much less alone when she is with me."

Even as Effie said the words, she realised how true they were. As badly as Lady Panovar's ball had ended, Effie was quite sure that it would have been a hundred times worse without Lydia's comforting figure at her back. Lord Blackthorn was very sincere, it was true; but he was terribly confusing and unpredictable, and Lydia's presence had helped Effie to remember that she had friends – *real* friends – even when people were not mistaking her for a lady.

Mr Jesson gave Effie a sympathetic smile. "Well, that is not so terrible," he said. "I am great friends with my butler, Mr Cotton – we drink together all the time, you know. He would have been here helping with breakfast, if he were not sick in bed today with that dreadful cough." His smile faded a bit. "I can see why some of the others here would be upset with you, of course. A maid cannot be a proper chaperone. I hope that you will both be more careful, Miss Reeves, if only for the sake of your reputation."

Effie let out a relieved breath at this. "We certainly shall, sir, yes," she assured Mr Jesson. "Thank you for your forbearance. It means ever so much to me."

Mr Jesson's manner relaxed again, and he fixed Effie with another fond look. "I cannot imagine how I could do otherwise," he told her. "It is the strangest thing, Miss Reeves – but when I look at you, I find myself thinking of the way this garden looks when it is in full bloom. Perhaps it is small, but it is my favourite garden in all the world. There is nothing that I like better than to walk here on a proper summer's day, enjoying the warm sunlight and the soft breeze." His voice took on a dreamy quality. "It would be lovely to have a companion with which to enjoy the scenery, though, wouldn't it? Why, if it isn't too forward of me, Miss Reeves, I would love to have you here again when the rest of the flowers have come—"

Mr Jesson cut himself off with a sound of surprise, as Lord Blackthorn took Effie's arm from his and interjected himself between them.

"The flowers here are nothing like those in Blackthorn," the faerie said. He had narrowed his leaf-green eyes at Mr Jesson; there was now a sharp edge to the scent of wild roses which he normally carried that hinted more at wicked thorns than soft blossoms. "The roses in Blackthorn are much larger, and they climb much higher. This garden is far too tame and too boxed-in – why, Miss Euphemia would suffocate here, I am sure!"

Effie found herself briefly at a loss for words. Lord Blackthorn had never exhibited the slightest bit of animosity in her presence before – but he was now all sharp edges and alien fear. The air around him shivered; the flowers in the garden seemed to lean in upon them with malevolent intent. She was reminded suddenly of the terrible stories about faerie lords and their tempers.

What on earth has set him off this way? Effie thought fearfully.

It must have been the garden, she realised. Mr Jesson had inadvertently bragged about his flowers in such a way that Lord Blackthorn must have believed he was comparing them to Blackthorn. Naturally, she thought, Lord Blackthorn had to be particularly sensitive about the land that owned him!

Effie dared to grasp at Lord Blackthorn's arm. "I am sure that Mr Jesson did not mean to imply that his garden ought to be *everyone's* favourite," she said quickly. "It is only his own favourite because it is familiar to him! Blackthorn is more familiar to *me*, and so I much prefer it myself."

Lord Blackthorn's cold enmity lessened at that, and he glanced towards Effie in surprise. "You do?" he asked. "Oh! But of course you do. Blackthorn is very fond of you as well, Miss Euphemia. I will take you back there this summer, and you will have plenty of sunlight so that you may grow properly."

The faerie's demeanour had returned to perfectly pleasant normalcy. Effie let out a sigh of relief, thinking how close poor Mr Jesson had come to being the victim of a cautionary faerie tale. "It is trees that require sunlight, Mr Jubilee," she reminded the elf. "Not human beings."

"But sunlight makes you happy, Miss Euphemia," Lord Blackthorn contradicted her. "And so you require it."

Mr Jesson snapped from the dazed confusion that had gripped him before. Now, he looked only vaguely troubled. The natural meekness which he had always carried reasserted itself, and his shoulders slumped. "I suspect I have insulted somehow," he said. "That was not my intention at all; I fear my mouth has run away with me. You must both forgive me, please."

Effie shot him a pitying look. "I do not think it was your fault, Mr Jesson," she said. "It was just a misunderstanding. And this gown is not doing either of us any favours."

Mr Jesson smiled weakly at Effie. "I remember now that I promised you a re-introduction to Mr Benedict," he said. "I am so embarrassed that it slipped my mind. Please, let me remedy the shortfall."

At this, Effie glanced warily at Lord Blackthorn. The elf still had her arm – and for a moment, she swore that he tightened his grip on her. But another distant emotion flickered across his face, and he let her go very slowly.

"I would not wish to be the cause of your misery, Miss Euphemia," he said softly.

"I do not imagine that you would be," Effie said, bewildered. But she remembered belatedly that Lord Blackthorn had said those words before, when they had been stuck in Blackthorn's

Folly. *Oh,* she thought. *He is speaking of the wager again. He is worried that he might have interfered again by frightening Mr Jesson off from his introduction.*

Effie smiled reassuringly at the faerie – but Lord Blackthorn had already turned back towards the table. With a few long, furious strides, he rejoined Lydia, who had been watching the entire scene with a chaperone's sharp eyes.

As Effie met Lydia's eyes, the other maid raised her eyebrows and mouthed something – but Effie could not make out the words, and so she shrugged helplessly.

Lydia turned her attention to Lord Blackthorn, who had settled into the chair just next to her in miserable silence. Lydia pursed her lips and opened her mouth, as though to speak – but she must have remembered just in time what a near-disaster her last slip of the tongue had created, for she shut her mouth again with a snap.

Mr Jesson took Effie by the arm once more, to direct them both towards Mr Benedict Ashbrooke's seat.

Benedict was already watching Effie and Mr Jesson as they approached his seat; rather, Effie realised, he was watching *her* with the most absorbed expression she had ever seen. The intensity of it left her just a bit breathless, so that she was barely able to speak when Mr Jesson introduced her once again.

"You remember Miss Reeves, of course," Mr Jesson said to Benedict.

"I remember," Benedict said. He looked directly into Effie's eyes as he said the words. There was a reverence in his voice, as though he had looked upon an exquisite painting rather than upon a woman. This did not help Effie's lack of composure at all – in fact, she found herself hiding very slightly behind Mr Jesson, unable to bear the full weight of Benedict's warm brown eyes.

"I must greatly apologise for the last time we spoke," Benedict said. "I fear that family matters absorbed me; I did not intend to be rude in the slightest." He stood and pulled out the empty chair next to him, gesturing in invitation. "Perhaps we might try again, Miss Reeves? The seating is informal today, and I feel the need to make up for lost time."

Had Effie's heart ceased to beat entirely, she would not have been surprised. The offer was something straight out of her daydreams; the expression on Benedict's face made her warm and fluttery. When Effie had been a maid standing just in front of him, Benedict had also been an entirely different creature – but his usual, politely bemused manner had now fallen away, and he looked her in the eyes without the least bit of hesitation.

"Please do say yes, Miss Reeves," Benedict asked fervently. "I am not sure if I could bear it if you said no."

Effie sat down in the chair, red-faced and frustratingly tongue-tied. Out of the corner of her eye, she saw Mr Jesson beam at her, and she thought that he must have been very proud to have made his introduction so successfully this time.

"Be careful of her chaperone, Mr Benedict," Mr Jesson advised. "She is quite the hawk." He tossed a wink at Effie, who nodded minutely in gratitude. Mr Jesson then turned to the older woman who had been sitting next to Benedict. "Would you care for a turn about the garden, Mother?" he asked.

"I cannot think of anyone with whom I would rather walk, Mr Jesson," the woman said. There was a kind, playful tone in her voice which suggested she was having fun with him. Mr Jesson pulled out her chair, and the two of them soon departed – leaving Effie neatly sequestered with Benedict, a few chairs away from any other prying ears.

"I am sure now that I cannot have met you before, Miss Reeves," Benedict told Effie. "You so easily outshine every other woman here. I look at you, and I suddenly forget that I am stranded in the country, away from all proper civilisation. Why, it feels as though I am in Italy again, admiring one of the statues in Rome."

Effie swallowed nervously. *This is all to do with the gown*, she thought. *Perhaps Benedict wishes that he were back in Italy, and I have reminded him of that.* Lady Hollowvale had suggested that Effie wear the gown for exactly that reason – but now that Benedict was truly looking at her, Effie could not help but feel the hollowness of his adoration.

"You are very kind, Mr Benedict," Effie said softly. "But it is my gown that makes you talk this way. If I were not wearing it, you would find me only a passing curiosity, if that."

"I cannot imagine ever overlooking you, Miss Reeves," Benedict promised her. "Please – where did you come from? I was told that you are Lord Blackthorn's ward, but I cannot remember ever meeting him before."

"You might remember meeting him if you spoke to him," Effie sighed. "But I have very humble roots, Mr Benedict. That you do not remember me is hardly a surprise."

Benedict reached out to take Effie's gloved hand. "Whatever has gone before," he said, "I hope that you will allow me to remedy the situation now, Miss Reeves. I want to know everything about you – indeed, it is my fondest wish."

Effie glanced up at him hopefully. There was no denying the way her hands trembled at the interest in his eyes. This, Effie thought, was everything that *she* had wished for. Lady Hollowvale had told her that the gown was only to catch Benedict's attention, however – if she wished for him to ever propose to her in normal dress, then he would have to fall in love with her for a reason other than the gown.

I have to take advantage of his attention while I have it, Effie told herself. *But the very next time that I see Benedict, I will wear the plainest frock that I can find.*

"I hardly know where to begin," Effie admitted. She could not possibly tell Benedict that she had been a maid all of this time; nor could she mention that she had been living at Hartfield, sleeping in the basement quarters. If she had been a lady, perhaps she might have spoken of the books she had read and the languages she knew – but Effie had only ever dusted the books in the library, and she could not manage even a fake French accent.

"Tell me about your family," Benedict said. "We shall start there."

Effie took a deep breath. He was still holding her hand. She suspected that this was far from proper – but Lydia was not really a chaperone, and both she and Lord Blackthorn had disappeared for the moment.

"I have three brothers," Effie said shyly. "But I only ever see my oldest brother. He has always looked out for me, and he even found me—" Effie cut herself off before she could say *he found me a job at Hartfield*. "– he found me my first embroidery hoop," she finished instead.

"How envious," Benedict said. "I have never been as close to my brothers as I would like, you know. They're both much more serious than I am, and I think they consider me a bit of a fool." He smiled wryly at her. "I am told that I am charming – but if I am, then that charm never quite seems to work on either of them."

Effie tightened her hand on his with a sympathetic look. "You are *very* charming," she assured Benedict. "You must not doubt that! And I'm sure that you are serious about the things you find important, even if your brothers do not realise it."

Benedict blinked at that. "I . . . suppose that I am," he said slowly. "I have a love for art and history. It's part of why I took so long on my tour of the Continent. But Thomas finds it all useless, and Edmund has accused me of learning only enough to converse with ladies on the subject."

Effie smiled weakly. "Surely you know more than enough to impress me for years and years of conversation," she said. "I know almost nothing of art *or* history. But I am sure that I could endlessly listen to you speak of both and never get tired, Mr Benedict."

The smile on Benedict's face became just a bit less dreamy and a bit more genuine at that, and Effie's confidence grew. *There is really something here*, she thought with relief. *I wasn't imagining it at all.*

"I would be happy to tell you all about Rome, Miss Reeves," Benedict said softly.

And for the next half-hour, he did exactly that.

Benedict spoke of the Pantheon and the Colosseum, describing the titanic structures with a lingering awe. He told Effie of the private collections he had visited, casually choked with paintings and sculptures from hundreds of years past. He had tried to learn painting himself, he said, but his hand was always less practised than his eye, and he had been forced to content himself with learning everything he could about the old masters and their lives instead.

He described Europe so vividly that Effie found she could almost imagine it in her mind's eye. For a beautiful few minutes, she imagined herself walking through Rome with Benedict, letting him explain all of the little details he had learned with the same sparkle in his eyes that he currently had. They could have breakfast just like this – but only the two of them! – and then she would ask him to paint something for her, even if he thought it was terrible.

Effie's daydreams were rudely interrupted, however, as a familiar voice spoke behind the two of them.

"Mr Benedict?" Miss Buckley asked. "It is you, thank goodness! I don't know very many people here, but Lady Culver said that you would surely keep me company if I asked."

Effie was sure that she saw a flash of exasperation cross Benedict's face – but he buried it beneath a polite smile and turned to address Miss Buckley. As he did, a strange expression overcame his face, and he seemed to lose his train of thought.

"Miss Buckley," he said. "Where on earth did you find that gown?"

Effie followed his glance. A moment later, her heart dropped all the way down into her stomach.

Miss Buckley was wearing Lady Culver's old gown – the very same one that Effie had embroidered herself.

Chapter Eleven

The sight of Miss Buckley in Effie's old gown was such an awful shock that Effie found herself barely able to speak.

Far worse, of course, was the fact that Miss Buckley looked *better* in the gown than Effie ever had. Her blonde hair was done up with real white roses today; her skin was smooth and creamy and her posture unimpeachable. She was wearing fine white gloves – but even if her hands had been bare, Effie knew that they would have been soft and uncalloused. Miss Buckley truly belonged in the garden here, wearing a gown of leaves and flowers.

"This gown?" Miss Buckley said – and Effie remembered that Benedict had asked her where she'd found it. "It's lovely, isn't it? You'll never believe it, Mr Benedict, but Lady Culver gave it to me. All of this embroidery must have cost a fortune, but she didn't even hesitate. I do not know if I will ever have a more generous friend in my life."

Every word dripped with sweet sincerity. Effie's stomach turned with nausea.

I am so angry, she thought. *I can barely breathe.*

Miss Buckley turned to look at Effie now, and she smiled uncertainly. "I am sure that it pales in comparison to some," she said. "My goodness, miss. I cannot imagine where it is you found your own gown. I have never seen anything so beautiful before in my life."

The insecurity in Miss Buckley's voice reminded Effie that she herself was wearing the very finest gown that any tailor in faerie could make. This should have made her feel better – in fact, it should have vindicated her. After all, Miss Buckley had clearly come to breakfast with the intention of securing Benedict's attention – but Effie had already stolen that out from underneath her, and the other woman had quickly grasped the whole of the situation.

But the crestfallen look on Miss Buckley's face did *not* reassure Effie. Nothing, she thought, could make up for the awful reality of seeing another woman in that gown. Effie had stayed up so many nights pouring her heart and soul into every stitch; she had spent far more than was prudent on the silk thread she had used for the leaves and flowers. Perhaps the gown had not been sewn out of wishes or handmade by brownies, but it was *her* gown. That Miss Buckley of all people should be wearing it was an inexpressible violation of Effie's soul.

Effie scrambled up from her chair, staring in horror.

"Is everything all right?" Miss Buckley asked curiously.

Effie's mouth worked soundlessly for a moment before she was able to croak out a reply. "I . . . don't feel well," she managed. "Please excuse me."

And then – to her utmost shame – she fled.

There was a tall willow tree some way outside of the hedges that blocked the breakfast from view; its long, drooping leaves had already sprouted, and so Effie hid herself away inside them, sitting down in front of the trunk. As soon as she was safely hidden, she found herself crying again – and this, in and of itself, was an insult. Surely, she had cried enough in the last little bit that she shouldn't be expected to cry *again*.

Effie's tears did not come from sadness, though – they were instead tears of such hideous, absolute rage that nothing she tried would stave them off. She started hoarsely:

> "Mistress Mary, quite contrary,
> How does your garden grow—"

But Effie could not finish the rhyme. She thought again of Miss Buckley, wearing that *gown*, and her throat closed up with fury.

"I would like to ask how Mistress Mary's garden *does* grow," Lord Blackthorn said from just behind her. "But you are terribly upset, and so it will have to wait for later."

Effie looked up from the cradle of her arms. She hadn't noticed the elf's approach – but of course, she thought, the grass and the trees would never give him away. They were all surely on his side.

Lord Blackthorn was looking down at her with obvious concern on his sharp features. Had Effie been in a more coherent frame of mind, she might have found that odd – for the first time that Lord Blackthorn had caught her crying in front of the hedge maze, he had only been delighted to find a subject for his experiment in virtue. Effie was not in any working state of mind, however – and so the strangeness went unnoticed.

"I do not want to talk to anyone," Effie choked out. "I am very angry, Mr Jubilee, and I might take it out on whoever is closest."

Lord Blackthorn did not seem at all concerned at this possibility, of course. He sat down next to Effie, still looking at her with worried eyes.

"I do not like seeing you cry, Miss Euphemia," he said. "Is there anything that I can do to help?"

Effie closed her eyes and sucked in her breath. The scent of wild roses suffused her, oddly reassuring. She had never needed her eyes to know when Lord Blackthorn was near – but she was now even more keenly aware of his warmth and his presence, as though her mind had begun to keep track of him without her permission.

Effie could not possibly explain to Lord Blackthorn all of the reasons that she was angry. There were so *many* reasons, and he wouldn't understand most of them without days of extra explanation. Instead, she threw her arms around him and pressed her face into his shoulder, hiccupping through her tears.

Lord Blackthorn did not stiffen or pull away, as Effie might have expected any proper English lord to do. Instead, he closed his arms around her and threaded his long fingers through her hair. There was not even a hint in his manner of the alien chill that he had displayed before; he was now all gentleness and care and full of warmth, rather like the sunlight in Blackthorn. His shirt was soft against her cheek – and for a moment, Effie wished that she *was* back in Blackthorn with him, far away from any shred of Lady Culver's constant, oppressive influence.

"I am powerless, Mr Jubilee," Effie told him miserably. "I wasn't sure until this very moment, but I am now. I am not a lady – I am not even a maid. I am *no one*."

"That surely can't be true," Lord Blackthorn said. Genuine confusion tinted his voice. "You are here with me right now, and so you must be *someone*."

Effie shook her head minutely against him. "You don't understand," she said, "because everyone is *someone* to you, Mr Jubilee. But here in England, to everyone who matters, I am nothing and no one. I am like the air or the wallpaper or the furniture. Do you know how I know that?"

Lord Blackthorn did not respond to this immediately. He tightened his arms on Effie, and she thought dimly that he was growing more concerned. But she could not have held the words in if she'd wanted to – they spilled out of her like a tide, as though he had used her name to compel them.

"I know that I am no one because ... because no matter what Miss Buckley or Lady Culver do to me, and no matter what they take from me, they will never face any consequences for it. I can get as angry as I like, Mr Jubilee! But at the end of the day, they are ladies, and they will give my anger as much consideration as they give to the wallpaper." Effie swallowed down a hard lump in her throat. "I wish that I did not have this anger. I wish that I *was* wallpaper. I would be less miserable if I didn't have to understand how unfair this all is. I am powerless, and this anger is good for nearly as little as I am."

"You are *not* wallpaper!" Lord Blackthorn's voice sharpened on the words. "You must not say such terrible things about yourself, Miss Euphemia. You are good for much, and you matter to many people. And ... " He struggled for a moment, as though searching for a thought. "And they will surely face consequences! It is only natural that they shall."

"Well, I have never seen Lady Culver face any consequences for anything," Effie said bitterly. "It is always the rest of us who face her consequences for her. And Miss Buckley! I hardly believe that she has faced any difficulty worth mentioning in all of her life." Her chest was tight and hard, even with Lord Blackthorn's comforting arms around her. Her next words came out small and tired and defeated. "Lady Culver gave her my *gown*, Mr Jubilee. Miss Buckley is wearing it right now."

At these words, Lord Blackthorn stiffened in such an odd way that Effie forced herself to look up at him. The worry in his eyes had deepened. "That is indeed a terrible thing," he said softly. "This will surely complicate matters, Miss Euphemia. I do not know if even a gown made out of wishes could compare to your masterpiece."

Effie knit her brow. Her anger was still hot and nauseous inside her, but her curiosity surged momentarily to get the better of her. "I don't understand," she said. "My gown is hardly a masterpiece, Mr Jubilee. It is fraying in places, and the lace is old."

Lord Blackthorn frowned down at her. An idea grew slowly across his features as something dawned upon him. "Is it at all possible," he asked, "that you do not *know* how fine your stitching is, Miss Euphemia?"

"I do not know why you call my stitching *fine,*" Effie sighed. "It is not fine, Mr Jubilee, it is ... adequate. Perhaps it is above average quality for a maid, but I am not a seamstress."

"But your stitching *is* very fine," Lord Blackthorn told her. "It is ... " He paused, and Effie saw that he was searching for different words than usual to use this time. "It is magical."

Effie nearly laughed aloud at this – but it occurred to her just in time that faeries could not lie. A cold chill broke through the fury inside her.

"That isn't possible, Mr Jubilee," she whispered. "I'm not a magician."

Lord Blackthorn winced. "But of course you would not know," he realised now. "You cannot even see a human soul, after all!" He shook his head at her. "You are indeed a magician, Miss Euphemia. You do magic, and so you are a magician. Is there any other definition of the word?"

Effie swallowed. "I have never heard of the magician that uses a needle and thread," she said. "The only magicians I have heard of in England read books and call fire and break curses!"

Lord Blackthorn became puzzled at this. "But there are all kinds of magicians all over England," he said. "Why, there is a man in London who talks to animals, and a woman in Devonshire who listens to gems! Why should it be strange for a maid to stitch souls with needle and thread?"

"Stitch ... *souls?*" Effie whispered. The madness of the statement made her feel faint.

"Oh yes," Lord Blackthorn sighed. "You create such beautiful things with your anger and your misery and your hopes and dreams. The brownies only wish that they could so casually stitch anger into frocks and handkerchiefs."

Effie thought of the faerie's many strange previous comments to her, and she buried her face into his chest with a groan. "When you said that you had never seen a more miserable tablecloth—" she began.

"– it *was* such a miserable tablecloth!" Lord Blackthorn said cheerfully. "Wherever did you put that tablecloth, by the way?"

"Oh *no!*" Effie moaned. "I have been stitching my anger into *everything* at Hartfield, Mr Jubilee! I have given it to Lydia and Mrs Sedgewick, and … and I only recently put stitches into Mr Allen's coat!" She released the faerie to scramble back up to her feet, wiping at her face. "I have to go and undo it all immediately!"

Lord Blackthorn blinked, pushing back up to his feet to join her. "But why would you undo it?" he asked. "It's all so delightful!"

Effie worked her mouth soundlessly for a moment. Lord Blackthorn had never been affected by any of her gowns, she realised. Oh, he had *commented* upon them, and he had called her lovely – but he had not begged for her opinion when she was wearing dignity, nor had he sighed wistfully in her direction when she had put on her gown of wishes.

"They are just art to you, aren't they?" she asked. "My stitches don't change the way that you feel at all."

Lord Blackthorn considered this. "Ah," he said sheepishly. "I see your concerns now. Yes, your hard work is rather … infectious to other mortals. I do not have a human soul, and so human emotions do not affect me."

Effie pressed her hands against her face. "This is all my fault!" she cried. "I am the reason that everything is so awful at Hartfield!"

"No, certainly not!" Lord Blackthorn assured her. He

reached out to grasp her by the shoulders. "Your anger is not ugly, Miss Euphemia – I did tell you that much, didn't I?"

Effie curled back out of his grip. "I have to go and undo it all," she said again. "I have to leave, Mr Jubilee. You must take me back right this instant."

Lord Blackthorn frowned. "But your wager—" he started.

"I must handle my wager later," Effie told him desperately. "I have hurt people, Mr Jubilee, and I must go make that right as soon as possible."

Lord Blackthorn did not seem to understand this idea at all – but Effie's distress *did* affect him, such that he eventually nodded. "If you are sure," he said, "then I will take you back."

Unfortunately, Lord Blackthorn's predictions about Effie's old gown were proven depressingly true; as Effie returned to the breakfast to search for Lydia, she caught sight of Benedict talking to Miss Buckley with an even more dazed expression than before. Effie's stomach turned uncomfortably as she watched the scene. Miss Buckley laughed politely at something in their conversation, and Effie found herself ashamed of her own gown of wishes.

I will take this off as soon as I return home, she thought. *I should never have worn it at all, even just to gain his attention. I am no better than some black magician, playing with someone else's mind.*

Miss Buckley smiled brilliantly at Benedict once more, and Effie turned away.

She found Lydia a short distance away from the breakfast table, talking to Mr Jesson. This conversation looked somewhat more business-like, which might have made Effie quite curious under other circumstances. Today, however, she quickly made her apologies to their host and dragged Lydia towards the carriage.

"We have to go back to Hartfield," Effie said worriedly, once they were safely ensconced inside. "I don't even know how to explain, Lydia, but I've got to undo all of the mending and sewing I've done for everyone."

Lydia shook her head quickly. "We can't go back, Effie," she said. "We've got to do our shoppin', or else Cookie *and* Mrs Sedgewick will have our heads."

Effie groaned at the reminder – but she knew that returning empty-handed would only get them both in trouble. *The stitching has been there for ages now,* she thought wearily. *It will have to wait for another few hours at least.*

"Now, since we're here," Lydia addressed Lord Blackthorn crossly, "may I ask what you meant exactly when you said I'd *caught* Effie's anger?"

Lord Blackthorn sighed. "I still do not fully understand the issue," he said. "But Miss Euphemia gave you her anger some time ago, and you are still carrying it about. In fact, I think you have made it mostly your own."

Lydia knit her brow. "I don't know what that means," she admitted. "Is it dangerous?"

Lord Blackthorn smiled at this. "I suspect it could be very dangerous for *some*," he observed. "But not for you, Miss Lydia."

Lydia shook her head. "As long as it isn't goin' to hurt me," she said. "All the rest of that faerie talk is over my head."

With the help of the carriage, Effie and Lydia were able to finish their shopping much more quickly than they otherwise would have done. They still got back to Hartfield around sunset, however, which left less time for Effie to search out her mending projects than she would have preferred. By the time they'd said goodbye to Lord Blackthorn, stashed Effie's gown and put away the shopping, there was barely any time left in the evening at all.

The only person Effie was able to find in good time was Mrs Sedgewick, who was rushing about as frantically as ever. Effie caught the housekeeper in the servants' passageways, just next to the green baize door that led to the rest of the house.

"Mrs Sedgewick!" Effie said breathlessly. "I need to ask you—"

"I am not in the mood for any requests, Effie!" Mrs Sedgewick snapped. Her face was tight, and there were dark circles beneath her eyes. "It is bad enough that we had to do without two maids today because of Cookie's last-minute requests."

Effie winced guiltily at that – but she forced herself to keep to the matter at hand. "I was only going to ask if I could check your gown over again tonight, after I'm done in the scullery," she said softly. "I thought I might do it as an apology."

Mrs Sedgewick blinked. A hint of the tension in her body lessened, and she paused. "That is . . . very kind of you, Effie," she said. "I suppose I could give it to you after you've finished some of the dishes, yes." The housekeeper drew in a breath. "You will want to check in on George as well. He's been so ill, Mr Allen told him to spend the day resting – though we can hardly afford to do without him."

Effie felt a spike of worry. "He hasn't got a fever, has he?" she asked.

"I truly don't know, Effie," Mrs Sedgewick said tiredly. "I have been on my feet all day, and Mr Allen has assured me that he has the matter handled. You may go and check for yourself – no one will protest you being in the male servants' quarters if you tell them you are helping to look after George."

Effie nodded at this. Had she the ability, she would have rushed off to see her brother immediately – but Hartfield had apparently been *three* servants short for the entire day, and there was so much work to be done that she couldn't possibly justify it.

Thankfully, Lydia was generous enough to help with the scullery again that evening. While they were cleaning, Effie explained the problem with her mending and her plan to undo the damage.

"Well, you can't undo the embroidery on my handkerchief," Lydia said, "seein' as I already wore it out."

"I know," Effie groaned. "I'm so sorry, Lydia. I truly didn't know that it would affect you that way."

Lydia shrugged. "I don't feel affected," she said. "But I guess I *would* say that, wouldn't I?" Still, she didn't seem nearly as concerned by the revelation as Effie had expected.

"I will have to ask you to redo the mending," Effie told Lydia glumly. "I don't *want* to ask it – but since I do not fully understand how I have been doing it in the first place, I'm not sure that I can sew anything at all that *doesn't* have a bit of soul in it."

"Lord Blackthorn doesn't seem to think your sewin' is a problem at all," Lydia said.

"Mr Jubilee also offered to *remove* all the other ladies from a ball on my behalf," Effie replied. "I like him very much, Lydia, but I do not think that he is a good judge of problems."

"You *do* like him, then," Lydia said, with a curious tone in her voice. "After all that talk of how dangerous faeries are."

Effie sighed heavily. "I can like him *and* believe that he is dangerous at the same time," she said. "Mr Jubilee does not have to mean bad things in order to *do* bad things. That is by far the most frustrating part."

Lydia breezed right past this answer, however. "I think he likes you too," she told Effie. "I think he likes you an awful lot, actually."

Effie managed a small smile at this. "I think he likes almost everyone," she said. "It is part of his charm."

"I don't think Lord Blackthorn likes Mr Benedict," Lydia observed. "He was askin' me today just what makes Mr Benedict so lovable. I wasn't sure what to say to that."

Effie shook her head. "Mr Jubilee is always trying to understand human things," she said. "It doesn't mean that he does not *like* Mr Benedict."

Lydia looked somewhat sceptical at this – but she did not belabour the matter.

Effie picked up Mrs Sedgewick's gown on her way to see George. She brought it with her as she headed for his room, which was as far away as possible from where the female servants slept at night. Normally, Effie would not have been able to walk here – Lord Culver had always been very keen on keeping the male and female servants properly separated, even before Lady Culver had taken over the household – but no one was really cruel enough to keep her from her brother while he was ill. Still, she knocked a few times very politely before letting herself inside.

George clearly had not moved from his bed for quite some time. Perhaps it was just the dubious lighting, but he did look awfully drawn and pale, leaned against his pillow. He managed a wry smile at Effie as she headed inside, though it was soon spoiled by a wracking cough.

"Well," he wheezed. "Now I'm gettin' visitors. Lucky me."

Effie settled down next to the bed, eyeing him with concern. "You look *terrible*," she said. "Thank goodness Mr Allen forced you to bed."

"Won't be for ever," George mumbled. "Lord Culver was already askin' where I was today. Mr Allen told him I'd be a nuisance since I'm coughin' too loud."

Effie narrowed her eyes. "Oh, is *that* the problem?" she asked tartly. "I suppose we wouldn't want you spoiling Lord Culver's morning by *coughing* too loudly."

George rolled his eyes at her. "Mr Allen wants me to get better," he said. "He's just a professional. He knows what the toffs need to hear in order to get what he wants."

"I know that Mr Allen is a good man," Effie said. "I am upset that *Lord Culver* doesn't seem to care what happens to you. You have worked for him for years now, George."

"It's *James*," George corrected Effie, with a grim sort of

laugh. "An' the next footman will be James too if I knock off from this cough."

Effie widened her eyes at him. "Don't you dare joke like that!" she said. "You're going to stay in bed and drink whatever Cookie gives you, and you're going to get better. I swear, George, you will even put those orange peels up your nose if that's what it takes!"

George narrowed his eyes at her. "You'll have to shove 'em up there yourself," he said. "An' I'm still bigger an' stronger than you."

"I shall have Mr Allen hold you down," Effie sniffed. "For now, however, I think I will go and get you some more of Cookie's tea."

Effie took a brief pause to do just that. She soon realised that she had underestimated the stench of Cookie's health concoctions – the tea smelled so awful that she had to hold it out in front of her as she walked back to George's room. Still, she forced him to drink an entire two cups before she allowed him to go back to sleep.

Effie continued to sit next to George's bed as she pried out those stitches which she had personally done on Mrs Sedgewick's gown. Eventually, she returned to her room, where Lydia took the gown from her to redo the most important stitches in her own hand. It was all Effie could do not to hover over her shoulder, worrying over the quality – and so, to distract herself, she pulled out Lord Blackthorn's coat and considered the stitches that she still owed him.

"Oh," Effie said suddenly. "That is why Mr Jubilee wanted me to embroider his coat, Lydia! The other faeries find things like human anger to be fashionable!"

Lydia chewed on her lip as she threaded another careful stitch through Mrs Sedgewick's silk gown. "Wouldn't surprise me in the least if he just wanted a big old rose on his coat," she observed. "But maybe you're right."

Effie frowned at the stitching she had already done. She couldn't see anything *magical* about it – to her eyes, it looked just like normal silk thread. But was there a hint of wistfulness there when she touched it? A feeling of contentment from the ball that she had just attended when she'd done the embroidery?

She searched out the thread made of wishes which Lady Hollowvale had given her and compared the sight. The spool glimmered in her hand with beautiful shifting colours, promising all of the things for which Effie so desperately wished. In that thread, Effie saw herself wearing lovely gowns all of the time; she saw herself walking through Rome on Benedict's arm, perusing all the fascinating history there; mostly, she saw the towering trees in Blackthorn and felt the warm, dappled sunlight there on her skin.

That last wish, Effie thought, was something that Lord Blackthorn might appreciate. It was this wish that she imagined – the memory of roses and butterflies and sunlight – as she pulled out her previous work and re-stitched it.

Eventually, she reached the new stitches that she owed the faerie. By now, Effie's thoughts had drifted to the memory of Lady Hollowvale's pianoforte, and the endless joy on Lord Blackthorn's face as they had danced. Her heart grew warm, and she knew somehow that this coat would be her masterpiece, even if she had no real sense of *how* she was doing her magic.

"There!" Lydia said, as Effie finished one of the rose's petals. "I think I've found all the spots you undid on Mrs Sedgewick's gown. You can mark at least one person off your list, Effie."

Effie set aside Lord Blackthorn's jacket and turned to look at Lydia's work. It wasn't quite as fine as hers normally was – but there was certain to be no *anger* in it, at least, and that was what mattered.

"Thank you so much for everything," she sighed, as she took the gown back from her. "I swear, I don't know how I'd have got this far without you, Lydia."

Lydia smiled softly. "We'll never know, now, will we?" she said. "Just promise that you'll treat all your maids real nice when you become a lady."

Effie snorted. "I cannot imagine doing otherwise," she said. "If I ever become like Lady Culver, Lydia, I give you full permission to poison my tea."

By the time Effie returned Mrs Sedgewick's gown to her and crawled beneath her covers, she was hopeful once again that she would somehow find a way out of all of her difficulties. She had finally had a conversation of substance with Benedict, after all – and even if Miss Buckley *did* have her old gown, Effie had proven to herself that she could sew something even better if she really put her mind to the task.

More than anything else, however, she found herself looking forward to Lord Blackthorn's reaction when she might eventually present him with his magnificent jacket.

Chapter Twelve

ffie's first inkling that something terrible had gone wrong
came when Mrs Sedgewick did not show up for breakfast.

"Mrs Sedgewick is still abed," Mr Allen informed Effie,
when she asked after the housekeeper in the hallway afterwards.
"She seems to be doing very poorly."

Effie thought of George, still under the weather himself. "Is
she sick?" Effie asked worriedly. "Has she caught that dreadful
cough, perhaps?"

Mr Allen shook his head. "I fear I do not know," he said.
"I did not hear her cough – but I have never seen her look so
dreadful. As difficult as it may be, we shall have to carry on
without her for today. Perhaps I can convince Lord Culver to
call a physician, if I frame the matter in the correct way."

"Perhaps Lord Culver ought to remember that a dead household cannot continue to serve him," Effie snapped. A moment
later, she realised she had said the words aloud rather than
thinking them silently to herself, and she blanched.

Mr Allen did not upbraid her, however. He smiled
humourlessly instead. "I do not credit Lord Culver with an
overabundance of intelligence," he said. "The rest of us must
trick him into doing what is best for himself and the others
around him."

Effie stared at the butler. These words were by far the most unprofessional that she had ever heard from him. Her eyes caught on the freshly mended edge of his coat, however, and she widened her eyes. *I forgot!* she thought. *I infected Mr Allen with my anger too!*

"Mr Allen," Effie said slowly. "I should really take another look at your coat when you have a moment—"

"Mr Allen!" It was Prudence – Lady Culver's personal maid – who interrupted them both. The lady's maid had just rushed downstairs; there was a wild look to her eyes which suggested something of truly apocalyptic importance. "Mr Allen, I can't rouse Mrs Sedgewick from bed, and I've got to tell *someone!* Lady Culver is in an absolute rage over it, and I don't know what to do!"

Though Mr Allen had already shown himself to be somewhat less professional than usual today, he now straightened his back and forced a reassuringly stoic expression onto his face.

"And what precisely has Lady Culver so upset?" he asked the maid.

Prudence gave him a despairing look. "It's her gowns, sir," she said. "They're all gone."

Mr Allen frowned. "Pardon?" he said. "You don't mean to say that we laundered *all* of her gowns at once? Surely the lady has *something* to wear?"

Prudence shook her head furiously. "No, sir," she said. "You don't understand my meaning, sir. *All* of her gowns are gone – and not to the laundry! They were in her wardrobe when I put her to bed, I swear – and this morning, when I went in to dress her, they had all disappeared! The wardrobe is empty. Her Ladyship is still wearing her shift, but I can't find her anything else – not even so much as a dressing gown!"

At this revelation, a horrible feeling of foreboding overcame Effie. All of this, she thought, was far too strange to be a coincidence.

Mr Allen stared at Prudence for a long moment; this

situation, Effie thought, must have finally been something outside even the esteemed butler's wide experience. Finally, he cleared his throat. "Lady Culver gave some of her old gowns to the maids during Christmas, didn't she?" he asked. "For now, see if you can find one of these spares for her. I will rally the staff to investigate her missing wardrobe. I cannot imagine that this is anything other than a strange misunderstanding."

Effie had already begun to edge back from this conversation; now, she hurried for the stairs, knowing that she might be conscripted at any moment to go searching for Lady Culver's wardrobe. She found Lydia in the house's entryway, sweeping the floor.

"Lydia!" Effie said breathlessly. "Please tell me you didn't call in another favour!"

Lydia blinked and paused to lean her broom against the wall. "Why would you think I'd called in a favour?" she asked.

Effie's heart sank even further at this. Much as she wanted to believe that Lydia was smarter than to call in her second faerie favour, it would have at least made more sense if she *had* done so. "All of Lady Culver's gowns went missing in the middle of the night," Effie said. "*All* of them, Lydia! She can't even get dressed to leave her bedroom! I don't understand it at all, but it must be Mr Jubilee's doing!"

Lydia let out a shocked laugh at this – though she had the decency to cover her mouth and stifle it after a moment. "Well, isn't *that* appropriate?" she said, with only a hint of remaining glee. "Lady Culver stole your gown, an' now someone's stolen all *her* clothing! Serves her just about right, I'd say!"

Effie stared at her in dawning horror.

No matter what Miss Buckley or Lady Culver do to me, and no matter what they take from me, she had told Lord Blackthorn, *they will never face any consequences for it.*

But he had assured Effie that the two women *would* face consequences. *It is only natural that they shall,* the faerie had said.

"This was *certainly* Mr Jubilee's doing," Effie whispered. "I all but begged him to do this, Lydia! I wasn't thinking. Why did I say all of those things? I *knew* that he was looking for an opportunity to be cruel to powerful people!"

Lydia frowned at this. "I don't see the problem," she said. "Lady Culver deserves a bit of cruelty. I for one won't give her a second thought."

Effie shot her a despairing look. "But that's just it, Lydia!" she said. "Lady Culver will be upset, of course – but in the end, she is only going to take her anger out on all of *us*."

Lydia scowled. "Oh, just let her try," she said darkly. "I'm tellin' you what, Effie, I've had just about enough of Lady Culver, an' I know I'm not the only one."

Effie groaned. "You're only saying that because I've infected you with my anger, Lydia," she said. "If you were in your right mind, you would never talk like this. Someone is going to get dismissed, and it's going to be all my fault—"

"Euphemia! There you are!" Mr Allen's voice barked from the doorway behind them. "And Lydia as well. I need the two of you below-stairs. I have asked all of the servants to assemble at once."

They both had little choice but to follow him. Lydia picked up her broom again with a long-suffering expression; Effie fell into step next to her friend with a sinking feeling in her stomach.

Mr Allen wasted little time explaining the situation to the staff. He asked whether anyone had taken Lady Culver's gowns to mend or launder – but no one had. Like a general directing his troops, Mr Allen next set them all to searching the manor, each of them in a particular area. Effie was assigned a few of the upstairs bedrooms; she did dutifully go to search them, though she knew that she would not find anything.

What do I do? Effie thought in a panic. *Surely if I call Mr Jubilee back, I can convince him to replace the gowns . . .*

"– absolutely incredible!" Lord Culver's voice snapped from

down the hall. The words filtered towards Effie as she switched bedrooms. "I swear, you are the only woman thick enough to lose all of her clothing at once, Eleanor! You can hardly expect me to pay to replace it all."

"I don't need you to replace *all* of it," Lady Culver replied – and Effie was surprised to hear a tearful note in her voice. "I only need *something*. You cannot expect me to walk around in my night shift, Thomas!"

Effie turned her steps towards Lady Culver's room, where the argument continued. Briefly, it occurred to her that she ought not eavesdrop – but then, a curious, nearly perverse idea overcame her, and she continued down the hall.

"We do not have the money!" Lord Culver said coldly. Effie saw him through a crack in the door, pacing Lady Culver's room with barely suppressed anger. "If you need to buy something, Eleanor, you may do so with the budget I have already given you. It is your duty as my wife to make that budget suffice – really, it is the *only* thing I ever ask of you."

Effie pushed open the door to Lady Culver's room and walked inside.

The full scene now displayed itself in front of her. Lord Culver had been pacing in front of his wife as he lectured her. Lady Culver sat on the edge of her bed, swathed in a housecoat she had borrowed from a maid. Incredibly, neither aristocrat paid any attention at all to Effie as she walked into the room, continuing her half-hearted search for Lady Culver's wardrobe. As always, she was entirely beneath their notice. A maid at work, Effie thought, could not eavesdrop ... because she was not a *person*. The idea crushed what little guilt she might have otherwise felt, as the two of them continued arguing in front of her.

"There *is* no more money in the budget, Thomas!" Lady Culver pleaded. "I cannot think where I will find the funds!"

"I suppose that depends," Lord Culver said, with sudden,

unnatural calm. "Which do you require more, Eleanor? Your clothing or your lady's maid? I am sure that you would hate to do without one or the other – but then, if you had planned things better in the first place, we would not now be having this conversation."

The contemptuous look on Lord Culver's face would have made most people quail; in Effie, however, it stirred the embers of a furious contempt in return. Effie still did not care much for Lady Culver – that she could be yelled at did not change the fact that she *also* yelled at servants and threw teapots at their heads. But Lord Culver's face currently expressed everything that Effie so hated about Lady Culver, except in even greater abundance. There was in his features a smug self-righteousness – a suggestion that he considered the person in front of him to be inherently more foolish, more childish and less valuable than he considered himself.

Lady Culver had probably grown very used to this expression; she slowly straightened her shoulders and shot her husband a hateful look which reflected the anger in Effie's heart. Lady Culver spoke with a new chill in her voice. "I am obliged to remind you, Thomas, that you appropriated a sizeable portion of our household funds for other purposes last year. I have already let go many of the female staff. Perhaps, since you cared so much for your *other* expenses, you should now do without a valet."

Lord Culver narrowed his eyes. For a moment, Effie wondered if he might strike Lady Culver – but he must have restrained himself. "If we have too many male staff," he said, "then perhaps you should dismiss one of the footmen, Eleanor. You shall simply have to do with one less handsome face about the manor."

Effie paused, partway through opening a drawer in Lady Culver's vanity.

Lord Culver's barb did not land quite as intended. Lady

Culver smiled flatly. "You are as wise as ever, Lord Culver," she said, with a sardonic bite to her words. "I do not know what we would ever do without your counsel. We shall have one less footman, then. Will that be all, or would you like to tell me again how foolish I am?"

Lord Culver whirled upon his wife with his hand upraised. Effie did not have much chance to wonder at her own impulses – before she quite realised what she was doing, she had leapt towards him to grab at his arm. As he brought his arm down, the sheer violence of the gesture was enough to haul her halfway off her feet. The blow which he had clearly intended for Lady Culver went wide; Effie stumbled against the bed, still hanging from his arm, as Lady Culver shrieked in surprise.

"What the bloody hell do you think you're doing?" Lord Culver roared at Effie. His face was now red and ugly; drops of his spittle marked Effie's face as he yelled.

Effie should have been terrified. Lord Culver was not a *large* man – in fact, now that she looked at him properly, he was only a few inches taller than she was. But there was a subtle, terrible energy to his stance which every servant knew instinctively on sight – it was the bone-deep conviction that he *deserved* things, and that correspondingly, anyone who denied him those things *deserved* to be hurt in any way he saw fit. Men who thought they deserved things were always capable of the worst sorts of violence.

But Effie was not afraid. Instead, she was *furious*.

"I think that you should leave," Effie said to Lord Culver. Somehow, she said it in a low, frigid voice in spite of her awkward position.

Lord Culver's eyes flashed with rage. The idea that Effie had not immediately cowered beneath his anger was even more offensive than the idea that she had denied him the violence that he *deserved*. But Effie used his arm to haul herself back up to her feet, and she looked him in the eye. She spoke once again, and her jaw trembled with rage.

"If you strike me," Effie told him, "be assured that I will not hesitate to strike you back. I am a dirty, mannerless maid, sir, and I have no standards. I will scream and kick and bite you until neither of us has any dignity left. Your brothers will surely come running, and they will see you rolling on the floor with a maid like a pig in a sty."

Lord Culver wrenched his arm away from her. For a moment, Effie saw him considering the brutality that he still desired. But the anger that she radiated must have convinced him that she was entirely serious, and possibly even more dangerous than he was – for he stepped back and curled his hands into fists at his sides.

"You are dismissed," he said. "Take your things and get out of this house within the hour, or else I shall throw you out myself. You will have no reference and no pay."

Effie did not dare allow his words to penetrate her haze of anger. She knew that if she did, she would lose all of her strength at once. "You cannot steal my pay," she said. "I have worked for months already, and I am owed that much."

Lord Culver curled his lip at her. "You may go and complain to a magistrate," he said. "If any will listen."

He turned on his heel then and stormed from the bedroom, slamming the door behind him with all of the violence that he had not discharged upon either Effie or Lady Culver.

Effie continued to stand where she was, staring at the door.

Behind her, Lady Culver slowly straightened, regaining her composure. Silence stretched between them, unbroken, until Effie finally turned around to regard her. The lady of the house did not meet Effie's eyes.

"You shall need to pack quickly," Lady Culver said. "You should leave before he changes his mind and comes back for you."

Effie shook her head in amazement. "That is what suffices for a thank you, I suppose," she said. "I should not be surprised."

Lady Culver flinched – not in guilt, but in surprise. It was clear that she had been expecting Effie to quietly disappear, just as she had suggested. "I did not ask you to interfere in my marital affairs," the lady said. "You made that choice all on your own. I do not have the power to shield you from the consequences."

Effie set her jaw. "I did not ask you to shield me from any consequences," she said. "I did expect some tiny sliver of gratitude, perhaps – but that was my own mistake." The absurdity of it all suddenly struck her, and she could not help but laugh. The anger within her rose and burned ever higher. "You do not even know my name," Effie said. "You have *never* known my name. And when I leave, you still will not know it. You are alone in your miserable little world, because you refuse to see the human beings who surround you. If you were not such a hideous person, Lady Culver, you might well have friends in this house. And that is entirely your own fault."

Lady Culver's expression cooled even further at this. "You are right," she said. "I do not know your name. And now, I certainly do not care to know it."

A dizzy faintness overcame Effie then, and she realised that there were no more consequences to be had. This, she thought, was as bad as it got. She would be tossed out onto the street with no references and no pay. Once Lord and Lady Culver spoke to the rest of the households in the area, she would never be hired again.

But there was a horrible freedom in all of it nonetheless. Effie felt as though a deep, dark weight had been pried from her shoulders; for the first time in ages, she was able to breathe properly. At least, she thought, no one would think to take their spite out on her brother in particular – for none of them knew *his* name, either.

"I am sorry that I ever washed your clothes," Effie told Lady Culver. "I am sorry that I ever swept your parlour or brought you tea. But I am *not* sorry for what I have just done, no matter how abominable you are – and that is really the most ridiculous part. For I know how little you care about me, and I am perplexed why it is that I should care about *you*. And still, I do." She shook her head. "It is your humanity which is lacking, and not mine. At least I know that for certain now."

Effie turned and left the room. And then, she went below-stairs to the room that she shared with Lydia, and she began to collect her things.

Chapter Thirteen

It did not take all that long for Effie to put her things together, sparse as they were. Her bag contained only her housecoat, the two faerie gowns which Lord Blackthorn had brought her, the embroidery hoop with his coat and the glamour which he had left with her – though she left Lydia's glamour where it was. Once Effie had finished stowing all of this, she settled her bag upon her bed and drew in a shaking breath.

"Juniper Jubilee," she said. "Juniper Jubilee, Juniper Jubilee!"

The scent of wild roses suffused the room even more instantaneously than it had done the first time she had called the elf's name. Effie became aware of Lord Blackthorn standing just behind her; she turned to regard him, with a hollow feeling in her body.

Lord Blackthorn was in his usual cheerful sort of mood – perhaps even more than was usual. His smile could not possibly have been brighter. "Miss Euphemia!" he said. "What a pleasant surprise! You have only ever called me once before!"

For once, Effie did not feel invigorated by the elf's exuberance. Instead, the anger inside her churned and sickened her. That he should be so pleased with himself while halfway responsible for the things that had happened to her was briefly unconscionable.

"You must bring Lady Culver's gowns back," Effie told him.

Lord Blackthorn blinked. It was clear that he had not been expecting this turn of events at all. "I must?" he asked. "But why? She has paid the consequences for her theft at least three-fold. How will she ever learn not to steal from others if I simply undo her punishment?"

Effie balled up her fists at her sides. "Lady Culver will not learn *anything* from this!" she said. "There is no point in punishing her, Mr Jubilee! She does not have the capacity to understand the connection – because she is a person, but I am *not* a person, and so the two situations are not alike to her. Our lord and saviour could walk into her bedroom and take his braided whip to her, and she would still only cry, *Why me?*"

Effie paused to take a deep, steadying breath. Her fury churned within her helplessly. "Lady Culver may well dismiss George so that she can buy more gowns for herself. And he is sick, Mr Jubilee. I cannot have it. I will not enjoy a useless revenge at the expense of my own brother. You must bring back Lady Culver's gowns."

Lord Blackthorn's bright expression dimmed at this; worry slowly overtook his smile. "But I cannot bring them back, Miss Euphemia," he said. "I have already given them away, as she gave away *your* gown."

Effie closed her eyes. The anger inside her could not be contained any more, no matter how she tried. For just a moment, she forgot the warm sunlight in Blackthorn, and the way her heart swelled when Lord Blackthorn spoke of how lovely she was, and how he loved her stitching. All of these things had been driven out of her mind by the keen and very present understanding that both she and her brother might be tossed out to sicken and starve.

"I will go and let Miss Buckley know that Lady Culver is in need of her gown," Effie said slowly. "They are such *great* friends, after all. I am sure that she will return the gift, now that Lady Culver is in need of it."

Lord Blackthorn cleared his throat uncomfortably at this. Effie opened her eyes and saw that his expression had now become openly anxious.

"About Miss Buckley," he said.

Effie waited, now resigned to expect the very worst.

Her feelings must have shown on her face, for Lord Blackthorn's posture wilted slightly. ". . . I fear that Miss Buckley is not in a state to entertain," the faerie said weakly. "I have put her to sleep for a hundred years."

Effie had *thought* she was prepared for his response . . . but this was so far beyond the pale that she had to sit down on the edge of her bed and bury her face in her hands.

"I am so sorry!" Lord Blackthorn said. And it was clear that he really *was* sorry – a fact which Effie might have found more interesting if she had not been so very miserable. "I am sure that we can come up with a solution, Miss Euphemia. True love's kiss will wake her, of course – I assumed that she had no true love, since she was so wicked – but I could ask Lady Hollowvale to do a divination—"

"I do not want you to do *anything* more, Mr Jubilee!" Effie burst out. "Don't you see that you have done enough? Every time you have meddled with my life, things have only become worse and worse! Your good intentions do not matter if everything you do still causes disaster!" She pushed to her feet, still trembling with the awfulness of the day. "The worst of it by far is that this is all my own fault. I *knew* what you were when I agreed to your deal. There is not a single English person who does not know that faeries cause trouble wherever they go. I am angry with you, Mr Jubilee, and I am angry with *myself*, because being angry with you is ridiculous – it is like stubbing my toe on a table and becoming angry with the table!"

Lord Blackthorn blinked quickly as Effie's voice grew more and more heated. The worry on his face passed into open alarm – and then into distress. He flinched at Effie's last words as though she had struck him, and he took a step back from her.

"I . . . I am sorry," he said softly. For a moment, Effie thought that he might say something more – but he stopped himself and fell silent instead.

The sight of real misery on Lord Blackthorn's face made Effie's heart twinge. *It is mostly the truth*, she thought. *But I did not have to be nearly so awful about it.* She looked down at her feet in shame, searching for the right thing to say.

"I will not help you any more, Miss Euphemia," Lord Blackthorn said softly. "Or rather . . . I see now that I *cannot* help you. You are right." He forced a smile, and the expression suddenly looked uncomfortable on him. "I certainly do not wish to be a table."

This innocent observation struck Effie with a particularly terrible force. She remembered her words to him only the previous day: *I am like the air or the wallpaper or the furniture.* It was true, of course, that Lord Blackthorn had brought disaster upon her. Unlike every other important person in her life, however, he had never once treated her like furniture. How could she have even implied that he was not human? Or rather – he was clearly not human, but he was certainly a *person*.

Effie swallowed against the lump in her throat. "I should not have said that, Mr Jubilee," she said. "Please won't you forget that I said—?"

But as she looked up once more, she saw that he was already gone.

~~~~~

Effie ran into Lydia on her way out through the servants' passageways. The other maid gave Effie a peculiar look as she noticed the bag over her shoulder.

"What's goin' on?" Lydia asked. "Did you talk to Lord Blackthorn about the gowns?"

Effie sucked in a deep breath. "I did," she told Lydia. "And he cannot bring them back. In any case, I have been dismissed. Lady Culver may well dismiss George too, if I do not find a gown to her standards. On that note – I don't suppose you can tell me where to find Miss Buckley's estate?"

Lydia's mouth dropped open; outrage kindled behind her eyes. "But – *dismissed*, Effie?" she asked. "How? Why?"

Effie tried to ignore the way the word made her feel, as Lydia repeated it once again. "Mainly," she said, "for Lord Culver's ego. But I will care about that later, Lydia. Do you know the way to Miss Buckley's estate or not?"

Lydia *did* know the way to Miss Buckley's estate – but she refused to tell Effie how to get there until she had heard the entire story from her. When Effie was done recounting events, Lydia was even more furious than Effie had been.

"This is ridiculous, all of it!" Lydia seethed. "Don't go waste your time on Miss Buckley, Effie! All of this has got to end, don't you understand?"

Effie threw up her hands. "I cannot think of what to do about it!" she said. "What, will you yell at Lord Culver next, Lydia? He'll only dismiss you as well!"

"Maybe I don't care if he does dismiss me," Lydia retorted. "I know you've had your hands full with Lord Blackthorn, Effie, but *I've* been shoppin' around. I talked to Mr Jesson, you know, after he found out I was a maid. He's lookin' for a housekeeper an' a maid at the very least, because Orange End is under-staffed. He asked if I knew anyone, an' I told him I wanted the job myself just as soon as you were married off."

Effie blinked. "I had no idea!" she said. "Thank goodness, Lydia. I'll be relieved to know that at least *you're* some-where better."

Lydia narrowed her eyes. "Well, I'm not just leavin' everyone else to hang," she said. "Maybe you don't want to fight this, Effie, but can you *imagine* this house now that you're leavin', an' I'm leavin', an' Mrs Sedgewick is too depressed to work—?"

"She's what?" Effie interrupted, confused. "I thought Mrs Sedgewick was ill?"

Lydia's face darkened. "I went to check on her, Effie. She's not sick – she just can't get up the will to get out of bed. She just started cryin' at the very mention of it. She said she'd rather die than face Lady Culver again." Lydia brooded on this. "You know what I think, Effie? An' maybe you won't like this, I don't know. But I think your anger was the only thing keepin' Mrs Sedgewick on her feet. An' now that it's gone, I don't know if she's got much else left."

Effie took this in uncomfortably. This possibility had never occurred to her at all. Mrs Sedgewick had always been Mrs Sedgewick – solid and reliable and ever so slightly insufferable. The idea that their housekeeper had been so ready to fold at any moment was a terrible revelation.

Effie took in a deep breath. "Bother all of this," she said. "Just give me a moment. I've got to think."

Her head pounded with emotion. Her chest clenched with anger. It was so hard to think with all of that *fury*—

"Oh," Effie mumbled. "Silly me. I've got more than enough anger to spare, haven't I?"

She pulled out her handkerchief – a white muslin square which she'd decorated with whitework leaves. She then unshouldered her bag and searched out one of the spools of wishes, along with a needle and thread. And then, right in the middle of the servants' passageway, she sat down and began to embroider a tiny thistle onto the fabric.

It was a terrible job, all things considered – certainly not worth the thread that she was using. But Effie was angrier than she had ever been before in her life; much as she knew she had begun a masterpiece in Lord Blackthorn's jacket, she *knew* that this would be a masterpiece too. She poured into that little thistle all of her indignation – her conviction that she was *not* a piece of furniture and that no one *else* should be treated as furniture either. She imagined, moreover, a world where no one would dare to treat her that way. She envisioned Lord and Lady Culver stripped of their haughty, self-righteous power, forced to acknowledge that other people mattered and existed just as much as they did. And as she stitched, Effie found that *this* was the single deepest, most desperate wish in her heart.

When she was done, she rose to her feet again and handed the handkerchief over to Lydia. "Give this to Mrs Sedgewick," she said. "I barely know what I am doing, Lydia, but maybe it will help."

A strange look came into Lydia's eyes as she took the handkerchief from Effie. "I think it *will* help," she said. "Oh, Effie. I feel like I could spit nails! Have you really been this angry all the time?" The question was awed rather than worried.

"I wonder if I have been," Effie said. "I've done so much stitching, Lydia. I imagine I must have had an *awful* lot of anger, since I kept having to give it away." She shook her head. "I don't dare stick around any longer. I might come back with Lady Culver's gown if I'm lucky – but I won't be back as myself, if you take my meaning."

Lydia nodded slowly. "If you really think that's best," she said. "I won't be leavin' till I'm sure George is sorted, Effie. If I've got to, I'll take him with me to Mr Jesson. He's a decent fellow, an' a bit of a doormat. I wager he won't complain."

Effie embraced Lydia tightly. "I expect I'll have to go to Blackthorn eventually," she said. "I can't imagine how I'll find the opportunity to marry Mr Benedict without a job or a home or a carriage. Just in case, I thought I should tell you goodbye and thank you, and what a wonderful friend you've always been."

Lydia smiled weakly. "Maybe faerie won't be so bad," she

said. "I've thought more than once that I'd rather work for Lord Blackthorn than Lady Culver, even if the work was ten times as hard. An' I *do* think he likes you an awful lot, Effie."

Effie sighed. "I will have to apologise to him," she said. "And I do want to apologise. But I don't dare call him up again until this is all sorted out, or else he might try to *fix* things."

Lydia squeezed Effie tightly. "You ought to go see George," she said. "What'll he think when you go missin' again?"

Effie shook her head. "George is sick enough as it is," she said. "I won't worry him with this right now. Once I'm sure his job is safe, I'll go to say goodbye – as a lady, if I have to. If I am somehow spirited away before then, you'll just have to assure him that I am gainfully employed elsewhere."

Effie released the other maid and hiked her bag up onto her shoulder. Lydia reluctantly gave her directions to Miss Buckley's estate.

And then – after many years of miserable service – Effie finally walked out of Hartfield.

Chapter Fourteen

☙

$\mathcal{I}$t was cold and rainy and muddy, all the way to Miss Buckley's estate. Technically, of course, it was not *Miss Buckley's* estate – the land and the manor upon it belonged to Miss Buckley's older brother, Lord Wilford. It took Effie most of the day to trek her way to Holly House – the name of Lord Wilford's manor. By the time she arrived, the sun had already set, and every inch of her clothing was miserably soaked.

Holly House was difficult to make out in the darkness, but there was still just enough twilight left that Effie could discern some of its details if she squinted. One detail in particular gave her significant pause.

The entire manor had been overgrown with briars.

"Drat," Effie said.

She rummaged through her rain-soaked bag, struggling to see its contents in the twilight. Finally, she pulled out the yellow rose which Lord Blackthorn had given her and twined it back around her neck. No one at this house, Effie thought, was likely to admit a drenched housemaid in from the cold. A drenched *lady* might perhaps have better luck.

Effie marched up to the manor's door, which was thoroughly entangled by thorns and white roses. She sighed heavily and addressed the thorns in much the same way that Lord Blackthorn had addressed the chair at the centre of his realm.

"I know that you are only trying to help," Effie said. "And I *do* appreciate it. But I have got to get inside – that is my goal, is what I mean to say. And I am very sure of that goal, because it is dreadfully cold out here, and I am wet and miserable. Would you please let me inside?"

Effie had not really been sure that this would work at all – but to her surprise, the thorns on the door slowly parted, rearranging themselves to either side of the stoop. She blinked and stepped forwards.

"Thank you," she told the briars. "That was very kind of you."

Perhaps it was only her imagination, but Effie thought that the roses blossomed just a bit more at this, as though they were pleased.

She rapped her knuckles firmly against the door.

Somewhere inside, a small dog began to yap loudly. Footsteps sounded as someone approached. "Who is it?" an old man's voice called from behind the door. "Is it the physician? You can't get through the front door; it's all blocked with thorns. You'll have to come around the servants' entrance, I'm afraid!"

Effie shivered and rubbed at her arms. "The briars are gone from the door!" she said. "Though I do not know for how long! Can I please come inside?"

The door opened abruptly. An elderly butler stood in the door frame, blinking at Effie over a candle. He had picked up a tiny pug dog, which wriggled and whined impatiently against his side. "My word!" he said. "A lady? At this time of night? But you must not come inside, miss – this house is cursed, and there's no telling if it will rub off on you!"

Effie frowned. "I suspect that the briars and I have an accord," she informed him. "I am here to try and *remove* the curse from this house, in fact. I was under the impression that Miss Buckley had fallen into a deep sleep – but I had not heard of the rest of it! What else is going on, sir?"

The butler blinked at Effie in bewilderment . . . but slowly, he stepped aside and allowed her to pass. "It's not just Miss Buckley," he said. "The whole of her family is asleep as well, though none of the rest of us seem to be affected. We've tried to wake the Family up, but nothing will do the job!"

Effie bit her lip. Lord Blackthorn had multiplied his punishment towards Lady Culver as well, so perhaps this turn of events should not have surprised her. "I don't suppose that there are *three* members of Miss Buckley's family in this house?" she guessed.

"Yes, that's correct," the butler told her. He closed the door behind her and let the pug back down to the floor – but its plaintive whines continued unabated. "Are you familiar with Lord Wilford, then?"

Effie paused in the entryway, still shivering, as she pried off her half-boots. "Not in the least," she replied. "Might I impose upon you for a cup of hot tea and something dry to wear, Mr . . . ?"

"Mr Fudge," the butler said quickly.

Effie nodded. "My name is Euphemia Reeves," she added, since she did not want to be rude.

Mr Fudge nodded. "I can find you both of those things, Miss Reeves," he said. "Please come into the parlour. And, er – please don't mind Caesar." He gestured towards the pug, which was still whining softly. "He'll calm down again eventually, I'm sure."

Effie was *very* relieved to find that there was a fire going in the parlour. She settled herself onto a chair just next to it, rubbing her hands together. Eventually, Mr Fudge returned with a heavy blanket and an entire pot of chamomile tea. Effie drank through three full cups of it before her limbs had thawed enough for her to move again. Still, she kept the blanket stubbornly around her shoulders as she stood up and addressed Mr Fudge.

"Where might I find Miss Buckley?" she asked.

Mr Fudge took Effie upstairs and showed her into a bedroom. It was a smaller bedroom than most family bedrooms she had seen, though it was still far larger than the basement bedroom in which she and Lydia slept. Briars crawled along the bedroom's walls here as well, interspersed with large white roses. The briars grew particularly thick around a single bed in the room, where Miss Buckley currently slept. As Effie drew closer, she saw that Miss Buckley was wearing Effie's old gown, and she still had her hair done up with roses as she had done at breakfast. The briars seemed to have grown from these cut flowers until they had overtaken the house.

"Miss Buckley fell asleep in one of the tea rooms," Mr Fudge told Effie, as he closed the door behind them. "We brought her up to bed – but then the flowers started to grow, and all of the *rest* of the Family fell asleep too. Do you really have an idea of how to fix her, Miss Reeves?"

A loud whine sounded outside the door, followed by insistent scratching. Effie knit her brow. "Perhaps you should let the dog inside?" she asked Mr Fudge. "He seems very distressed."

Mr Fudge sighed. "Caesar's been out of sorts since this whole thing began," he said. "We've had to keep him out of Miss Buckley's room so he doesn't hurt himself on the thorns."

Effie nodded, nearly dismissing this statement entirely . . . but then, she paused. "Could it be that Caesar is Miss Buckley's dog?" she asked.

Mr Fudge smiled wryly. "He is technically Lord Wilford's dog," he said. "But that dog's been in love with Miss Buckley since the first time she picked him up."

Effie stared at Miss Buckley. *Surely, it can't be that simple,* she thought.

But there was little harm in testing the theory, after all. And so Effie went back to the door and opened it. Caesar bolted past her legs like a shot – but she scooped up the pug as he passed her, lifting him towards the bed where Miss Buckley currently slept.

Mr Fudge watched with a furrowed brow as Effie carefully settled the dog right next to Miss Buckley's beautiful sleeping face. Caesar whined one more time – and then, he stuck out his tongue and gave Miss Buckley's face a long, mournful lick.

Miss Buckley stirred in her sleep.

"What the devil?" Mr Fudge exclaimed.

"A faerie told me that true love's kiss could wake Miss Buckley," Effie told him. "I cannot think of any truer or more unconditional love than that of a dog."

Miss Buckley mumbled something in her sleep. Caesar's whimpers faded into curiosity, and he nudged at her cheek with his wrinkled nose. He licked her again – and this time, she yawned and sat up in her bed.

"My word!" Miss Buckley sighed. "How late did I sleep?" Caesar barked and wriggled his way happily beneath her arm. Miss Buckley scratched absently at his ears. She blinked at the other occupants in the room. "Oh dear! I didn't realise I had company!"

Mr Fudge let out a loud sigh of relief. "Thank the lord!" he said. "You've been asleep for more than a day, miss!"

Miss Buckley blinked around at the thick rose briars, which had even now begun to shrink sulkily away, disappearing back to who-knew-where. "I must still be dreaming," she said. "This is exceptionally odd."

Effie glanced towards Mr Fudge. "Would you mind giving us a moment of privacy?" she asked.

The butler nodded reluctantly. He retreated through the door, leaving the two of them in silence.

"You are not dreaming, Miss Buckley," Effie told the lady wearily. "You were faerie-cursed. Your dog has kissed you awake and broken the curse. I *hope* that it shall suffice to break the curse on the rest of your family as well – I don't know if Caesar loves any of the rest of them quite enough to wake them up."

Miss Buckley widened her eyes. "Faerie-cursed?" she asked. "Really? I have heard of people being cursed before, of course, but I have never seen it before with my own eyes! What could I have done to upset a faerie, though?" She frowned as she recognised Effie. "But you were at breakfast, weren't you? You were the lady I saw talking to Mr Benedict."

Effie looked away. "I was," she said. "And I cannot say that I am very fond of you, Miss Buckley, whether that is any of your fault or not. But I am *not* a faerie, and a hundred years of slumber seems to me to be a ridiculous sort of punishment." She drew in a breath. "The gown that you accepted from Lady Culver was stolen, and that is ultimately why you were cursed. If you give it to me now, I will return it to her, and I believe that you will no longer be troubled by any faeries."

An unexpected misery flickered across Miss Buckley's face at this, and she hugged her dog closer to her chest. "I should have realised it was to do with the gown," she said. "It is the only reason that Mr Benedict showed any interest in me, isn't it?" She glanced down, unable to meet Effie's eyes. "I do not know what I will do if he does not marry me. I have so few prospects, miss. Whichever faerie this gown was stolen from ... do you think they might be merciful enough to let me keep it for just a little while longer?"

Effie stared at her. "You want to keep the gown until Mr Benedict marries you?" she asked slowly. "Don't you wish to find out whether he really cares for you first?"

"But he clearly *doesn't* care for me," Miss Buckley said. "I can live with that – goodness knows, he probably spent more than his fair share of time with ladies in Venice whom he did not care about at all. I will be a good wife to him, at least. All I wish is that I will not be wed to some old creature that my brother chooses out of desperation!"

Effie pressed her lips together. "Thank goodness your dog loves you so much, Miss Buckley," she said, "for that is the most odious thing that I have ever heard, and I cannot imagine anyone *else* loving a woman who would express such a sentiment. I had a magical gown too, you know – but I never would have accepted a marriage proposal in it!" She shook her head. "You do not have to charm a man into marrying you with a magical gown, nor do you have to marry some old creature. You have *many* other choices open to you, but you refuse to see them. You could run away from your comfortable life and become a governess – or even a very proper lady's maid."

Miss Buckley recoiled at this. "A *maid?*" she repeated incredulously.

"Oh yes," Effie said. "A maid. Is that very terrible, Miss Buckley? Could it be that maids are not treated very *well* in your household? Are they, in fact, treated so very poorly that you would rather wed a toothless old man than become a maid?"

Miss Buckley fell silent. Effie did not really think that her words had penetrated; rather, she thought that Miss Buckley was worried that Effie was *herself* a faerie, and that any further argument might lead to her being cursed once again.

"Give me the gown," Effie said curtly. "I will lose my patience entirely with you if I stay any longer." She paused. "And take very good care of that dog, Miss Buckley. He is a kinder creature than you are by far."

Effie waited in the parlour while Miss Buckley changed out of her gown. As she did, she heard the rest of the Family puttering about, making sudden loud demands of the servants. Eventually, Mr Fudge came down with the gown. The expression he gave Effie was now something halfway between fear and gratitude, and she suspected that Miss Buckley had convinced all the *rest* of them that Effie was a faerie as well.

I am not a faerie, Effie thought. *But I am apparently a magician, which I suppose is close enough as to make no difference.*

Effie accepted the gown from him, eyeing it glumly. The idea of giving it back to Lady Culver made her stomach hurt – but George needed his job far more than Effie needed the gown.

Yearning hopes whispered to her from the stitches in the leaves and flowers, however . . . and Effie set her jaw stubbornly. *At least*, she thought, *I will not give up my dreams to Lady Culver.*

"May I borrow some embroidery scissors, Mr Fudge?" Effie asked the butler.

Mr Fudge was very quick to fulfil Effie's request. He soon returned with the scissors, then settled himself carefully against the wall, pretending not to watch as she snipped away at the embroidery on the gown.

There were only a few stitches, Effie found, that were imbued with special significance. Now that she knew what to look for, she could feel those brief moments of wistfulness as her fingers trailed over the fabric. It was these stitches that Effie cut away, one by one – until the only thing that remained was a well-worn gown with a painstaking amount of very normal embroidery.

"Please, Miss Reeves," Mr Fudge said, as she inspected her work. "Can we offer you anything else – anything at all? We would not wish you to find our hospitality lacking."

Effie sighed. She could not bear to look any more at the normal, boring gown in her lap. "I could use a carriage back to Hartfield, Mr Fudge," she told him. "I do not fancy walking all the way back in the rain."

"Of course," the butler stammered. "Yes, we will fetch you a carriage at once. It will be difficult in the mud, of course, but I hope you will forgive us the trouble."

"I am not going to curse you, Mr Fudge," Effie informed the butler coolly. "I suspect that working in this household may be curse enough. But I would still appreciate the carriage, for it has been a long day, and I still have much to do."

It was a sign of the household's awe that they *did* fetch Effie a carriage, even on a dark and rainy night. Had she truly been a lady, she would have tipped the coachman quite richly for his troubles – but she only *appeared* to be a lady. In reality, she was a common maid without a household or a reference, and without a penny to her name.

She thanked the coachman profusely instead, as he dropped her off in front of Hartfield. Effie stomped her way through the mud all the way up to the front door – and she knocked.

Chapter Fifteen

*E*ffie had to knock again a few more times – it was far past the hour where any proper visitor ought to be expected. But eventually, Mr Allen answered the door.

"Miss," he said, with a hint of peevishness. "It is after sundown. May I ask what is so very important?"

Effie blinked – she was unused to being addressed so tartly by the butler. She coughed in surprise. "I . . . I'm very sorry," she said. "I heard of Lady Culver's difficulties. I have come with a spare gown that she may use."

A flicker of unutterable relief crossed the butler's face. "Have you indeed?" he said. "Well, please come in, miss – it is dreadful outside. We shall settle you somewhere warm and dry while I take your gift up to Lady Culver. Do you have a calling card?"

Effie forced a smile. "I fear I do not have one with me," she said. "I was not expecting to visit today."

Mr Allen ushered her inside and closed the door behind her. "I will inform the lady of your arrival then," he said. "Your visit is very unusual – but then, these are very unusual circumstances. I am sure that she will wish to thank you personally for your concern." He paused. "Might I have your name, miss?"

Effie hesitated at that. There was no reasonable way to avoid giving her name to the butler. But surely, he would recognise the name, even if he did not recognise *her*?

Silence stretched between them. Just as it began to become uncomfortable, Effie sighed. "My name is Euphemia Reeves," she said. "I am primarily acquainted with Mr Benedict."

Mr Allen knit his brow at this. "Euphemia Reeves?" he repeated slowly – as though he wasn't sure that he had heard Effie properly.

Effie did her best to look composed. "Yes," she said. "That is my name."

Mr Allen looked at her very closely. *Please don't let him cause trouble*, Effie thought at the rose around her throat. The flower trembled nervously beneath the butler's gaze.

"Curious," Mr Allen said finally. "We have a servant here by that name. What are the odds, do you think?" But his eyes became unfocused, and he seemed to overlook the matter.

The rose at Effie's throat relaxed again, and a bit of tension drained from her shoulders.

Mr Allen led Effie to the Blue Room and took the gown from her so that he could bring it up to Lady Culver; shortly thereafter, Lydia appeared with yet another pot of tea, and Effie found herself in a very bizarre position indeed. The other maid did not seem to recognise Effie at all, in spite of the fact that she had surely been expecting Effie's return. In fact, Lydia did her very best to pretend that she could not see Effie as she set up the table in front of her.

"Lydia?" Effie whispered.

Lydia jumped. She stared at Effie, wide-eyed. "Um. I . . . do not speak Eengleesh," she attempted, in the very worst French accent that Effie had ever heard.

Effie barely swallowed a giggle. "It's Effie, Lydia," she said. "I'm wearing my glamour. But . . . oh! You're not wearing yours. That must be the problem." The rose at her throat began to flutter again, but Effie reached up to calm it with her fingers. "What do I look like to you right now?"

Lydia knit her brow as Effie spoke. She squinted and tried to focus more keenly. "You ... look like a lady," she said dubiously. "But that doesn't make sense. You're not even wearin' a nice gown. I just *feel* like you must be a lady, somehow."

Effie nodded. "I suppose it doesn't really change the way I *look*, then," she mumbled. She shivered and let out another cough. "Ugh. I suppose I will need that tea. I've already had most of a pot tonight, but that walk was *terrible*."

Lydia poured a cup for Effie, and she sipped on it gratefully, letting the heat soothe her throat.

"I gave Mrs Sedgewick the handkerchief," Lydia told her. "No tellin' whether it's helped just yet, but I really think it will. You'll check on George afore you leave?"

"I will," Effie said. "I doubt that anyone could stop me."

The door to the Blue Room opened then, and Lydia turned away, pretending once again to be invisible. Benedict entered, walking just a bit more quickly than normal – he was dressed more casually than he had been at either the ball or the break-fast, with his neck cloth loosened and the top button of his waistcoat undone. His warm brown eyes settled on Effie, and he frowned in sudden concern.

"Miss Reeves," he said. "My goodness, you look awful! Please tell me you did not *walk* here to save Lady Culver from her misfortunes?"

Effie coloured at the observation – but there was only shock and concern in Benedict's tone, and not disapproval. "I fear I walked to Miss Buckley's residence earlier," she said. "It was not my most intelligent moment. But Lord Wilford was kind enough to send me here with his carriage."

"But Lord Blackthorn has a carriage!" Benedict said. "Why would he send you out in the rain? And – oh. Your chaperone is absent?" He sounded sheepish now, as he realised how inap-propriate their current situation was.

Effie looked down. "I have had a falling out with Lord Blackthorn," she said. "I am sure that it is temporary. But because of that, it was not possible to borrow his carriage. My chaperone is otherwise occupied, and so I had to go out unaccompanied today."

She tried very hard not to look at Lydia as she said this, aware of the heavy irony inherent in their situation.

"This is dreadful," Benedict declared. "I have never heard of a guardian acting in such an inappropriate manner. Why, I am tempted to call him out, Miss Reeves!"

Effie coughed on her tea. She had to clear her throat a few times in succession before she could speak again. "I do not think you want to do that, Mr Benedict," she said. "Truly, I beg that you don't even try. Lord Blackthorn is mostly very kind, but I doubt that anyone here would come out the better in a duel with him."

Steps sounded just down the hallway – and before Benedict could properly answer this, Lady Culver swept into the room. She was wearing Effie's old gown; her hair had been hastily done up, and she was smiling in a way that suggested her troubles had unexpectedly melted away in the rain. "Miss Reeves!" she said. "I cannot express how touched I am. Did you and Mary concoct this idea together, perhaps?"

Effie knew that she ought to respond, but the glowing, beatific smile on Lady Culver's face took her so much aback that she couldn't find the words. Never – not once in her life – had Lady Culver ever *smiled* at her.

"Lady Culver," Benedict said respectfully, filling in the sudden silence. "Miss Reeves walked through the rain to retrieve this gown from Miss Buckley, I am told. She has only just come here by carriage – but as you can see, she is ragged and unaccompanied! Her guardian has all but abandoned her!"

Lady Culver's mouth dropped open in astonishment. "Well, that is unconscionable!" she said – and there was real anger in her voice. "I have never heard the like!" She narrowed her eyes at Effie. "Men are just terrible, aren't they?"

Benedict opened his mouth to protest, and Lady Culver waved a hand at him. "Present company excluded, of course."

Somehow, Effie found the strength to speak. "Yes," she said slowly. "All of that is true. I was left out in the rain, Lady Culver, without even a carriage. I was told that I had only an hour to leave my home. I am sure that the person who sent me away does not care at all what happens to me – in fact, I suspect that they would not much care if I had died."

Lady Culver shook her head incredulously. "This is awful," she said. "I am outraged on your behalf, Miss Reeves. You can be sure that everyone I know will be hearing about this. A lady ought not to be treated in this manner, not ever."

"Perhaps," Benedict interjected, "Miss Reeves might stay with *us* for a time, Lady Culver? We could not possibly put her back out into the rain, after all. If there is no other room prepared, then she can have mine. I will sleep in some unprepared bed instead."

Lady Culver scoffed at this. "Of *course* we will not put her back out into the rain, Benedict," she said. "But I'm sure that the servants can prepare a new room—"

"– that is absolutely not necessary," Effie interrupted her quickly. "Please, please don't ask the servants to do that. It's far too much trouble." She meant this in the most literal way, of course, for she knew very well how much work it was to make a room habitable when it had gone unused for so long.

Lydia swept up next to Lady Culver and murmured something to her quietly. Lady Culver nodded, and the maid disappeared from the Blue Room.

"The servants have already started preparing a room," Lady Culver said. "And so it cannot be undone. You will stay with us until your guardian comes to his senses, Miss Reeves. And I am *certain* that he shall! He will be unable to show his face in polite company without being reminded of his boorishness by everyone who hears of this."

Effie did not respond to this. How *could* she respond? She could not help but feel that she had somehow wandered into faerie and met some mirror image of the real Lady Culver. It was just as Miss Buckley had said – Lady Culver's instant, instinctive generosity was a sight to behold. If Effie had not worked for the woman for so long, and endured so many bitter, biting words from her, she might have been instantly smitten by her manner, convinced that she had just made a lifelong friend of impeccable virtue.

Another cough tickled its way up Effie's throat; she released it nervously, swallowing more tea to confound it. Benedict reached out to touch her shoulder in concern.

"You really must get to bed, Miss Reeves," he said. "I begin to be worried for your health. My bed has already been heated – I will take the other room when it is ready."

"Thank you," Effie said quietly. "I am … overwhelmed, I'm afraid. I cannot find the words to describe how I feel about all of this."

Benedict went upstairs to clear some of his effects from his room. As he did, Lady Culver stayed with Effie, sipping from a cup of tea. "Take heart, Miss Reeves," she said encouragingly. "All is not lost. I have nearly been in your position before, myself. Now look at me – I am happily married, and in possession of a very respectable title."

Happily married? Effie wondered. But she did not dare to say the words aloud. "I must admit, Lady Culver," she said, "I do not understand how you can take me into your house so easily."

Lady Culver sighed. "You remind me awfully of myself," she said. "I suppose – in a very small way – I feel as though I am helping some other version of me."

Effie nodded dully. The explanation was more telling than Lady Culver probably intended it to be. *She only treats me as though I am someone because she thinks I am like her,* Effie thought. *It is the same with all of the nobles, I suppose.*

Eventually, Benedict returned to let them know that he had vacated his old room. He and Lady Culver led Effie upstairs and tucked her into a soft, warm bed with hot bricks at the end of it. Lady Culver watched from an appropriate distance as Benedict smiled at Effie and reached out to brush back her hair. "I am glad that you came to our door, Miss Reeves," he told Effie. "I would have been heartbroken if anything had happened to you."

Effie smiled back up at him in spite of herself. "I am surprised that you did not forget me the very moment that I left your sight," she admitted.

Benedict frowned at this. "How could I possibly forget you?" he asked. "I must tell you something, Miss Reeves – it may sound incredible, but I must say it anyway." He paused to gather his thoughts. "I had never felt before that anyone had really seen me. I don't mean to say that I am invisible, certainly – but when people see me, it is not *me* that they are seeing." He smiled wistfully at Effie. "It was so wonderful to be seen for once. I will always treasure that feeling."

Effie's heart gave a wistful twinge at the words.

"Benedict," Lady Culver said. Her voice held a hint of fond reproval. "Stop being inappropriate and let the lady rest, please."

Benedict's smile turned helpless at that. He inclined his head towards Effie. "Goodnight, Miss Reeves," he said.

He and Lady Culver left Effie to sleep then. And – as much as Effie's mind reeled from all of the day's events – she did indeed fall into an utterly exhausted sleep.

Chapter Sixteen

*E*ffie awoke early the next morning in a feverish haze, wondering why Lydia had not yet budged her up to handle the fireplaces.

Her bed was softer and warmer than it should have been. The room was bigger and less claustrophobic. Strong sunlight trickled in around the edges of the curtains in her room, informing her that she had slept far later than expected.

Even as Effie remembered her strange situation, someone knocked politely at her bedroom door. She blinked dimly, before realising that the person on the other side was waiting for her response. "Er," she said. "Come in!"

Lady Culver stepped politely inside, dressed in her borrowed housecoat. She smiled at Effie. "I hope you got a bit of rest," she said.

Effie shrank down into her pillows instinctively, though there was no hint of acrimony on Lady Culver's features. "I think I must have," she said. "I'm so sorry."

Lady Culver shook her head. "Benedict was right," she said. "You don't seem well, Miss Reeves. It's best that you get as much rest as possible. I've asked the staff to bring some food up for you soon, rather than having you eat with the rest of us." She sat down on the edge of Effie's bed, considering her with curiosity. "I went to visit Mary this morning to thank her for returning the gown. I asked how the two of you had come to know one another, but she would not say much – except to say that you *were* acquainted, and that she would not utter a word against you."

Effie coughed – whether from nervousness or from her scratchy throat, she could not tell. "That is ... very kind of her," she said.

Lady Culver tilted her head. "I wonder if there is anything else I can get for you, dear? I know I am always dreadfully bored when I am forced to stay in bed."

Effie had never been *forced* to stay in bed before, as far as she could remember. Privately, she thought that she would never dare complain at being told to rest as much as she liked. "I cannot think what I would ask for," Effie admitted. "Though it is generous of you to ask."

Effie reached up to rub at her throat as though she might banish the soreness inside it – but as she did, her fingers caught on the rose there, and she snatched her hand back again. Soon after, an alarming thought surged to the forefront of her mind.

I have been a lady for hours and hours now, she thought. *Who knows how many stitches I owe Mr Jubilee?*

"I do have an embroidery project which I would like to finish," Effie said suddenly. "I am sure that I brought it with me."

Lady Culver nodded. "The maid has put your things away somewhere," she said. "I will ask her to find your embroidery for you." She paused. "Benedict would like to see you. I have been putting him off for the sake of your health, but he is most impatient on the matter. I will be frank, Miss Reeves – I have never known him to show such a fondness for any woman before. But I would like to assure you that you may put him off without consequence, if that is your wish."

A warm tingle spread through Effie at the observation. In spite of everything, she realised, she had caught Benedict's attentions after all. But Lady Culver's suggestion made her knit her brow. "And ... would you *like* me to put him off, Lady Culver?" she asked slowly. "I know that you have promised to ingratiate Miss Buckley to him."

Lady Culver blinked. "Oh," she said. "I see that you and Mary *do* talk. Well, Miss Reeves ... the truth of the matter is that I have always thought that Benedict was incapable of settling. And he has made it clear so far that he has no interest in Mary whatsoever. I truly do not think that she will be happy with him." She considered for a moment. "I would normally warn you away from Benedict for the sake of your own happiness. But he is such a different man around you that I begin to wonder if you could settle his less disciplined tendencies. If that *were* the case ... then I suppose that all parties involved might benefit from his sudden attachment."

This was, Effie realised, Lady Culver's way of giving her blessing. The very idea was inconceivable.

I cannot believe this is the same woman who made my life a living misery, Effie thought. *There was a time when I would rather hide in faerie for ever than face her even one more time.*

But the truth remained that Effie still had a wager to fulfil – and Lady Culver's tacit approval was almost certainly necessary if Effie wished to see Benedict at all while she was a guest at Hartfield.

"I would not like to put off Mr Benedict at all, then," Effie admitted. "As long as you have no complaints. He is excellent company, and I do enjoy talking to him."

Lady Culver nodded. "I will let him know that he may visit you, then – as long as I am present, of course. Do let me know if he becomes an imposition, however, and I shall send him away at once."

"Thank you, Lady Culver," Effie said. "Your kindness knows no bounds." She had to stare very furiously at her pillow as she said these words – but they seemed to have the intended effect, for Lady Culver beamed with delight for the entire rest of their conversation, until the moment that she finally departed.

Lydia came up not long after, carrying with her both breakfast and Lord Blackthorn's jacket. She grimaced as she saw Effie. "You don't look well," she said. "Between your time with George an' that walk in the rain, I think you must have caught whatever he has."

Effie frowned down at her lap. Her body felt hot and flushed, and the tickle in her throat had quickly climbed its way deeper down into her chest. "I am being given the most solicitous care available," she said. "If I *am* sick, then I could not possibly ask for better accommodations. But how is George, Lydia? I want to go and see him, but they're keeping such a close watch on me!"

Lydia did not respond immediately. Effie looked up at her face and saw that it was uneasy. "Lydia," Effie repeated. "How is George?"

Lydia sighed. "He isn't *well*, obviously," she said. "But we're all doin' our best to keep him from havin' to work. You ought to focus on yourself for now. I promise, I'll let you know if he takes a bad turn." She set the embroidery hoop on the table just next to the bed, eyeing it worriedly. "Are you still plannin' on finishin' that, even while you're sick?"

Effie stifled another cough. "Embroidery is one of the few things I *can* do from bed," she told Lydia. "And I really must. I am far behind on stitches ... but more importantly, I will not call Lord Blackthorn back until I've prepared a proper apology for him. I have decided that I am going to finish his jacket entirely."

Lydia nodded. "I'll get you a pot of Cookie's special tea. She's makin' it for George all day, so another pot won't be a hardship." She smiled wanly. "I don't guess you'll be wantin' to put orange peels up your nose, though."

Effie choked on a laugh. "If I get much worse, I suppose

I'll have to," she said. "If only because I told George that he must as well."

Lydia had work to do, of course – more work than ever, in fact, since Effie had been dismissed – and so Effie was left alone with her embroidery for a time. Once she had finished with breakfast, however, she did not immediately take up her stitching again. Instead, she considered the jacket very seriously, thinking on what she ought to stitch into it.

So far, Effie had been embroidering her own wishes into the coat. And this had been fine enough, when the jacket was only meant to be payment. But the things that she had said to Lord Blackthorn had been blind and self-centred, and Effie knew that she ought to offer him a better apology than a handful of her own fond wishes.

I should think of what Mr Jubilee might wish for, Effie thought. *I should embroider his wishes onto this coat, instead of mine.*

But what would Lord Blackthorn wish for? Effie chewed her lip, thinking on the matter. The obvious answer was that Lord Blackthorn wished to be virtuous – at least by his own definition of the word. But Effie could not bring herself to try and stitch virtue into a jacket; she had only ever been able to stitch things that she had herself in abundance, and it seemed very arrogant indeed to assume that she had an abundance of virtue.

But Effie remembered then what Lady Hollowvale had said about Lord Blackthorn: that what the faerie really desired was simply to *grow.* Effie knew that she had grown plenty, especially in the last few days. She had left Hartfield and *chosen* to accomplish something on her own, rather than because she'd been told to do it. She had spoken her mind to several powerful people, though the consequences had been dire. And she had chosen to do magic on purpose, rather than by accident, though she barely understood the way it worked.

Effie picked her needle back up and began to stitch again.

This time, she imagined herself as a tree – feeling the

sunlight on her leaves, wishing to grow taller and taller in the hopes that she might touch the sun itself. She thought of how difficult it must be to feel constantly that she had *almost* made it to her goal, only to be told that she had somehow been growing in the wrong direction the entire time.

But you can grow, Effie thought. *You have already grown, in fact. You simply haven't noticed it because you are constantly looking at the sky and not back down at your roots.*

Lord Blackthorn was already an aberration of the best kind. Perhaps he had not helped Effie as much as he had hoped, but he had truly *meant* to help her, and that was not nothing. He had tried so hard to understand her – and while he had failed, perhaps, to help Effie secure a husband, he had still brought hope and happiness and comfort into her life, right when she'd most needed it. *You are someone,* he had said to her.

It was this very sentiment that Effie coiled into her needle as she stitched. *You are not a table,* she thought. *You are also someone. And you are growing faster than you think.*

Effie quickly lost track of the time as she worked. The embroidery was tiring, but oddly therapeutic. She was nearly disappointed, in fact, when Lady Culver returned with Benedict and she was forced to put the embroidery aside.

"I brought you a book," Benedict told Effie, after he'd settled next to her bed. "I thought you might like to read more about the Italian masters. There are no pictures, of course, but this is one of the books that inspired me to want to see their art in the first place."

Effie blinked at him. There was an eager expression on Benedict's face which reminded her almost of Miss Buckley's puppy. Benedict was clearly hopeful that Effie had decided to share his passion for the arts. The thought made her warm – it was obvious that he'd had few people to talk to on the subject in the way that he would like, and he had placed a certain trust in her by bringing it up once again.

Unfortunately, Effie was absolutely certain that her skill at reading was not up to the task of the book in his hand. "I fear I am a bit tired to be reading a book of that sort," she said softly. "But if you were feeling very generous, Mr Benedict, perhaps you could read it *to* me?"

This suggestion made Benedict smile so broadly that Effie felt it all the way down to her toes. "I could not think of a better way to spend the afternoon," he said.

There was a dreamy sort of quality to the whole scene – Effie could not help drifting off just a bit, as Benedict read to her in his low, rich voice. Every once in a while, she found her senses just enough to ask him questions about the content, which he answered with both expertise and enthusiasm.

She was greatly embarrassed when she later awoke, having fallen asleep somewhere in the middle of chapter four. But Benedict returned that evening after supper to bid her goodnight, and Effie knew from his manner that he did not hold it against her.

Still, her fever grew worse, and her coughing got stronger. She was only able to finish a hundred more stitches that night before she had to sleep. By morning, Effie found that she could barely talk at all, because her throat was so sore. The idea that she might soon not be able to call Lord Blackthorn at all troubled her, so she continued her embroidery over breakfast, knowing that she would feel far lighter and rest much easier once she had properly apologised to him and given him his finished jacket.

I wish for your happiness, Effie thought at the stitches this time. *And I wish for Blackthorn's happiness too, since it is so important to you.*

So focused was she on the work, in fact, that Effie found herself at an abrupt loss when there was no more work to do.

The rose on the back of the jacket was complete – she had even added a trailing stem and some fanciful leaves to make it feel less stark. The thread made of wishes glimmered and shifted, so full of heartfelt hopes and dreams that they could not possibly be contained. Effie was so sure that it was the best thing she had ever embroidered that she nearly cried at the sight of it.

She cut away the extra linen with care, keenly aware of her shaking hands. A little voice in her head insisted that she ought to finish the ragged edges with proper stitches before calling the faerie, but she could tell that she was unlikely to have the strength for it until she'd recovered. *I can finish off the edges later,* she thought. *I have waited long enough to apologise.*

Effie glanced around the empty bedroom, then cleared her throat as best she could. "Juniper Jubilee!" she tried to say. The words came out in a hoarse whisper, along with a cough. "Juniper Jubilee! Juniper Jubilee!"

For a moment, nothing happened – and Effie worried that perhaps she had not spoken loudly enough. Or worse – what if Lord Blackthorn had been too insulted to ever return?

But soon, the scent of wild roses drifted up around her. Effie wondered if the aroma was a bit more subdued than usual – but it was hard to tell, since her nose and throat were so raw.

"Miss Euphemia." Lord Blackthorn spoke softly from the other side of the bed, and she turned to look at him. There was not much cheer in his voice today; rather, he looked sad and anxious and a bit dejected. The rose at his throat had closed itself most of the way into a tight bud, and his leaf-green eyes would not meet hers.

Effie's heart twinged in her chest. "Mr Jubilee," she coughed. "I'm – I'm so sorry. I said awful things to you. I would take them all back if I could, but I know that I can't."

Lord Blackthorn raised his eyes as she spoke, and Effie saw a hint of alarm within them. "You do not sound well, Miss Euphemia," he said. "Have you been getting enough sunlight?"

Effie smiled helplessly. "I have been sick in bed for the last few days," she rasped. "But that's not why I called you back. I really must apologise, Mr Jubilee. I will not talk of anything else. You have been nothing but kind to me, and you have always tried your best. You are not a table, do you understand?"

Lord Blackthorn managed a wan smile. "But *I* must apologise," he said softly. "You were very angry, Miss Euphemia. And I was surprised – but I should not have been. I have had time to think, and I have talked to Lady Hollowvale. You *were* right to be angry, I mean to say. How could you be otherwise? You have made a dangerous bargain, and I have made that bargain more difficult for you. You have much to lose – and I have nothing to lose. Why should it matter to you that I *meant* well, if I am always the cause of terrible trouble for you?"

Effie blinked slowly. These were possibly the most sensible words that she had ever heard the faerie utter – and so it was difficult for her to decide whether or not she actually *agreed* with them.

"I truly believed that everything was fine," Lord Blackthorn told her. "But because you became angry, I have realised that everything is *not* fine. Lady Hollowvale told me that I do not consider the consequences of my actions – that I must think of what will happen *tomorrow*, and the day after that. And so I have tried to think ahead for once."

The faerie produced a handkerchief – and as he did, Effie saw that someone had embroidered upon it, very messily, the words: *Think about tomorrow*.

Effie coughed on a laugh. The revelation touched her deeply, for all that it was a bit nonsensical. "That is very clever of you, Mr Jubilee," she said.

Lord Blackthorn managed a smile at that. "I hope that it will suffice," he said. "But you must tell me if I upset you again, Miss Euphemia. I do not wish to make your life difficult."

Effie reached out to take his hand. "I will tell you," she promised. "But you must also accept my apology, Mr Jubilee. Even if

I had some justification, I was harsher than I should have been. It *does* matter that you mean well. You have put so much effort into my troubles. I cannot imagine someone like Lady Culver walking below-stairs and asking how to help me."

Lord Blackthorn closed his fingers around hers. The rose at his throat unfurled just a little bit, as though with hope.

"I wanted to apologise correctly," Effie told him. "I know that I cannot give you a gift exactly, so I have finished your jacket early instead. I promise I will do the edging as soon as I am feeling better."

She unfolded the coat from her lap and showed it to the faerie. Lord Blackthorn stared at it for a long moment, and she could not quite make out his reaction – but as he released her hand to take the coat from her, his eyes misted up with awe.

"I have never seen anything like it before," he whispered. "Why – I think it must be the most beautiful thing that I have ever seen."

Effie blushed with pride and embarrassment. "I hoped that you would like it," she said shyly. "I wanted you to know that I think the world of you, Mr Jubilee. Whatever trouble you have caused, you have also made my life much better with your presence. I enjoy your company and your good cheer and your refusal to ever give up. I do not know if that is what you would call virtuous, but it is important to *me*."

Lord Blackthorn blinked at Effie as though she had struck him over the head. In fact, as consumed as he had been by the jacket, he was outright flustered by Effie's declaration. "Oh," he said. "I . . . I think quite highly of you as well, Miss Euphemia. Really, I always have."

Effie smiled again. "I know," she said. "You have said so. And you do not ever lie."

Lord Blackthorn hesitated. The rose at his throat had blossomed again – but there still seemed to be something he was finding difficult to say.

A polite knock at the door interrupted them.

"Miss Reeves?" Benedict's voice floated over. "I was hoping to have a word, er . . . in private. I understand if you would prefer otherwise."

In private? Effie wondered. Certainly, that had to be improper. There were only so many circumstances under which a man might speak to a woman alone. But she was not *actually* a lady, and so she said, "You can come inside. Though I am not in private, er, *precisely.*"

Benedict opened the door. He was dressed with surprising neatness for a man still at home; he was wearing the fine golden waistcoat she had seen on him before, and his neck cloth was done up in a more fashionable manner than usual. He glanced between Effie and Lord Blackthorn, and Effie saw his eyes cloud over somewhat.

"Ah!" Benedict said, with a hint of confused irritation. "The nerve of you, sir! I suppose you have finally been shamed enough to come collect your ward."

Lord Blackthorn blinked. "I don't quite understand your meaning," he said. Effie could tell that the faerie was very unused to receiving such a reaction, given how often people breezed past the complexities of his existence.

"Well, you needn't worry either way," Benedict informed Lord Blackthorn, as he strode towards the bed. "I would call you out, but Miss Reeves has made it clear that she would prefer otherwise. Instead, I shall take her off your hands entirely."

Benedict took Effie's hand and knelt down next to the bed. "These are the words that I meant to say regardless," he told her seriously. "I doubt that I shall ever meet another woman who suits me so perfectly, Miss Reeves. I begin to worry that if I do not make an offer, you shall disappear." He met her eyes with his, and Effie's heart stuttered at the open affection that she saw within his gaze. "Please say that you will marry me, Miss Reeves."

Effie worked her mouth soundlessly for a moment. Finally, she found some semblance of her raspy voice. "I ... I would love to marry you," she said. "But—" A terrible memory of Miss Buckley's insistence returned to her, and Effie felt a hint of fear. How could she possibly marry a man while he thought her better than she was? "I am not a lady, Mr Benedict," she admitted. "I have no money and no status."

Benedict shook his head. "I am not interested in either money or status," he said. "I fell in love with you for other reasons – and I have remained in love with you, even when you showed up at our door with neither a guardian nor a penny to your name. I know that my life shall be very dull and stationary from here on out, now that I must settle and stay in England – but I could bear all of that, I think, if you were by my side."

Effie smiled beatifically at this – and for a moment, even her aching lungs failed to trouble her. "Then I will marry you, Mr Benedict," she said. "On the sole condition that you must give me the dance that you promised me."

Benedict laughed with relief. "I will accept that condition, Miss Reeves," he said. "You may be sure that you will have a ring on your finger the very moment that I can steal you away to a proper ball." Benedict glanced towards Lord Blackthorn. "Unless, of course, your guardian objects?" His tone made it clear that he was prepared to object in return, if Lord Blackthorn became troublesome.

Lord Blackthorn looked, if possible, even more bewildered by this turn of events than Effie was. He glanced between Effie and Benedict, blinking very quickly. "Well, I ... " He furrowed his brow and tightened his hands on the jacket he was holding. "That is, I ... of course. I am most concerned for Miss Euphemia's happiness. She may marry or not marry whomever she would like."

The faerie sounded less certain of these words than Effie might have expected. She wanted very much to ask him what the matter was – but she could not do so with Benedict in the room.

"We shall have to make sure that you get your rest, then," Benedict told Effie, with a fond look that stole her attention. "I will inform Lady Culver that we have a wedding to plan."

Chapter Seventeen

Effie did not get a chance to speak again to Lord Blackthorn. The next few hours were a blur of smiles and congratulations; she was especially put off when she received a paternal sort of visit from Lord Culver, who patted her on the hand and thanked her for turning his youngest brother half-way respectable. Among all of this chaos, Lord Blackthorn was suddenly nowhere to be seen.

Eventually, however, Effie's illness got the better of her, and Lady Culver shooed the rest of the Family away in order to give her some space.

"I *am* glad that Benedict proposed," Lady Culver sighed. "But how irresponsible of him to excite you while you are still sick! We are going to have to call you a physician after that stunt of his."

Effie tried to respond – but she coughed so hard this time that she was now gasping for breath. Lady Culver smoothed back her hair and tucked her back into bed. "Don't worry, dear," the other woman said. "I'll take care of all your preparations. I was expecting to have to arrange Benedict's wedding in any case. See to your health for now."

Lady Culver left the room then – but she must have called for extra help, because Lydia soon arrived in her place, carrying more hot bricks for Effie's bed.

"I don't like any of this at all," Lydia told Effie grimly, as she tucked the bricks into place. "On top of everything else, I thought you had more sense than to marry that toff, Effie."

"What—?" Effie devolved into coughing again. "What do you mean?"

Lydia smacked her arm. "Stop talkin'," she ordered. "You an' George are both as bad as I've ever seen. You'd better spare your breath before I go an' get those orange peels." She paused. "I *meant* you've been so stuck on Mr Benedict that you've gone an' missed the obvious. But that's no business of mine, I guess. You'll do what makes you happy."

Lydia pulled the curtains closed against the evening. "Lord Blackthorn told me you're free to keep the glamour since you've won your wager. You're a lady now, Effie. Lady Culver's already talkin' about how we'll need to have an engagement ball."

Effie blanched at this. "I—" Lydia shot her a warning glare, and Effie shut her mouth again, quailing against her pillow.

I asked for a dance, Effie thought. *But I didn't mean to imply that we should have yet another ball at Hartfield! Lydia must be furious with me, with us so many servants short.*

The rest of what Lydia had said finally penetrated, however, and Effie widened her eyes. "Lord Blackthorn is gone?" she managed breathlessly.

Lydia rolled her eyes. "Of course he's gone," she said. "You won your wager, he got his jacket an' you're all ready to get married. I wouldn't stick around for that if I was him, either."

"I didn't finish his jacket," Effie mumbled very softly. "The embroidery is all ragged at the edges."

Lydia shrugged. "I thought it was strange too," she admitted. "But Lord Blackthorn said he intended to always be an unfinished person, an' so he liked the reminder."

The other maid poured Effie a fresh cup of awful-smelling tea. "Drink up. It's goin' to be a rough few days, Effie. Mrs

Sedgewick's back on her feet, an' she's become a real dragon."
Lydia smiled oddly at this. "You're not too attached to that
engagement ball, I hope? I like to think I know you, so I assume
you're not."

Effie nodded slowly in affirmation.

"Good," Lydia said. "Cos it might or might not happen. We'll
have to see how sensible the Family's feelin' that day."

Lydia left long before Effie had the breath to ask her what
exactly she meant by that.

The next few days *were* rough – but only because Effie couldn't
tell them very well apart. She woke up dizzy and miserable,
barely able to breathe and unable to tell the time. At one point,
she was dimly aware of a man standing over her bed, talking in
an officious sort of manner; he checked her pulse and investi-
gated her mouth, and she realised that he must be the physician
that Lady Culver had called.

" . . . hard to tell," he informed Lady Culver as Effie closed
her eyes again. "I've seen a few instances of this particular
cough now – mostly among servants, actually, but she might
have caught it from one of them."

"By which you mean, we would not be in this mess if some
servant had been more responsible," Lady Culver said with
obvious exasperation. "Well! We shall handle it regardless.
What do you recommend?"

Effie did not hear just what the physician recommended,
however. Instead, she opened her eyes and realised that it was
evening again, and that she had somehow slept the day away.

It was the scent of roses that had woken her, she understood
a moment later – for Lord Blackthorn had settled on the edge
of her bed to hold her hand.

Effie could only barely make out the green of his eyes in the darkness. The warmth of his fingers was like sunlight, though, and she clung to his hand with hers.

"You're here," she mumbled distantly. "I'm so glad that you're here."

Lord Blackthorn tightened his fingers. "I am, of course," he said softly. "I have been concerned for you, Miss Euphemia. I asked Blackthorn what I ought to do. It sends its best. I hope that is enough."

Effie did not entirely understand his meaning – but he soon pressed a warm teacup into her hand, and she looked down at it in confusion. The tea there was dark and pungent, and it did not smell like anything that Cookie had ever made before. It smelled instead of wet leaves and deep roots and slippery green mosses.

It was clear that Lord Blackthorn meant for her to drink from the cup – but Effie frowned at it worriedly. "But George –" she mumbled. "He's worse than me, I think—"

"Mr Reeves is on the mend," Lord Blackthorn told her. There was a strange note to his voice as he spoke. "It is possible that I forgot another cup of tea just next to his bed. And, well, he might have mistaken it for *his* tea. I cannot blame him for that, since I was the one who left it there."

Effie blinked back sudden tears. She had been so convinced that Lord Blackthorn had been insulted or upset by something she had done – or else that he had disappeared for ever now that their wager was complete – but he had really been off finding a way to help her and her brother.

"How can I ever repay you?" she whispered.

Lord Blackthorn pressed her hand around the cup again. His fingers lingered upon hers. "I will accept your happiness, Miss Euphemia," he said. "Er – I don't mean that I wish to *own* your happiness. But I would like for you to *be* happy. I hope that is a fair price to pay."

Effie blinked blearily. "That does not seem like a very fair deal," she mumbled. "I would not like to cheat you."

Lord Blackthorn looked away from her. "It is a fair price to *me*," he said. "I find your happiness very valuable, in fact. So it shall have to suffice."

Effie lifted the cup to her lips and swallowed down as much of the tea as she could. The flavour was strong, but not unpleasant – in fact, it had a taste like wood and roses. It was instantly soothing against her scratchy throat, and she relaxed with a sigh.

The warmth of the tea overtook her body – and she soon found herself blinking tiredly again. "Are you upset about something, Mr Jubilee?" she asked hazily.

Lord Blackthorn blinked. "What a strange question," he said. "What would I have to be upset about? I am certainly not—" He cut himself off and knit his brow. "I mean to say, I am quite—"

He fell into an uncomfortable silence.

He cannot lie, Effie thought. *He is upset about something.*

Her mind was growing more and more distant, however, and she couldn't focus very well upon the problem. She meant to ask whether there was anything she could do to help.

But the hazy heat of the tea overcame her, and she fell instead into a very deep, very restful sleep.

Effie awoke the next morning feeling nearly like herself. The very first thing she did was to leave her bed, which she had come to associate with that awful illness. She pulled on her frock and guiltily rang a bell, hoping that Lydia would be the maid to answer it.

Thankfully, Lydia *did* soon appear – and in much better spirits than Effie had ever seen her. This greatly confused Effie, given that the servants had to be more overworked than ever, but she was entirely too anxious about her brother to spend any time asking about it.

"George must be doing better this morning as well, mustn't he?" Effie asked hopefully.

Lydia hummed cheerfully to herself as she stripped the sweat-stained sheets from Effie's bed. "George is doin' *quite* well," she said. "He's not up an' around just yet – but then, I don't see as he'd strain himself even if he could. Lady Culver told Mr Allen to dismiss him just this mornin'."

Effie widened her eyes. "What?" she asked. "But Lady Culver has her gown back! She doesn't *need* to dismiss more staff! And surely, Mr Allen has told her that we can't do with any fewer servants—"

"Don't you worry about it," Lydia said to Effie. There was a hint of glee in her tone. "We're all well an' truly done with Her Ladyship, Effie. A bunch of us were already talkin' about doin' somethin' – but now she's gone an' nailed her own coffin shut. Once she dismissed George, the last holdouts came around. Every single one of us is so angry, Effie, you've got no idea – an' it's *glorious*."

Effie blinked. "But ... what does that *mean*, Lydia?" she asked. "Being angry won't change the fact that she has so much power over us."

Lydia laughed. "I promise," she said, "I'll make sure you're there to see it when it happens. I'm sure you'll want to see George, though, an' I think you should be able to do that now. I know Lord Culver *said* you were to leave an' never come back, but everyone's so upset with the Family right now that they all agreed they'd look the other way if you wanted to visit George."

The words lessened another terrible pressure that Effie had been carrying around in her chest, and she sighed in relief. "I'm surprised that Mrs Sedgewick would allow that," she admitted. "I have never known her to bend the rules, especially when one of the Family specifically ordered something."

Lydia snorted. "Mrs Sedgewick is bendin' a lot of rules

lately," she said. "You won't believe it, Effie – it's like she's even more Mrs Sedgewick than usual, except she's pointed all of her Mrs Sedgewick-ness at the Family. I actually *like* this version of her."

Lydia went out to check that the hallway was clear before leading Effie down the stairs towards the green baize door. The moment that they entered the servants' passageways, Effie carefully removed the glamour from around her neck. After having worn it for so many days, she now found its absence very strange.

Stranger still was the general atmosphere below-stairs. Effie was used to feeling trapped and harried within the narrow passageways – but today, all of the servants whom they passed had an excited cast to their manner. Effie was especially surprised when they passed Lady Culver's maid, Prudence, who nodded towards them. Normally, Prudence would not have given either Effie *or* Lydia the time of day, since she was a lady's maid and therefore much more refined than either of them – but today, Prudence gave them each an enigmatic smile, and her eyes flashed with camaraderie, as though all three of them shared some sort of thrilling secret.

Effie realised a moment later that when Lydia had said that everyone was angry, she had truly meant *everyone*.

"Even Prudence is upset with Lady Culver?" Effie asked Lydia softly. "But I never mended any of Prudence's things – and Lady Culver treats her the best out of all of us!"

Lydia shrugged. "Prudence was one of the last holdouts," she said. "But now that Lady Culver's dismissed George, everyone knows they might be next. What if Prudence gets sick? Lady Culver probably won't remember how much she likes her lady's maid if she stays in bed an' out of sight for too long."

Effie widened her eyes. "And Mr Allen?" she asked.

Lydia did not even need to respond to this question – for as they passed the servants' hall, Effie saw Mrs Sedgewick and Mr

Allen sitting at the table inside. Even as she watched, Mr Allen said something to the housekeeper and smiled at her – and Mrs Sedgewick *laughed.*

Effie stopped to stare. "My God," she said. "They're getting along?"

"Thick as thieves," Lydia confirmed. "We're all on the same side now, Effie. We've been snipin' at each other cos we didn't feel like we could do anything about our *real* problems – but that's not how it is any more. Mr Allen told Mrs Sedgewick he'd help us come up with a plan. He's heard all kinds of stories about angry servants an' the trouble they cause on account of his work in town. Mrs Sedgewick has been sweet on him ever since, sayin' how lucky we are to have such a professional among us."

Mr Allen caught sight of Effie then, just over Mrs Sedgewick's shoulder. The butler's smile broadened for a moment – and then he *winked* at her.

"I feel as though I've wandered into faerie again," Effie said faintly. "Everyone is so different, Lydia. It's almost *pleasant* down here. I don't understand how that's possible – I thought my plague had turned everyone too angry to be pleasant."

"Oh, we're angry," Lydia assured her. "But we're all angry at the same time, an' in the same direction! It's funny how that makes everything more pleasant, isn't it?" She smiled serenely at Effie. "Anyway, don't mistake me – we'll be plenty unpleasant to *some* people soon. But right now, we're goin' to see George."

As they came to George's door, Effie knocked there carefully. "George?" she asked. "It's me, Effie. Are you halfway decent?"

"I'm all dressed!" George called back from inside. There was a strong, cheerful note in his voice. "Come on inside!"

Effie opened the door – and blinked.

George was indeed awake and fully dressed. He looked quite hale, in fact – but he had settled himself lazily back upon his bed with a carefree look on his face. In his hands, he held one of the books from Lord Culver's library, though Effie knew that he was about as literate as she was.

"You look . . . quite well!" Effie managed. "When Lydia told me you'd been dismissed, I thought that you would be . . . er . . . "

"Upset?" George asked. "You know, I really should be. But I wasn't goin' to stick around anyway, after what happened with you an' Lord Culver. Imagine that! Waitin' hand an' foot on that popinjay, always thinkin' about how he nearly attacked you!" He shook his head. "I'll be goin' with Lydia to ask Mr Jesson for a job. I'll offer to do a maid's work an' take a maid's wages instead if I have to. Till then, I don't have to do anything I don't want to do."

Effie managed a smile at this. She left the doorway and threw herself onto the bed to hug her brother. "I'm so glad you're feeling better," she said.

George patted her fondly on the head. "Lydia said you got a better job too! Good on you, Effie – that accent of yours is workin' for you already! I'll be sad not to see you so much, but you'd better send letters, at least."

Effie's smile turned awkward at this. What *would* she put in her letters to George once she was married? Would she have to lie to him about her life from now on? Surely he would never believe the truth.

"I'll send letters, of course," Effie promised, though she wasn't yet sure exactly what they would contain. She was suddenly keenly aware that this might be the last time she saw her brother for a very long while. "Why don't you tell me what you've been reading?" Effie asked.

George glanced down at the book in his hand. "Oh, this?" he asked. "Somethin' about the fall of Rome, I think. I can't read half the words, but it's still fun to try."

Effie lit up at this. "I've learned so much about Rome lately," she enthused. "My . . . new employer is very fond of the subject, and he talks about it often."

George looped his arm around her shoulders. "Tell your big brother all about it," he said. "We've got the time, after all."

Lydia had to leave very quickly, given the amount of work in the household, but Effie and George talked for another hour, at least. Effie knew that she probably shouldn't stay for so long – surely someone from the Family would go searching for the lady who had disappeared from her room – but time with her brother was such a rare commodity that she couldn't help but savour it.

Eventually, however, she convinced herself to leave him to his book, with one last very tight hug.

Effie carefully replaced her glamour as she exited the servants' passageways, crossing back beyond the green baize door. She began to make her way back towards her bedroom – but partway there, she heard tense voices filtering out from the entryway. Effie paused just next to the door below-stairs, halfway obscured by the hallway.

". . . a *small* engagement party, Benedict," Lady Culver was saying. "We do not have the budget for more. I have had to buy a better replacement gown for the event, and we are already stretched quite thin."

Lady Culver stood not far from the doorway, with her arms crossed and her expression dark with displeasure. She was wearing Effie's old gown again, since she still had nothing else available in her wardrobe.

Benedict had just come in from the outdoors – even as Effie watched, he carefully discarded his muddy boots at the door once again. His hair was attractively tangled, and his cheeks were flushed from the brisk spring air; looking at him, it occurred to her that very soon, he would be her *husband*. The thought stirred a flurry of strange, conflicting emotions inside of her, and she paused to examine them in bewilderment.

"I don't understand," Benedict said. "Thomas agreed—"

"Thomas does not handle our finances!" Lady Culver snapped abruptly. "He says yes to whatever he pleases, Benedict – and then, he asks *me* to make it happen. I am telling you, regardless of what Thomas has told you, that we do not have the funds."

Benedict knit his brow, caught halfway between confusion and concern. "I'm sure that something can be done," he said. "It can't be all *that* bad."

Lady Culver's eyes flared with anger. "That is just like you," she hissed. "Have you any idea how much money your little jaunt to Europe cost us, Benedict? Even then, when you sent back to tell us you'd gone all the way to Rome instead of returning home, Thomas *insisted* on sending you more money. Did you think that money would appear out of thin air? Because it certainly did not. It came from our household, Benedict. It came from our staff and from my wardrobe and from the groundskeepers! I had to dismiss good help to make up for your little side-trip!"

Effie's heart froze in her chest. She stared at Benedict's face, hoping to see some hint that Lady Culver was exaggerating the situation. But her husband-to-be's expression was neither surprised nor penitent – it was instead vaguely annoyed.

"I was a stone's throw from seeing things I've dreamed of seeing since I was a child," Benedict shot back. "And we both know that I will never have the chance to get that close again. Now that I'm home, Thomas expects me to marry and settle and ignore any hint of adventure until the day I die. And I will do that, since it is my duty – but I will not apologise for fulfilling that one dream before I do so!"

Lady Culver threw up her hands. "You have had your adventure then, Benedict," she said. "But we paid for it very handsomely indeed – and so you will not have the engagement ball that you were hoping for. If you are going to settle, as Thomas expects, then you had better start settling *now*. You will have a ball – but it will be modest. Goodness knows I shall have to organise it all on my own, as usual."

Benedict shook his head incredulously. "As you like," he said. "But *you* will have to explain the situation to Euphemia. I will not do it for you."

Lady Culver sighed. "That girl is just happy not to be ruined, Benedict," she said. "Her guardian abandoned her, and she has been staying in a house with an interested party with no one to chaperone but his sister-in-law. I would love nothing more than to give her one proper party before she goes off with you to the lodge. But I content myself knowing that her story has a relatively happy ending." She turned to head back up the stairs. "Now, if you will excuse me – I have already sent out the invitations, so I have very little time to waste."

Effie watched her go in shocked silence.

Benedict shook his head once more, running his fingers back through his hair. The conversation had not weighed upon him quite so much as it had weighed upon Lady Culver, however – and so, he soon brushed off the disappointment and started for the stairs himself.

Effie knew that he was heading to *her* room. As upset as she was by the conversation she had overheard, she knew that there was no putting off the obvious – he would soon find her room empty and start searching the house for her.

"Benedict," she said.

Her voice was still a bit raspy – but Benedict turned at the sound of his name. His face broke out into a smile as he caught sight of her, and he quickly crossed the distance between them, taking her hands in his.

"There you are!" Benedict said. "You're practically all better! I'll admit, I was sceptical, but that physician really earned his fee!"

Effie stared at him. Much as she desperately wanted to, she could not banish the memory of Benedict's apathy as Lady

Culver had told him she'd dismissed people to make up the shortfall from his travels. The dreamy look on his face as he had described ancient works of art; the soft, low sound of his voice as he had read to her about the Italian masters; the pleasant daydream she had once held of walking the streets of Rome with him – all of them were now irrevocably tainted. Instead, she could not help but think of the weary way that she had dragged herself out of bed every morning, dreading yet another day of life at Hartfield. Effie remembered the breathless way that they had all tried to keep up with Lady Culver's balls short-handed . . . and the cough that her brother had caught when he could not get enough sleep.

Benedict frowned down at her with sudden concern. He pressed his hands gently to either side of her shoulders. "Perhaps you're not quite *that* well," he said worriedly. "You're looking a bit pale. Here – let's get you back up to bed."

Effie wrenched herself free of his grip before she could stop herself.

"Your trip to Rome," she said hoarsely. "Do you have any idea how terribly the servants here suffered for it, Benedict?"

Benedict blinked. Whatever he had been expecting Effie to say, this clearly had not been anywhere on the list.

"I understand your concern," he said slowly. "But you mustn't listen to Lady Culver. She gets into these moods, Euphemia, where she blames everyone and everything but herself. I am hardly the only person in the family who has spent a tidy sum of money. Thomas regularly indulges in expensive French imports. Edmund has . . . well, let's not speak of what he has, since it isn't very polite. Let us just say that he has bought an endless number of gifts for an unattached widow. And Lady Culver, of course – she must have new gowns all the time. It must gall her terribly to wear the same thing every day."

Effie breathed in deeply, trying to calm herself – but there was an anger inside of her that would not be denied, no matter how she tried.

"*Wind the bobbin up*," she muttered to herself. "*Wind the bobbin up . . .* "

"Er?" Benedict said. "I'm sorry, I can't understand you. What were you saying?"

Effie exploded.

"All of you are to blame!" she yelled. "All of you, Benedict! What difference does it make to the maids who were dismissed that everyone else in the Family overspent as well? Every time one of you has made a mistake with your finances, it has been the *servants* that pay the final price, and not you." She sucked in a deep, trembling breath. "If you had shown even an inch of remorse, then perhaps it would be different – but we are clearly not worth even a second thought to you!"

Benedict took a bewildered step back. The confusion on his face was now mixed with alarm; the situation had spiralled so quickly out of his control that he barely knew what to do with it.

Effie swallowed hard. "I cannot marry a man who cares so little for me," she said. "I cannot *love* a man like that."

Benedict's mouth dropped at this statement. "I don't understand at all what you're talking about," he started warily. "But, Euphemia, you will be ruined if you call off this wedding—"

"There is no wedding," Effie told him sharply. "I said that you would have to dance with me before I accepted your proposal, Mr Benedict. We have not danced; and now, we never shall." She shook her head. "I am taking my things and leaving. I have a place waiting for me in Blackthorn, though it is a painfully modest one. At least there, I will have a master I respect."

Effie whirled up the stairs and ran back to her room. She heard Benedict's footsteps behind her – but she shut herself inside the bedroom and leaned back against the door.

"Juniper Jubilee!" she gasped out quickly. "Juniper Jubilee!

Juniper Jubilee! I have given up our wager! You must come and spirit me away to Blackthorn immediately!"

Effie waited with bated breath for the scent of wild roses to materialise . . . but the air remained defiantly musty and *normal*, and no elf appeared to steal her away.

Lord Blackthorn had not heard her – or else, he simply was not coming.

Chapter Eighteen

"Euphemia." Benedict's voice came from the other side of her bedroom door — both pained and painfully reasonable. "I do not know what has happened. But whatever it is, I am sure that we can discuss it."

Effie closed her eyes. *How can I discuss the fact that you and your family worked me and my family nearly to death for the sake of Rome and gowns and fine French imports?* she wondered. *How could I possibly reconcile myself to that sort of oblivious cruelty?*

In no world could she imagine having a *reasonable* conversation with Benedict on the matter.

Effie reached up to the glamour at her throat and pulled it neatly free.

Benedict blinked at her as she opened the door. His brow knit, and he glanced past Effie for the woman he had been chasing. "I'm terribly sorry," he said earnestly. "I need to speak to Euphemia."

Effie shook her head at him. "Euphemia does not wish to speak to *you*," she informed him. "But you may keep trying if you like, Mr Benedict." She swept past him to the hall then, as invisible as the wallpaper. Behind her, Benedict headed into the bedroom, calling her name as he searched for her.

"You!" Lord Culver's cold, angry voice snapped the word from further down the hallway. Effie turned in surprise — only to find herself hauled nearly off her feet by a strong grip on her arm.

Lord Culver's eyes blazed down at her with fury. "I told you to leave and not come back," he hissed. "Now I find you skulking brazenly around my house! What – have you come back to steal from me, you little animal?"

Effie tried to pry his fingers from her arm – but there was no breaking the sharp, pinching grip of his fingers. "I came back to get my *own* things," Effie told him hotly. "Now let me go, and you'll never see me again."

"Your own things?" Lord Culver scoffed. "I suppose you stashed them in one of the guest rooms, then?"

Effie flushed. There *was* no good way to explain her presence on the upper floor. At best, she was about to be thrashed – at worst, Lord Culver might well call a magistrate to have her arrested for thievery. If she could find a moment alone, perhaps she could put back on the glamour just long enough to escape—

"Lord Culver." Mr Allen's voice sounded from behind Effie, at the top of the stairs. "I am afraid that I require your immediate attention downstairs."

Both Effie and Lord Culver turned to blink at the butler. It was rare indeed for Mr Allen to venture upstairs unasked; he had certainly never dared to interrupt the lord of the house before, for any reason at all.

Lord Culver knit his brow, though he kept his hand stubbornly closed around Effie's arm. Effie could tell that his first instinct was to snap at the butler – but he must have realised that Mr Allen would never bother him in this way for anything short of an emergency. "What is going on?" he asked instead.

Mr Allen spoke directly to Lord Culver – but he glanced at Effie as he did. "Lady Culver has just informed the servants that they have barely a week to plan another ball," he said. "To put the matter bluntly, Lord Culver – your household staff have resigned their positions."

Lord Culver dropped Effie's arm at once. "What?" he demanded. "You can't mean *all* of them?"

Mr Allen kept his face admirably professional and unaffected. "I fear so, sir," he said. "They are packing up to leave as we speak."

Effie's mouth dropped open at this; for just a moment, she thought she saw a twinge of amusement on the butler's face.

Lord Culver shook his head. "If they want to quit – then let them quit!" he said. "We will find new servants."

Mr Allen cleared his throat delicately. "About that, sir," he said. "The invitations for the ball have already gone out. It is possible, I suppose, that you might replace your entire household staff within a week – though that is unlikely if word spreads among the locals that the entire staff has left at once. It is certainly impossible to hire all new servants *and* plan a ball, however."

Lord Culver blinked very quickly at this – and Effie saw that he was at a loss.

Effie took the opportunity to creep back from him, searching for her glamour. Unfortunately, she quickly discovered it on the floor, crushed beneath Lord Culver's foot. She winced, and stifled a very unladylike swear word.

"The servants have laid out a list of demands," Mr Allen informed Lord Culver helpfully. "It is possible that they might still be convinced to stay. But I would not recommend that His Lordship wait for them to leave. We might still manage to contain word of the situation – but that will be very difficult as soon as even one of them departs. It does not take very much for rumours to spread among other households, sir."

At this, Lord Culver recovered his dignity, scowling in distaste. "I am not going to negotiate with *servants*," he said. "Go and ask Lady Culver to meet with them."

Mr Allen shook his head. "One of their demands is that they will not meet with Lady Culver," he said, with exaggerated apology in his voice. "I truly do not wish to speak ill of the Family, sir. But she has made a terrible mess of things. I have never seen such a crisis in all of my years as a butler."

Lord Culver worked his mouth soundlessly for a moment. Finally, he said, "Why don't *you* handle their demands, then?"

Mr Allen blinked. "Me?" he asked. "But, sir, I have no authority over the household budget. I cannot begin to address their concerns."

"Well, I am clearly in need of a steward," Lord Culver snapped, "since I cannot rely on my wife to do the sole job that I ask of her!" He straightened angrily and took in a deep breath. "You have been promoted, Mr Allen. You are a professional – I trust that you shall negotiate on my behalf."

Mr Allen inclined his head respectfully. "As you say, sir," he replied. "I will go and head this off as soon as I can. I shall need your signature soon, though, I am sure."

"Go and get it done," Lord Culver said shortly. "I will sign whatever you manage to negotiate." He turned back to Effie with a renewed fury in his eyes, and she knew then that he was intent on taking out his new troubles upon her. But Mr Allen interrupted once again.

"May I suggest, sir, that this is a poor time to be punishing one of your old maids," the butler said. "It will make things much more difficult, I assure you. If you hand Miss Euphemia into my care, I shall ensure that she is carefully searched and thrown out of the house."

Lord Culver stared down at Effie, clearly torn between practicality and frustration.

"That is my professional advice as your steward, sir," Mr Allen said solemnly.

Lord Culver shoved Effie back towards the butler. "Get her out of my sight," he spat. "If she shows up here again, you're to hold her until she can be arrested."

Mr Allen caught Effie by the shoulder. He nodded

deferentially to Lord Culver – but he squeezed Effie's shoulder reassuringly, where the lord of the house could not see it. "Of course, Lord Culver," he said. "Please, do not worry yourself overmuch with the situation. I shall resolve everything appropriately – so you may put it all from your mind."

Lord Culver whirled down the hall. In the storm of his passing, Effie caught sight of Benedict standing in the doorway of her bedroom, staring at both her and Mr Allen.

"Miss Euphemia?" Benedict repeated slowly, as though he was not certain he had heard the name correctly.

Effie shook her head at him with a sigh. "My name is Francesca," she said.

She turned down the stairs with Mr Allen and left Benedict behind them, without so much as a backwards glance.

"So that is what Lydia meant when she said that you were all planning something," Effie observed to Mr Allen, once they had safely descended into the servants' hall. The butler had sat her down and poured her a generous glass of French brandy, which she drank with shaky gratefulness. "But Mr Benedict's fiancée has called off the engagement. There is no longer any need for an engagement ball. Won't that be a problem?"

Mr Allen shook his head. "The invitations were still sent out," he said. "It is bad enough that Mr Benedict's fiancée has jilted him; if all the servants suddenly leave as well, then Lord Culver's financial instability shall become a matter of instant speculation. It is true that he is financially unstable, of course . . . but he will be desperate not to let people *know* that it is true."

Effie let out a long breath. She looked down at her hands, where they rested against the glass of brandy. "I cannot believe that Lord Culver simply handed you all his authority like that," she said.

Mr Allen shrugged. "I will admit," he said, "I was not expecting that turn of events. But it does make things somewhat simpler."

"You blamed Lady Culver," Effie said in a small voice. "But all the Family have been overspending, Mr Allen. She is still a terrible woman – but they have only given her their dirty work and pretended as though they are not responsible for all of these problems."

Mr Allen nodded tiredly. "All of that is true," he said. "But a man like Lord Culver will not change his ways when he is confronted with his own failures. It is far easier to tell him that it is mostly his wife's fault, and only a little bit his own. He will not listen to Lady Culver when she tells him that he cannot cut the household budget any further – but he will likely listen to his steward."

Effie took another long, miserable swallow of brandy. "That is terribly unfair," she said. "He will take it out on her, Mr Allen."

"The world is unfair, Effie," Mr Allen informed her. "But it is far more unfair to the servants that Lady Culver threw out on the street than it is to her. I have chosen to prioritise them as best I may with what tools are available to me. I write regular letters back to her aunt – if things truly become intolerable, I shall encourage her to flee back home."

Effie leaned her chin into her arms. "But things are not at all fixed at Hartfield, are they?" she asked.

"They are not," Mr Allen agreed. "Lord Culver shall attempt at every turn to fall back on his old ways. But we shall do our best to prepare for that eventuality. If he cannot change, then he really shall lose his entire household, *and* his reputation." He smiled grimly. "Lord Culver is very used to getting his own way. But he has backed down once now. The servants here know that he is not all-powerful. For now, that shall suffice."

"Oh! Well, if it isn't Effie!" Mrs Sedgewick swept into the

servants' hall with a joyful click-clack of wooden heels, beaming at both Effie and Mr Allen. "I was *very* worried about you, young lady," Mrs Sedgewick told her sternly. She glanced towards Mr Allen. "Well? Did you indeed secure a reference for Effie, Mr Allen?"

Mr Allen smiled sheepishly at this. "I have secured a job as the house's steward," he admitted. "I have been told to make all of Lord Culver's problems disappear by whatever means necessary. And so, in a way, I have secured Miss Euphemia's reference."

Effie blinked at Mrs Sedgewick. The housekeeper could not possibly have seemed more different from her usual self. Her stride was less harried and more confident. Her back was straighter – and it was only now that Effie realised Mrs Sedgewick had been slouching at all before. The rest of Mrs Sedgewick's words penetrated, and Effie flushed.

"Surely, you didn't cause all of this trouble just to get me a reference," Effie said.

Mrs Sedgewick smiled ruefully. "No, not *just* for your reference," she admitted. "But it was certainly on our list of grievances. If Mr Allen is truly empowered to do as he sees fit, then we shall be sure that you have a very fine reference to see you employed elsewhere—"

"I do not need a reference," Effie told her. "I ... I don't *believe* that I do, in any case. I have already promised to work for someone else. But I am truly touched that you thought of me, Mrs Sedgewick."

The housekeeper sniffed. "It was a travesty all around, what the Family did to you, Effie," she said. "It is likely for the best that you go somewhere kinder. But we who are still here do not intend to brook any *further* travesties. I know that I certainly do not." Mrs Sedgewick scowled at the very idea. "I tell you, Effie, I have been on my very last nerve for the entire last year. I had nearly given up entirely before Lydia came to check on me. But I had a revelation – something like divine inspiration! I realised how very much we all deserved better than this! It would have been a shame if I had simply let myself waste away in misery, rather than taking a stand."

Effie managed a misty sort of smile at this. "I am glad that you found your anger, Mrs Sedgewick," she said softly.

Mr Allen pulled out another two glasses and topped them all off with a generous amount of brandy. "I believe this calls for a toast," he informed the two of them gravely. "We must celebrate our small victories – for there will be many battles ahead for all of us, I am sure."

Mrs Sedgewick picked up a glass and clinked it against the other two. "To small victories!" she declared. "To any victory at all, in fact! It is one more victory than I ever had before, Mr Allen."

Mr Allen smiled warmly at this – and all of them drank down their brandy with relish.

The other servants all began to filter into the servants' hall in short order, deeply curious about the results of their small rebellion. Effie watched as a few more glasses of brandy were passed around – but while she took the opportunity to congratulate her fellows, there was another matter pressing at the very back of her mind.

"I really must go, George," she told her brother, as she gave him one last hug. "I am so proud of all of you – but I have a promise that I must keep."

George raised his glass of brandy and winked at her. "I hope your new employer is better than this one," he said.

Effie smiled helplessly. "He is incalculably better in every way," she said. "I believe that I will be happy just to see him again, in fact."

George leaned down to kiss her on the top of her head. "I'm sorry that I ever recommended you for Hartfield," he said. "It's treated us both so badly, Effie. But I'm glad you were just plain angry enough to claw your way out."

Effie blushed at this. "I have always had somewhat *too* much anger, George," she said. "By which I mean to say ... I will always be happy to share it, whenever you need it."

George laughed at this, and let her go.

Effie could still hear the sounds of celebration behind her as she headed into the hallway. To her surprise, Lydia soon joined her.

"I've got your things packed up already," Lydia said, with a hint of smugness. "I had a feelin' you'd be leavin' soon."

Effie blinked at this. "You did?" she asked. "But how?"

Lydia rolled her eyes. "I *hoped* you'd be leavin' soon," she admitted. "You're goin' to call up Lord Blackthorn, aren't you?"

Effie pursed her lips at this. "I tried to call him earlier," she said. "He did not answer, Lydia. But I have a wager to fulfil, and I will not let him back out of it! I know the way into Blackthorn, and I will walk there myself."

Lydia nodded sagely. "Let's go an' get your bag, then," she said. "I'm sure you'll need your embroidery hoop, at the very least."

They went to secure Effie's few belongings. After that, Lydia walked Effie out behind the house, to the very edge of the hedge maze.

"That's the way into Blackthorn?" Lydia asked in surprise.

"We are in Mr Jubilee's backyard," Effie said primly. "So he cannot possibly be surprised when I show up to pay him a visit." She hauled her bag up over her shoulder. "If we do not speak again, Lydia, then I am probably stuck trying to sweep an entryway in the middle of a forest for all eternity. But I can think of far worse prospects, if I am to be honest."

Lydia snorted. "I'm sure that's not goin' to be the case," she said. "But if it is, by chance, you ought to remind Lord Blackthorn that you accidentally infected a whole household with your anger the last time you were mistreated."

Effie straightened her shoulders. "I did do that," she said.

"And do you know what, Lydia – I would do it all over again, if I had the chance." The statement made her feel for a moment as though she weren't a maid at all, but a powerful magician to be crossed only at one's own peril.

No, she thought. *I am both a maid and a powerful magician. There is nothing wrong at all with being a maid.*

As Lydia looked on, Effie spun triumphantly three times in place, counter-clockwise – and then, just because she could, she spun a few more times, enjoying the last rays of sunset and the cool air upon her face.

Only once she was terribly dizzy did Effie stumble backwards into the hedge maze, clutching at her bag and thinking very furiously of the faerie whom she wished to see.

Chapter Nineteen

✢

*E*ffie knew the moment that she crossed into Blackthorn proper. The air around her grew heavy with the scent of wild, woody things, and the reddish sunset light which trickled past her shoulders became dappled and unsteady.

She turned herself forwards once more, forcibly calming the fearful beat of her heart in her chest. It was one thing for Effie to declare to Lydia that she was going to demand her wager from Lord Blackthorn – but now that she found herself wandering alone through faerie, her confidence began to flag.

The reality of the situation squeezed at her certainty. Effie was here to do something terribly arrogant, after all. She was not even sure how to word her explanation to Lord Blackthorn yet. And what if he did not *want* to fulfil their wager? That, Effie thought, would be simply humiliating. She was not at all sure what she would do if that were the case.

Effie passed the entryway to Blackthorn, where fireflies had begun to swarm in the darkness. The air was still chill, and she crossed her arms over her chest with a shiver.

"I am looking for Mr Jubilee," she addressed the realm. "We have unfinished business, you know."

Effie was not at all certain that Blackthorn had heard her. But she continued walking anyway, carefully watching her feet to avoid tripping herself up in the flickering light of the insects.

Her thoughts kept straying to what she was here to do, however, and her heart grew more and more afraid – and so, perhaps she should not have been surprised when she looked up and saw that she had walked into a forest clearing with only a single, large chair at the centre of it.

Effie sucked in a breath. "I do not need a chair, thank you," she told Blackthorn. "I know that I might seem uncertain, but I am *not* uncertain. I am a little anxious, it is true, but it is only natural to be anxious in a situation like this. I would like to see Mr Jubilee, if you do not mind."

Even as Effie said these words, however, a dark shape moved upon the large chair – and a familiar voice spoke in bafflement. "Miss Euphemia?" Lord Blackthorn asked. "Oh dear. What are *you* doing in Blackthorn's Folly?"

Effie jumped, and let slip a small squeak of surprise. A handful of fireflies startled away from her – and in their light, she saw Lord Blackthorn's tall form, fully outlined upon the chair. He was still wearing his mostly finished coat – but he had loosened his waistcoat buttons, and his black hair was a frightful mess, as though he had run his fingers through it far too many times.

Effie's heart went immediately soft and wistful and longing, and she knew without a doubt that she had made the right decision.

"I am sure that Blackthorn thought I needed to sit and think," she admitted. "Or else – well, perhaps it did take me where it was I wanted to go. I was looking for *you*, Mr Jubilee. I desperately wanted to see you." She paused, however, on a sudden thought. "But what are *you* doing here?"

Lord Blackthorn groaned miserably. "I have been stuck in Blackthorn's Folly ever since I last saw you," he said. "I have argued with Blackthorn for days and days, as faerie time goes. But every time I try to leave, it simply sends me right back here!"

The elf forced himself unsteadily back to his feet. "But you are here for a reason, of course. Has something terrible happened? I know that I am not always the greatest help, Miss Euphemia – and I fear that I have already unbecome a lord – but I will do my best to be virtuous, either way."

Effie smiled shyly. "You are truly Mr Jubilee now, then," she said. "I think that is even better. But you must be very careful what you promise, Mr Jubilee. I *am* in trouble – and you could certainly help me if you so chose."

Mr Jubilee paused, and Effie had the impression that he had blinked at her. "Oh dear," he said. "What trouble is it? It must be quite something for you to come all this way."

Effie crossed the distance between them, carefully stepping over roots and snags. Finally, she came close enough to see the elf properly among all the little fireflies. The sharp edges of his features no longer unsettled her; rather, Effie found that she had come to feel a great affection for his slashed cheekbones and his pointed ears and his far-too-vivid green eyes. The flickering light of the fireflies around them made him seem even more unearthly than usual – but even so, there was a softness to him as he looked at her which made her feel warm and cherished.

"I have been a terrible fool," Effie admitted to him. "From the very beginning, I was convinced that I was in love with Mr Benedict. But I was *not* in love with him, Mr Jubilee. I was ... " She looked down in shame, searching for the right words. " ... I was in love with the way that he made me feel. Because he was rich and important and *someone* – and because, for just an instant, I thought that he saw me as a person. That day, I got to borrow his importance for myself ... and what I really yearned to do was to borrow it again."

The faerie hesitated at this. "You are *not* in love with Mr Benedict?" he asked uncertainly. "But you said that you were. I heard you say the words, Miss Euphemia."

Effie winced. "Humans can lie, Mr Jubilee," she told him. "We are especially good at lying to *ourselves*, I'm afraid." She drew in another breath. "I do not mean to imply that I felt nothing at all for Mr Benedict. He has many qualities which are quite lovable. And perhaps I was right that I might finish falling in love with him, under the correct circumstances – but I have now realised that I never really knew him at all. I had such a limited impression of who he was. And now that I know him better, I can say with certainty: I do not love him. Not one little bit."

Mr Jubilee took a moment to absorb this. Effie suspected that the part about lying was very difficult for him in particular, and she felt a wash of sympathy.

"If I married Mr Benedict," Effie said, "then I would lose my wager, Mr Jubilee. You said that faerie deals must always be fulfilled to the letter. I had a hundred and one days to marry the man that I love. Since I do not love Mr Benedict – indeed, I do not think that I *could* love him – I am now in a fresh bit of trouble."

Mr Jubilee sighed heavily at this. "Ah," he said. "I see. Well – we shall have to find a man that you can love. Do not fear, Miss Euphemia: we still have some time left to us." He did his best to sound confident, but there was a bit of gloominess to his tone which Effie had not ever heard before.

Effie took his hand. As she did, she was surprised to feel his warm skin directly against hers; his gloves had likely gone the way of his waistcoat buttons while he had been trapped and frustrated in Blackthorn's Folly.

The faerie glanced down at her hand. Slowly – hesitantly – he curled his fingers around hers.

"Mr Juniper Jubilee," Effie said softly. "I would be very obliged if you would marry me."

Mr Jubilee blinked very slowly at this, as though he was not quite sure that he had heard the words correctly. Effie could not help it; the absolute shock on his face made her break out into nervous laughter.

"I ... you do not have to, of course!" Effie managed. "But I am *quite* certain that I am in love with you. And so, if you would not like the inconvenience of searching out some other man, you could just as easily help me win my wager yourself."

Mr Jubilee tightened his hand on hers. He spoke very carefully now, with a bit of a tremble in his voice. "I am ... so very fond of you, Miss Euphemia," he said. "I must admit – I suspect that I have been stuck in Blackthorn's Folly because I was upset at the thought that you might marry Mr Benedict. But I ... I am not sure that I know what love is. It might be best if you were to find some human who is sure to be more practised at it than I am. After all, I have barely even begun to understand anything about virtue, let alone about *love*."

Effie smiled uncertainly. "Perhaps it would help if I told you why I am in love with you," she said. "For I am sure this time that I am in love – it is part of how I realised that what I felt before could not possibly have been love." She swallowed nervously. "Mr Benedict treated me like someone for only a moment, Mr Jubilee – but you have always treated me and all of the other servants as though we were someone, even though you could have easily ignored us. I cannot say that it has always been strictly to our benefit ... but it is one of your very best qualities. You are always so quick to help others, and to see the best in every situation. And you are determined to become more than you were before, each and every day. I am in awe of you, Mr Jubilee. And the longer that I spent with you, the more I began to realise that I desperately wanted to stay beside you to see how much you continue to grow each day." She smiled worriedly. "In a way, I suppose ... you have become even more *someone* to me than everyone else is. I would like for you to be happy, and to accomplish all of your goals. And that is why ... well, if you do not love me back, then that is fine. I will handle my wager in some other way – but I will still hope that you eventually learn to love someone else. Because I think that you greatly deserve to be loved."

Mr Jubilee drew Effie's hand upwards to clasp it against his chest. Effie dared to look up at him – and she saw that there were tears in his bright green eyes.

"You are very much someone to me, Miss Euphemia," he said. "I fear that I am not yet virtuous enough to let you marry someone else for a second time. If I am not capable of love – then I shall simply *learn* how to love. And until then, you shall always have the closest thing to love that I can manage."

Effie's heart leapt in her chest. She threw her arms around his neck and held on tightly. Mr Jubilee wrapped her up in his arms – and he sighed with the same sort of heavy, heartfelt relief that Effie felt herself.

"Perhaps you are no longer a lord," Effie said. "But I shall embroider you so many lovely things that every other faerie is always dreadfully envious, Mr Jubilee."

Mr Jubilee smiled against her hair. "I do not care how envious all the rest of them are," he said. "I suspect that none of them will ever understand the things that truly matter to me, in any case."

They perched themselves upon the chair in Blackthorn's Folly for quite some time, watching as the fireflies drifted on the breeze. And as Mr Jubilee held her close and Effie leaned her head upon his shoulder, she realised that she had indeed discovered a faerie tale where a maid could have her happily ever after.

Epilogue

The Royal Post did not deliver to Blackthorn. But somehow, a few very discreet wedding invitations still managed to find their way into the right hands.

One could not call the wedding very fashionable or very rich, especially since it took place in the middle of a forest in faerie – but every one of Effie's family somehow managed to attend, along with both Lydia and a number of curious butterflies. All in all, Effie could not imagine a happier occasion for herself.

Effie's family was very befuddled by the entire affair, of course. George spent most of the ceremony trying to get a look at Mr Jubilee's ears, and Effie's mother could not be convinced that the wedding was anything much more than a very pleasant dream. But Lydia and Lady Hollowvale cried enough for all of them combined – in fact, the two of them were forced to share a handkerchief, since Lydia had forgotten hers.

And though Mr Jubilee had been convinced that love would be difficult for him, Effie quickly decided that he was such an excellent study as made no great difference. In fact, she often told him, she suspected that he had an *abundance* of love, in the same way that she herself had an abundance of anger.

Of course, Hartfield did continue to have terrible problems. And perhaps it would be lovely to say that the servants always managed to hold their ground, and that they eventually battered the Family into learning some modicum of respect for their hired help. But as formidable as Mr Allen and Mrs Sedgewick were between them, there were certainly some sad losses along the way, as there are in every worthy war. At the very least, however, they were never again overwhelmed by the magnitude of their problems – and since the servants at Hartfield had learned to fight side by side rather than one by one, they met with much more success than any other embattled household in England could have expected.

And perhaps Mr Benedict, at least, eventually learned some sense of responsibility towards others. But perhaps he did not. And in either case, it is too often true that the rich and powerful have too much space devoted to the telling of their stories – so it is hardly necessary to expound any further upon the lives of either him or the other Ashbrookes.

Miss Buckley's fate remains similarly unnecessary to our story – but the reader will be particularly pleased to know that Caesar the dog lived a long and very happy life, full of love and treats and excellent days running around after squirrels. In this respect, at least, one creature may be said to have received exactly what he deserved.

Mr Jesson, it turned out, was so desperate for household help and so inept at finding it that he soon hired Lydia as his housekeeper rather than as his maid. Thankfully, Lydia showed uncommon forbearance by using the flower merchant's easily bullied disposition only to improve his circumstances and not to take advantage of him. She hired George as a footman nearly at once – and while the work of keeping a house was as difficult as ever, the small group of servants at Orange End regularly laughed and drank with Mr Jesson, and none of them ever felt the need to escape their employment. Moreover, they were all encouraged to enjoy the sunlight in the gardens exactly as much as they liked.

As a natural consequence of this, perhaps, Lydia found

herself in the tulip gardens one day at the very height of summer; and when Mr Jesson joined her for a walk, the two of them discovered that they were actually quite fond of one another. Thus did Mr Jesson's housekeeper eventually become his wife – and for her remaining favour from Mr Jubilee, Lydia asked only that the tulips in the garden should always bloom the broadest and the brightest of any flowers in the country.

But while Effie and Mr Jubilee were indeed as blissfully happy as any faerie tale couple, Effie had firmly decided that she was still a maid at heart – and since Mr Jubilee still longed to try on a more useful job, the result was perhaps inevitable. For not long after the wedding in Blackthorn, a maid and a footman applied for work elsewhere in the countryside. Both of them arrived with impeccable references from a noblewoman named Lady Hollowvale. The maid, who boasted quite the skill at mending and stitching, was hired on the spot. The footman was somewhat less convincing – but he still managed to secure a trial period for himself, for which he was truly, endlessly grateful.

In very short order, of course, terrible disasters began to befall the household. And then, in no time at all, the servants somehow ended up in open revolt, demanding to be treated with far greater care and respect than they had previously been afforded. But by the time the matter had been settled, neither the maid nor the footman could be found anywhere – nor, in fact, could anyone seem to remember their names.

Off in London, the Lord Sorcier eventually noticed that he had received a surprising number of distressed letters about faeries with a predilection for instigating trouble among the servants at various country estates. But even as he began to consider investigating the matter, his wife assured him that it was not deserving of the least bit of their time.

And so, to this day, the English sometimes tell stories of meeting a man in a very strange coat and a woman whose stitching is oddly enchanting. How these faerie tales end is a matter of some speculation – for the two mysterious strangers are very fond of maids, who never seem to fare any worse for the meeting. But it is also safe to say that the rich and powerful are rarely so lucky.

Which is to say – in a roundabout sort of manner – that Mr Jubilee may have finally obtained all of his wishes, after all.

Look out for...

Longshadow

Book THREE of the Regency Faerie Tales

Keep reading for a sneak peek!

Afterword

I have such a complicated relationship with the story of Cinderella.

I knew, even as a child, that there was something wrong with it. Maids, as they say, simply do not marry noblemen. In fact, in almost every version of Cinderella I have ever read – including lesser-known versions, such as *Princess Furball* or *The Goose Girl* – Cinderella is not actually a maid. Rather, she is a noblewoman, unjustly cast down from her natural life of luxury. From at least one perspective, the story of Cinderella tells us only that women born *rich* do not deserve to be maids – otherwise, Cinderella's rightful status would not be so central to the story.

But why do so many less wealthy women deserve to continue being maids, if it's really so easy for their masters to abuse them? I can understand, of course, that Cinderella was so desperate to escape her situation that she did not always think very hard about that question. But if the prince were really such a fantastic fellow, then why did *he* only decide to go and save a maid once he finally got attached to one?

The faerie godmother, I decided, was really the most admirable character in the whole story. She was the one, after all, who saw an injustice and tried to fix it. And I am sure that Cinderella was not the only maid that she ever saved.

Thus did *Ten Thousand Stitches* eventually become a story about a Cinderella who was an actual maid, and not a noblewoman forced to temporarily become be a maid – a Cinderella who was not always perfectly nice, and who struggled with her perfectly reasonable anger over how all the servants she knew were treated. And of course, since I had the utmost respect for the faerie in the story, Cinderella eventually decided to run away with her faerie godfather, rather than marrying the handsome but questionably bland sort of prince.

That said, it was very important to me that Lord Blackthorn should not be a magical solution for the servants at Hartfield – because the other thing that Cinderella teaches us is that the world shall magically ensure a happy ending for women who remain sweet and compliant and who never get angry even when they should. And that is not something that I ever see in the world around me either. Rather, when villains mistreat us, they shall almost always continue to mistreat us until someone forcibly stops them. If you are powerless, then it is almost impossible to stand up to your villains – but when you and other powerless people finally become angry on each other's behalf and stand up together, it is far more difficult for villains to get their way.

As with anything worth fighting for, of course, there are days when you shall all lose together, because you have chosen to fight together. But history progresses at those times when people choose to risk the fight anyway, because they believe that the reward is worth it.

As always, I must give special thanks to my husband, whose love is so abundant that I must admit to basing Mr Jubilee's better parts upon him. My alpha readers, Laura Elizabeth and Julie Golick, are the constant voices of support which kept this book on track even when I was tired and discouraged from constant lockdown. Lore was kind enough to help me research all things related to historical stitching. My fellow historical fantasy authors in the Lamplighter's Guild, Jacquelyn Benson and Rosalie Oaks, not only kept me on track but also offered suggestions when I was stuck or chewing on plot problems. My historical nitpicker, Tamlin Thomas, is responsible for many important suggestions and corrections – and furthermore, he sent me a package of the most fantastic coffee I have ever had.

But I must also make special room this time to thank my father, who always believed that I would be a writer someday, and who did not hesitate to tell me so at every juncture. In so many ways, I would never have managed to end up writing this book right here and now without his support.

And thank you, reader, for finishing *Ten Thousand Stitches*. It means the world to me that so many people seem to find so much hope in my writing. I do not dare to assume – but I hope that this book might serve as an adequate balm for at least one other person.

Lord Elias Wilder, Regency England's court magician, regularly performs three impossible things before breakfast – but the one thing he cannot do is raise a daughter. As Theodora Wilder continues taking children under their roof, however, Elias is finally forced to confront his dark familial past and the matter of his dubious faerie father.

This short, exclusive novella, written from Lord Elias Wilder's perspective, takes place just after the events of *Half a Soul* and includes glimpses of the Lord Sorcier's childhood in faerie. Visit the link below to subscribe to *The Atwater Scandal Sheets*, and read *The Latch Key* today!

https://oliviaatwater.com/newsletter

extras

orbit

meet the author

OLIVIA ATWATER writes whimsical historical fantasy with a hint of satire. She lives in Montreal, Quebec, with her fantastic, prose-inspiring husband and her two cats. When she told her second-grade history teacher that she wanted to work with history someday, she is fairly certain this isn't what either party had in mind. She has been, at various times, a historical reenactor, a professional witch at a metaphysical supply store, a web developer and a vending machine repairperson.

Find out more about Olivia Atwater and other Orbit authors by registering for the free monthly newsletter at orbitbooks.net.

if you enjoyed
TEN THOUSAND STITCHES

look out for

LONGSHADOW
Regency Faerie Tales: Book Three

by

Olivia Atwater

Proper Regency ladies are not supposed to become magicians, but Miss Abigail Wilder is far from proper.

Abigail Wilder's father may be the Lord Sorcier of England, but that does not mean that society is willing to accept her as a magician. When a dark lord of faerie threatens London, however, Abigail is determined to uncover the truth and save Lord Longshadow's victims—and neither good manners nor her father's worries will stop her.

Abigail is not the only one investigating the terrible events in London, though. A street rat named Mercy soon insists on joining her cause—and while Mercy's own magic is strange and foreboding, she may well pose an even greater danger to Abigail's heart.

Prologue

Miss Abigail Wilder was not supposed to use her magic in front of the tea ladies. *Never use your magic in front of the* ton, her father had told her. *Once you do, they'll never let you rest – you'll be doing useless magic tricks until you're old and grey.*

Eighteen-year-old Abigail greatly suspected that the tea ladies were exactly the sort of nobility her father had warned her about. Once every month, the tea ladies met in her Aunt Vanessa's sitting room for tea. Ostensibly, the ladies were there at Aunt Vanessa's invitation in order to discuss the charity she intended to set up – but in practice, they rarely did much other than take their tea and gossip about the rest of the *beau monde*. Often, in fact, their conversations turned to the subject of Abigail's father, Lord Elias Wilder – England's court magician, sometimes known as the Lord Sorcier.

"Won't you tell us at least a *little* bit of what your husband is up to, my Lady Sorcière?" Lady Mulgrew asked. She was a thin, pinched-looking woman with a high, reedy voice – Abigail sometimes thought she looked a bit like a horse. Lady Mulgrew had been a tea lady for months now, ever since Aunt Vanessa had started their meetings. As one of the few ladies who had donated any real money so far, Lady Mulgrew carried herself with a certain air of importance, enjoying Vanessa's increased attentions. She always sat in a spot of honour at tea, just next to Vanessa herself.

Abigail's mother, Lady Theodora Wilder, did not respond immediately to the query. In fact, she continued sipping at her tea for a long while, as though she hadn't heard the question at all. Abigail knew that her mother *had* heard the question, despite her lack of reaction – she was simply thinking through the implications, trying very hard to formulate an appropriate response. Lady Theodora Wilder had only half a soul, which skewed her social acumen somewhat. Long silences never bothered Dora in the way that they bothered most other people – and since Dora's first instincts always suggested that she should be utterly honest and forthright, she often required those long silences in order to engineer a more appropriate, diplomatic reply.

Lady Mulgrew blinked over her tea. "I'm not certain if you heard me, my Lady Sorcière," she observed very slowly, as though she were talking to a deaf woman. "I said—"

"Oh yes, I did hear you," Dora assured Lady Mulgrew. She set her teacup down on the table in front of her, buying herself further time to think. Dora turned her mismatched green and grey eyes upon Lady Mulgrew, considering her gravely. "I know much of my husband's business," Dora said finally, "but I do my best to keep it to myself. It is his duty to protect England from black magic – and from worse sometimes. One never knows when a stray word might have unintended consequences."

This was not, of course, what Lady Mulgrew wished to hear. She leaned forward in her seat of honour. "But surely," she insisted, "nothing terrible could come of sharing some small news of interest with *us*. We are hardly the sort of people from which the Lord Sorcier must protect England!"

Abigail snorted into her teacup. Dora shot her daughter a sideways look – and though Dora rarely showed emotion on her face as other people did, Abigail knew that they were sharing the same thought: Lord Elias Wilder *often* implied that the aristocracy were worse than any black magicians.

Aunt Vanessa probably had the best of intentions asking Abigail and her mother to tea. Abigail was, herself, the product of Good Charity – as anyone could surely tell. For though Lord Elias Wilder *called* Abigail his daughter, and though he had loaned her his surname, he was truly just fostering her as his ward. And while Lady Theodora Wilder had dressed Abigail in creamy muslin and done up her hair with a green taffeta ribbon, Abigail's skin was still covered in old pockmarks, and her blonde hair was lank and straw-like. Abigail had made half an effort to improve her accent, mostly just to please her old governess – but she had to speak very slowly and with great concentration in order to manage her elocution.

Aunt Vanessa thought that the tea ladies would be more willing to help other children if they saw how much Abigail had benefitted from similar charity. Abigail was…less convinced. But Aunt Vanessa had asked with such lovely, naive sincerity that it was difficult to turn her down.

Which all went a very long way to explaining why Abigail Wilder was currently settled in her aunt's sitting room deflecting attempts at gossip, rather than practising magic with her father as she would have preferred.

Dora picked her tea back up – and Abigail realised that her

mother didn't intend to respond to Lady Mulgrew's comment. Abigail sipped at her own tea, contemplating a reply. She had found Dora's tea-sipping strategy to be terribly helpful herself – for Abigail often felt tempted to say very *honest* things aloud just to see how people might react. The tea, she found, stifled that impulse somewhat.

What Abigail thought was: *You will spread the slightest bit of gossip all over London regardless of the consequences, and my entire family knows it.*

But Abigail swallowed down the words along with her tea. What she said aloud was: "Magicians can scry upon people and conversations from a distance. Naturally, everyone here can be trusted... but I don't believe that Aunt Vanessa has any magical protections cast upon her sitting room."

Abigail worked to keep her vowels crisp and rounded – but she knew from the way the other women shifted in their seats that something was still subtly *wrong* with her diction.

"I have no such protections, of course," Aunt Vanessa said with a smile. "I have never felt the need to hide my social gatherings from strange magicians." Vanessa reached up to tug self-consciously at one of her blonde curls, however, and Abigail suspected that her aunt found the topic of conversation a bit discomfiting. Aunt Vanessa was a very proper woman, and she disliked the idea of prying into other people's business. Lady Mulgrew was the only tea lady to have shown genuine interest in Vanessa's charitable endeavours so far, though, and so Vanessa's attempts to deflect Lady Mulgrew's gossip were often half-hearted.

"You must know much of magic yourself, Miss Wilder?" Miss Esther Fernside piped up. At seventeen years old, she was the youngest lady present. Miss Fernside was a recent addition to the tea ladies. She had only joined them for last month's tea – and even then, Abigail couldn't remember her having said a word. She was a young, mousy woman of quiet demeanour and large, dark eyes; her curly brown hair had already mostly escaped its neat bun after only an hour of tea, and her smile was dim and hesitant.

"It would be strange if I didn't know *anything* about magic, wouldn't it?" Abigail replied carefully. The last thing Abigail needed was for Miss Fernside to realise that she could do magic – the resulting conversation would probably derail the entire tea.

"Oh yes, I suppose that would be strange," Miss Fernside admitted sheepishly. She looked so embarrassed by her own question now that Abigail felt a moment of pity.

"I've read many of my father's books," Abigail elaborated. "We talk about magic an awful lot. There are two kinds, you know – mortal magic and faerie magic. Almost all magic done in England is mortal magic, but faeries work the strangest spells by far."

This distinction was one of the very first things any magician learned – but it tended to impress people who knew nothing about the subject. Miss Fernside brightened at the discussion, sitting up in her chair once more.

"I knew that!" Miss Fernside assured Abigail. "My mother used to read me faerie tales. She said that faeries are wild and dangerous and wonderful. She said they can do just about *anything* if you pay them the right price."

Abigail shivered with sudden unease. Miss Fernside had no way of knowing that Abigail herself had been stolen away by a faerie – it wasn't precisely common knowledge. But the reminder did little to improve Abigail's already lacklustre enthusiasm for tea.

"Faeries *are* dangerous," Dora said softly. "And…yes, wild and wonderful. Which is why you should hope never to catch their attention."

Dora, too, had been stolen away to faerie. Abigail could still remember the day they'd met, in the awful halls of Hollowvale's Charity House. At the time, Abigail had been convinced that they would never leave again. But Dora had assured her that they would escape... and then, of all things, Dora had killed their cruel faerie captor.

No one in the sitting room – Aunt Vanessa included – would ever have imagined that mild-mannered Dora was capable of murdering a faerie. But Abigail *did* know... and in fact, it was one of the things she loved most about her mother. None of the other women here, Abigail thought, would have dared to do what was necessary to save her from Charity House.

"Faeries are *terribly* dangerous," Lady Mulgrew interjected, in an attempt to regain control of the conversation. "Why, I've heard other ladies and gentlemen of our acquaintance specu- late that the recent deaths in London are to do with a faerie. I assured them that the Lord Sorcier was surely looking into the matter... but of course, no one here could possibly confirm such a thing." Lady Mulgrew smiled specifically at Dora, with only a hint of annoyance.

"What recent deaths would those be?" Abigail asked wor- riedly. She fixed her gaze upon Lady Mulgrew, discarding her other thoughts.

Lady Mulgrew raised her eyebrows. "Why, I assumed that you would know, Miss Wilder," she said. "Such awful busi- ness. We have lost several fine ladies in the last few weeks. They pass overnight, in their sleep – with the western window open."

This last statement should have meant something to Abigail, perhaps. But she didn't dare admit that it had gone entirely over her head. Abigail glanced at her mother – but Dora's expression was, as always, blank and serene.

"Is it possible that the Lord Sorcier is *not* investigating these tragedies?" Lady Mulgrew asked Dora archly.

Dora looked down at her empty teacup with vague surprise. "Oh," she said. "I have finished my tea."

And then – with absolutely no preamble – Dora stood and smoothed her gown. Abigail hurried to follow suit, just as her mother turned to leave the room.

"We have an appointment," Abigail lied. It was barely an excuse – but it was something, at least.

Aunt Vanessa smiled ruefully at Abigail. She knew, more than anyone, how different Dora's social perceptions were. "It was lovely having you both here," she assured Abigail. "I appreciate that you came."

The words held more meaning than most of the tea ladies likely appreciated. Aunt Vanessa had almost surely noticed Abigail's discomfort today.

Abigail curtsied awkwardly, and left to join her mother.

if you enjoyed
TEN THOUSAND STITCHES

look out for

WILD AND WICKED THINGS

by

Francesca May

*In the aftermath of World War I, a naïve woman is swept
into a glittering world filled with dark magic, romance,
and murder in this lush and decadent debut.*

*On Crow Island, people whisper that real magic
lurks just below the surface.*

*Magic doesn't interest Annie Mason. Not after it stole her future.
She's on the island only to settle her late father's estate and,
hopefully, reconnect with her long-absent best friend, Beatrice,
who fled their dreary lives for a more glamorous one.*

Yet Crow Island is brimming with temptation, and the most mesmerizing may be her enigmatic new neighbor.

Mysterious and alluring, Emmeline Delacroix is a figure shadowed by rumors of witchcraft. And when Annie witnesses a confrontation between Bea and Emmeline at one of Crow Island's extravagant parties, she is drawn into a glittering, haunted world. A world where the boundaries of wickedness are tested, and the cost of illicit magic might be death.

Welcoming the Dark

R. Crowther

Mabon—Autumn Equinox

There is a new witch at Cross House.

Perhaps it is the girl I have seen at the last few gatherings, silently lingering at Priscilla's feet like a ghost, her dark eyes watchful and her angular face solemn, but I cannot be sure. I don't trust my judgement after what I have seen tonight.

I suppose I don't have the taste for any of this anymore. Since the fighting began Priscilla's nocturnal soirees have grown vicious and wild; I should have known better than to be tempted to attend another, but I have always been weak when it comes to wanting to be around my own kind. Still, I couldn't stomach the debauchery for long, all that cowardice in one room, and I fled onto the beach beyond the house, where the sand was pale under the prickle of autumn starlight.

I wandered along the cove until I grew tired. And there—a young woman, I think, but with no childish softness or feminine curves, only sharp edges and long limbs, dressed in a boy's shorts and a man's shirt rolled at the elbows.

She picked herself up off the sand, where rocks grow out of the ocean all jagged and slippery with dark sea moss, and limped a step backwards. I only noticed because I felt *it. It was like a blade scraping against the back of my teeth, its edge skimming my tongue. I could taste it, like nothing I have tasted before. Earth, salt, and an iron tang, bright and startling. And strong, so strong. It flooded me and I froze, letting the darkness smother me with her cloak.*

The girl did not see me. She inspected her palm, holding it up to the silver moon like an offering. Blood trickled, dark against the rocks. The magic I could taste was untamed—fierce and angry. She lifted her hand to her mouth, tongue hungry, and when she pulled it away her lips were smeared bloody red.

My own blood sang in response. I coveted that power, wanted it so desperately that I almost went to her. Almost begged on my knees for a sliver of that dark gift. Yet as the moment stretched, the singing in my blood morphed into a scream, a primal urge. Stem it, wrap the wound, stop the spill. *The girl only bared her teeth at the moon.*

I did not care if she watched me flee. I could not stay, could not allow myself to become captivated. There is so much to be done and so many more men will fall for peace. I have vowed to help them. I cannot be like the others, cannot squabble for that taste of power. Oh Goddess, how I nearly forgot the way true power tastes.

Tonight, truly, I am glad I came here. With the scent of the witch's blood still lingering on my tongue, I am relieved I left before I could hurt them. They will not share this fate.

extras

Priscilla is the strongest witch on Crow Island. Until tonight I thought she needed no guidance from the likes of me—and certainly she would not take it. Now I am afraid for her.

This girl… Whoever she is, she has a darkness inside her and it glitters like broken glass.

Chapter One

Annie

Rumour had it that Crow Island was haunted by witches.

As I saw it for the first time, I understood why. People said the witches who had first discovered the island lived on in the bodies of the crows that flocked on every street corner and bare-branched tree. They flew high above as the boat drew closer to the shore, a constellation of black stars against the bright summer sky.

Tucked away beyond the murky water off the east coast, the island's crescent-moon shape gave it the appearance of a curved spine, a body curled secretively away from the mainland. Yet up close the properties, built to resemble American plantation houses and crumbling Georgian manors, dispelled this illusion of secrecy. They loomed large, like spectral grey sentries guarding their land.

On Crow Island, people had whispered to me back home, real magic lurked just below the surface. Wealth seeped from the place like honey. They said that it had a reputation, that here the law looked the other way.

My mother hadn't wanted me to come, but I had pleaded, surprising both of us. It was my father's final request, which felt vital somehow, and I was compelled in a way I never had been before. He had wanted me to do this, to travel to a place I had never been, to sort through and sell his belongings, although I had hardly known him. And I had thought I could do it. I thought, at least, I should try.

I was no longer sure. I had never been away from home, had never slept anywhere but the squat back bedroom in the little stone terrace house I shared with my mother. The thought was both light and sharp. I inhaled a lungful of the salty ocean air, which tasted different here than it did back home, and reassured myself that I could be brave. Crow Island might be haunted, but it couldn't be much different than the rest of England had been since the war, life trudging on despite the ghosts. I would be fine.

In the harbour the final traces of Whitby drained away: here was no Mam to guide me; there were no familiar street corners to remind me of sunny afternoons with Sam and Bea; there was not even to be the routine of the shop, of cosy evenings by the fire or Sunday afternoons visiting the gallery in town. It was an unwritten story. I had never had so much freedom, or felt so timid.

There was a car waiting for me by the harbour office, a swanky hayburner unlike anything I'd ever dreamed of driving, with a paper slip bearing my name tied to the steering wheel. I approached hesitantly, placing my palm flat against the sun-warmed metal. It felt, for a second, like I could feel the heartbeat of the island, the same thundering under my skin I sometimes swore I could feel when I scavenged shiny polished stones on the beach back home. I pulled my sweating palm back and glanced around nervously.

The harbour had long since emptied and I couldn't see another soul. The office loomed ahead, its windows mirrored by the sun. In the letter I had received before leaving I'd been told I would have to go inside to collect the key for my father's car, but some force held me locked in place. It wasn't the office itself that scared me, more the idea that once I had the key—what then?

I stood for a minute watching the occasional cloud scud across the dark glass of the office windows. Two minutes. Five. My thoughts trickled towards my father. I should be more upset by his death, but I was almost indifferent. Perhaps I was being harsh, perhaps he *had* loved Mam once, but she had never said. She had shed his surname as if even the suggestion of his love was painful for her. I almost preferred to think that he had never loved her. After all, what kind of man would abandon his wife and newborn daughter for an *island*? Still, this was my inheritance—money that could mean everything for Mam and me.

The sun beat down on my shoulders and I was hot and impatient with myself. Sam would have thought I was silly. Bea would laugh if she saw me. But Sam wasn't here and Bea was probably still angry with me. My irritation grew. A roaring sound began inside my ears, the same sound I always heard when a panic came on—like ocean waves. Like drowning. I closed my eyes, squeezing them tight, blocking out the sensation of swirling water that clogged my mind.

"Are you...well, miss? Do you need a doctor? Papa says it looks like you might faint."

A girl of no more than ten had appeared, red-haired and freckled, wearing a grey smock. Concern etched her forehead. I must have been standing here for longer than I'd thought.

"I'm—a little lost," I said, fumbling for an excuse. "I think this is my car but I don't have the key...?"

The girl's face sagged in relief and she snatched at the handwritten slip tied to the wheel plus the paper I handed her, my own messy scrawl in the margins of the note my father's lawyer had sent me. When she returned them, it was with a small key ring, which she thrust at me.

"Thank you," I managed, finally able to breathe.

The girl disappeared as quickly as she'd come. I gazed at the car for a moment more, remembering the illicit runabouts in Sam's dad's jalopy. I'd hated them at the time but was glad

273

now, although I was worried that it would be harder here than roaring along the winding, empty country roads at home.

I didn't want to think of Sam, or of home, and that spurred me into action. I threw my meagre belongings into the car, and once I was on the road it came back to me little by little. It was easier than I remembered, or perhaps the car was simply better. The air tasted of tree sap, the future shimmering ahead like a mirage in the heat.

The reality of Crow Island stretched and grew around me as I drove, lavish houses making way for smaller dwellings as I headed away from the harbour, and quiet, crooked streets peeling off the main road through the town known as Crow Trap. I took in the freshly whitewashed shops and the bright, shiny windows. I hadn't seen such a lush air of festivity since the parties we'd thrown after the armistice. The bunting was fresh and neat, fluttering between lampposts, and the children who ran in circles outside the small bakery wore clean aprons and shoes.

It was beautiful, and yet I couldn't help the nervous way my palms itched at the sight of the wooden boards outside shops peddling *Genuine Palm Readings* and *Holidaymakers' Charms for Good Fortune,* and at the windows that offered a glimpse of trailing greenery, framing small signs that proclaimed the vendors' license to advertise faux magic.

It had been this way since the prohibition began after the war. Licenses, posters, and provisos, silly games that danced on a knife-edge as far as the law was concerned. Back home I hardly thought about magic except to avoid the advertisements at the back of the newspaper where faux mediums passed public messages to the great beyond. In Whitby there wasn't much cause for meddling with magic, real or otherwise; most people barely had enough money to put food in their bellies, never mind extra to waste on trifles.

And it wasn't worth the risk.

Mam always said that real magic was cunning and it was best to steer clear. Fake magic was a joke, a party trick for rich people who had nothing better to do, so it was best to steer clear of that too. Her most well-worn bedtime caution over the last two and a half years was the story of a girl in York, Bessie Higgins, who'd been hanged for selling poppets that turned out to have dried monkshood in them, although she'd sworn she had simply picked the weeds near the river.

There must be more to Bessie's story, but talking about magic had always made Bea act foolish, so we never did.

Magic seemed different here. The licenses and advertisements were light, funny. These signs offered a glimpse into the future instead of the past. Perhaps the rich could better enjoy the soft scares of make-believe fortune-telling, since they hadn't lost as much as the rest of us.

I counted seven of the island's famous crows as I headed back towards the coast. They were perched on rooftops and in trees, one more on the pinnacle of a lamppost, her beady eyes and sharp little beak shining in the May morning sun. I acknowledged each one under my breath like a prayer, the hazy words of a half-remembered poem in the back of my mind.

One for malice,
Two for mirth...

The stretch of coastline where I'd rented a house for the summer was a jungle of grand houses and sprawling estates, the odd cottage like mine annexed from wealthy land a long time ago. I drove down roads shaded by hedgerows growing verdant and wild and speckled with dark thorns. It was a relief to easily find the cottage, nestled less than five minutes' slow drive away.

It sat atop a sloping lawn, surrounded on three sides by so many trees you could hardly see the sky, or the ocean, or anything but tangles of green. At the back of the cottage the lawn dipped until it fell away into a sandy stretch looking out to the North Sea. I'd used some of my new inheritance for the privilege of being able to see water. That was why outsiders came to Crow Island after all, wasn't it?

There was a man waiting for me outside the cottage when I arrived. He was tall and broad shouldered with greying rust-coloured hair and a cheerful, ruddy face. He smoothed the jacket of his immaculate herringbone suit and smiled.

"You must be Miss Mason," he said, shaking my hand warmly as I climbed out of the car. "Your father spoke very highly of you. My name is Jonas Anderson—it's a pleasure to finally meet you. I'm very sorry about your father. Such a shame to have lost him so unexpectedly."

This was my father's lawyer. The man he'd left in charge of his estate. He was the one who had written after my father's heart attack and begged me to come. *It's what your father wanted. The only thing he asked for.* He was the one who had given me an advance on my father's money—for the cottage. I hadn't expected him to be here, and his presence made my muscles bunch nervously.

"Mr. Anderson," I said, smoothing my hair flat under its scarf. I didn't like the idea that my father had spoken about me at all when it hardly seemed like he'd remembered I existed, but I tried to keep that from my voice. "How nice to see you in person—but I'm here so early. I thought we weren't scheduled to meet until next week."

"No, but I wanted to, ah, welcome you to the island," he said, still smiling. "I wanted, really, to make sure you found the car without trouble, and the cottage..." He pointed vaguely.

"I was surprised you chose one over here, but I can understand why. It's lovely, isn't it? Anyway, I know it can be daunting to find your feet in a new place. Especially one like this." He gestured at a single crow that had perched itself comfortably on the bonnet of my car. "So, if you need anything, you mustn't hesitate to let me know. Particularly if it's about your father or his things. We were good friends, you see. I'm sure you must have questions, though I understand if you're too overwhelmed today. I thought perhaps that was why you came early. I can try to speed through the necessary paperwork, but I'm more than happy to give you this week to get settled if that's preferable."

I blinked away the unexpected tightness in my throat at his kindness and nodded as he talked, allowing myself to settle into this new world and agreeing gratefully to keep in touch. Once he was gone I slipped into the cottage, shutting out the sunny warmth to set about unpacking my few belongings.

Now that I was alone, the cottage seemed big and rambling. Frivolous. It wasn't like it was even my money I was spending yet. It was strangely quiet too, the sound of my footsteps muffled by the distant rush of the ocean and the caw of a crow. And there was a different quality to the quiet; it felt like the blackest part of a shadow, coiled and waiting.

I had never been alone like this before. I had spent all my early years with a gaggle of other neighbourhood children, Sam and Bea and a snotty girl called Margot at my heels as we ran and played in the streets behind my mother's chocolate shop. Later, when Sam was gone, I had Mam and Bea, and then Mam. What would I do with all this space? I could walk from one side of the cottage to the other without tripping over Mam's knitting basket or having to slow for Tabs and her kittens. I could swing my arms and not hit a single thing if I wanted to. I didn't want to.

I wasn't sure I wanted to be here.

Until Sam was deployed I'd never thought about leaving Whitby. After he left I thought about it constantly. I was still trying to convince my mother to let me sign up to nurse when we found out he'd died. Just—died. Gone.

It felt like a warning. *This is what happens when you dream.* This is what happens when you get ahead of yourself. For two years Bea and I hardly spoke of him, and when we did we pretended that he was still away, travelling the world and collecting experiences he would bring home to share with us. He never came home. And when Bea had left last spring—when she'd come to this very island—without saying goodbye to me, it felt like I was doomed to lose everything, each part of me slowly chipped away until there was nothing left.

I stayed with Mam, pretending I was content. I did what it felt like I should do, going through the motions like no war had ever happened. How was my loss any different from anybody else's? My life became a pattern of dance halls on the weekends, more out of obligation than anything else, and the shop during the week. Trips to the gallery and the dull excitement of a new sewing pattern. Mam never said so, but eventually she expected me to marry. It had been four years since Sam died, and my inevitable future grew closer every month. I couldn't put it off much longer.

And then...?

That was the part that scared me. The picture of a life already lived, so predictable I could write it point by point in my journal and tick it off. Marriage, babies, hard work, and never enough money to stretch...The problem was, as much as my father's death felt almost like a windfall, coming to the island scared me too.

Standing here, in this cottage that wasn't mine, I told myself it didn't—*couldn't*—matter that I was afraid. This felt like my last chance to change my path; I needed to grasp it with both hands, pull the opportunity up at the roots, and carry it with me, ready to plant, or else the life back home was all that waited for me.

It seemed like fate that Bea was here. I'd been thinking of her a lot since I set out on the ferry, wondering if she'd truly missed me like her letters said. Whether she was still angry with me. The hole she'd left in my chest ached. If only we could be friends again—true friends—maybe I wouldn't feel so lonely.

Bea and I had been so close, once. Both of us had grown up without fathers, although hers had died when she was just a baby, and we often joked that we were fierce enough not to need them. It felt strange, after all our jokes, all the secret longing we'd hidden behind our bluster, that I was here today because of my father.

Perhaps he had hoped coming to the island would be good for me. Perhaps he had hoped that the island would jostle my soul and wake me from a slumber he recognised—that it would cut this stunted part of me free. Perhaps he hadn't thought of how it would affect me at all. I wasn't sure which possibility I liked the least.

The late-afternoon air in the cottage was loaded with my questions. I wanted to know about his life, about his friends, his work, and his hobbies. I wanted to know why this place had captivated him so much that he had left us without a second thought. And most of all, I couldn't stop the small voice in my head that asked the same thing I'd been returning to for weeks—at home, on the boat, seeing that shiny car for the first time...

Why now? Why had my father only wanted me to come to Crow Island once he was dead?

Follow us:

f **/orbitbooksUS**

𝕏 **/orbitbooks**

▶ **/orbitbooks**

Join our mailing list
to receive alerts on our
latest releases and deals.

orbitbooks.net

Enter our monthly
giveaway for the chance
to win some epic prizes.

orbitloot.com